Hornito

Hornito

my lie life

Mike Albo

HarperCollins*Publishers*

Parts of this book appeared on Word.com, on Stim.com, and in *Queer 13,* published by Rob Weisbach Books.

HarperCollins books may be purchased for educational, business, or sales promotional use. For information, please write: Special Markets Department, HarperCollins Publishers Inc., 10 East 53rd Street, New York, NY 10022.

FIRST EDITION

Designed by Joseph Rutt

Library of Congress Cataloging-in-Publication Data
Albo, Mike.
p.   cm.
Hornito: my lie life/by Mike Albo—1st ed.
ISBN 0–688–17436–1
1. Gay youth—Fiction   2. Suburban life—Fiction   I. Title.
PS3551.L268 H67 2000
813'.6—dc21
00-38669

00 01 02 03 ❖/RRD 10 9 8 7 6 5 4 3 2

For my family
And for Virginia

Acknowledgments

A deep, deep thank-you to my agent, Tina Bennett. A huge thank-you to my editor, Robert Jones.

Indepted thank-yous to Colin Dickerman and Rob Weisbach for their support and initial work on this book, John Jusino, Fiona Hallowell, Cliff Chase, Rose Kernochan, Margie Borschke, Michael Ian Kaye, and Erica Freudenstein.

Constant thank-yous to Lorraine Tobias, Virginia Heffernan, Larry Shea, Lisa Archambault, Victor Silveira, Gregg Guinta, Nell Casey, Maud Casey, Cary Curran, Gary Baura, Maria Russo, Brenda Shaughnessy, Scott Zieher, Hilton Als, Jack Louth, Michael Burkin, Tori Rowan, Darcy Cosper, James Cavera, Ned Malouf, Jill Weidman, Erik Mercer, Jim and Nancy Heffernan, Pamela Lawrence Svendsen, Libby Hiller, John Osthaus, Karen Lawrence, Maureen Ratel, and Will O'Bryan.

And thanks a million, of course, to Mom, Dad, Steve, Dave, Cathy, and all Albos.

Hornito

I'm in the car waiting for my parents, parked in the Springfield Plaza with its mock-wood awning and signs lit from behind—Morton's and Color Tile and Baskin-Robbins and Circuit City and Today's Man and a CVS drugstore, where today I had to secretly get the A-200 crab-removal system because I am home for Labor Day weekend with my bag of laundry and everything-is-fine smile.

I felt those little crabs on the entire bus ride down from New York City, but I stupidly didn't really notice them until I was crammed into the seat by the bathroom in the back of the Peter Pan bus, breathing the stuffy air, the sun magnifying into the side of my face and thigh, a chewed-up piece of Wrigley's Spearmint gum cooking in the windowsill's black rubber craw and giving off a nauseating saliva-mint fume. An awful, tubby man in front of me yanked his seat all the way back and snored the entire time, and then, halfway through the ride, went to the bathroom. When he opened the door, the hideous fusion of waste and gum and blue chemical disinfectant made me swallow hard.

I was up all night last night, and I quietly left the apartment this morning so Benny wouldn't come out of his room and confront me, and I hauled my duffel bag to Port Authority and got on the Peter Pan bus.

I sat next to a little peach-fuzzy fourteen-year-old who was listening to Sugar Ray very loudly, his earphones seeping tinny cimbal crashings into the stale air. He looked out the window the whole trip with his arm on the thin window ledge, and it looked like a cylinder of butter with little glinting hairs on it. *Oh ho, if you knew what was ahead of you,* I thought. *Whatever you end up being attracted to, little boy, in twelve, thirteen, fourteen years you will be sitting here, like me, and you will be as shocked as I am now that you are twenty-eight and the kind of person who says "Oh, if you knew what was ahead of you" to yourself and has crabs.*

For four hours I read through my diary from this summer—a documentation of day after humid day, malarial rain and softened asphalt, my stupid temp job at the American Liver Association, stops at the ATM machine, all the bars and clubs filled with guys I tried to fixate on, my wicked roommate Benny's fucked-up loyalty, and of course beautiful, slippery Eric, who floods my mind if I let him. When I looked at these wheezy entries I had no cool detachment; I wanted him all over again. His powder his blondness his beautiful shoulders his calligraphy body. I read words I wrote about him and headed right back into that zone of poetry where he is suspended, humming and warm. The fact that Eric has a boyfriend is dry, empirical data, as unsatisfying as dusty crackers. My fantasies don't have solid floors or sober bulb wattage. An image of seeing Eric on 6th Street in daylight becomes redder and warmer and bottomless and shifts into kissing and kissing and then becomes completely unreal as we make it to our Virgin Atlantic Premium Economy seats, taking another trip to Umbria because my good friend Jorie won't be at her villa until October.

I think the kid next to me tried to peek at my diary, but it's his fault if he was freaked out reading through my pathetic slippage into love, only to come home to Springfield in itchy defeat.

When I got to the house I said hello to my parents, who seem so stable and bifocaled now. *Hey, I'm gonna borrow the car!* I said, pretending to jingle change happily while I secretly itched myself, and then I drove their new Cutlass to CVS. I walked in through the automated doors as efficiently as possible, trying to detect A-200's location with a casual face—past the It's a Spooky Halloween! paper plates, paper cups, and paper picnic tablecloths; past the Back to School shelves with their spirals and crayons and glue; the shampoo shelves, gel shelves, conditioner shelves, black-hair shelves, cotton balls, astringents, foot care, skin care, moisturizers, exfoliators, replenishers, removers, testers, to the subject of lice, below Band-Aids and Mercurochrome. I bought it, and as the cashier teen bleeped the scanner gun and nicely stapled the receipt to the bag, I thought again, *Oh, if you knew what was ahead of you.*

I took my crinkly CVS bag up to my bathroom, with the familiar maroon-and-foil wallpaper and salmon cups and toothbrush stand. The bathroom where I believed I was being observed for social-sexual-scientific experiments when I was seven, where I saw my pubic hair grow, where I ran and hid from my brother Mark, where I scrambled when I saw him getting a massage from Ken Fenning, where I danced and moussed my hair and tried my mother's eyeliner and wore satin shorts.

I applied the lice killer, waiting ten minutes, shampooing, combing out nits, until my genitals ached. The Crabs of Guilt. The Crabs of Embarrassment. I am embarrassed that I actually thought there was an honest pathway to my lie of a life: a simple existence with

Benny as a friend and me falling in love with Eric, when in actuality Benny is a skulking freak and Eric is probably enjoying a fulfilling sexual fiesta with his boyfriend right now.

A-200 is clear and soapy and smells of some old-fashioned witch hazel tonic that you'd find at your grandparents' house. They must make A-200 smell nostalgic so that when you use it your grandparents float around you like ghosts, and you feel even more dirty as you rid yourself of crabs.

Crabs are the lamest STD of all, because you see them, dots on your body, and their pinchy needle legs squeal, "You are dirty! You are a whore! You are single!" until you blast them out with radioactive A-200, which is so toxic it makes your skin throb, and then you sit there and glow like shameful uranium. Crabs are visual and concrete—not like the noxious, ever-present fumes of AIDS. It hovers like gas. It is the air that I breathe and surrounds my body. I monitor myself constantly—Was that a night sweat? Am I fatigued? Are my glands swollen? Is that what thrush looks like? Am I practicing "safe(r) sex"? I lie in my bed the night after a sex act and ask question after question, putting myself through a brochure of risks until my terrifying investigation begins to tire me and I have to slump in a chair and find comfort in the idea that I will soon be too dead to care. Then I will wake up forgetful and go out and start all over again, giving blow jobs with the same mouth that says *God I have to get tested again soon.*

I also have this strange lump in my left breast. Since it has no basis in sex, it is a parent-approachable ailment. Tumors are acceptable. My mother says it is just a fibroid—"Don't worry about it." I guess cancer is okay to die from. . . . No, I don't mean that—I'm sorry God. I don't want to sound so falsely rebellious, because I am not like that anymore. Maybe I am I don't know I am such a freak.

I went downstairs, pelvis burning, and my brother Mark and his wife Ann are watching *The Towering Inferno* on TV. Richard Chamberlain is about to get fried. *He is such a big raving queen, isn't he?* I said, and Mark laughed, because now, after twenty-eight weird years, it is finally fine for us to laugh about sexuality. "Hey, do you want to go to Dave's with us? He's got a pool," he says, and I say, *Sure,* and we drive to Dave's house.

It's been two years since Mark got married. His wife loves crafts. Ann knits constantly, and makes cushions for everything, blanketing every semipermanent surface: knife handles, tissue boxes, remote controls. They have a baby, and Ann is sitting with the baby beside her, actually knitting little footsies on the physical infant itself. My niece's name is Amanda-Jennifer. Recently I held her and told her, in her tiny, fascinated ear, to watch out because people are weird about love and sex in the world and they try to contaminate you with their damaged desires and make you as rotten as they are. *BE CAREFUL, Amanda-Jennifer, don't let them shell-shock you.*

We get to Dave's house. Dave is Mark's frat friend from college. "Hey, Mike," he says.

Hi, Dave. Oh, hi dog. . . . What's your dog's name?

"Cheeto," Dave says. We sit down to tan by their pond-shaped pool and I get really sunburned.

Hi, Jenn, I say. Jenn is Dave's wife. She drags lounge chairs over the cement, and the sound gives me chalky chills. The automated pool cleaner twists toward me and sucks by my side. I sit there with my legs apart, nervous that someone is going to suddenly make an AIDS fag joke and I will be forced to stand up for myself. But that never happens. It's as if everyone read a sidebar article about my sexuality in the *Springfield Excite Community Magazine*. Everyone knows and smiles and never says a thing.

"Hi Mike, what's up? How's New York?" asks Jenn.

Okay.

Cool! What do you do?

This and that. I have this really annoying lump in my breast.

Oh, my God.

My mom says it's just a fibroid.

"Maybe it's a child. Maybe you're pregnant," Mark says, smiling.

They say that some tumors have actual hair and teeth in them, like little extra nonpeople, I say. I don't even know if that is true. Everyone is silent.

"Did you know," Jenn says, "that babies who immediately cry when they are born have already had souls when they were fetuses, and babies who are dazed and confused when they come out receive souls right when they get out of the womb?"

"No, I didn't!" Ann says.

"Are you interested in reincarnation theory?" Jenn asks me.

I don't think I believe in souls. All their faces faintly fall.

"That's sort of bleak," my brother says.

"Baby baby baby baby baby," Amanda-Jennifer chants. She runs to Cheeto and falls in a little slap of flesh onto the cement. Time stops. Everyone watches her to see if she will cry, and soon a wail is released from deep inside her. Cody, Dave and Jenn's baby, wails. Simultaneously Ann and Jenn rise, the plastic lattices of the seats striping the backs of their thighs. They sweep up their children and expertly rock and rock.

"It's funny what things will upset them."

Yeah, it's weird.

We sit and drink beer, picking from a Fiestaware party boat filled with Tostitos and salsa, my brother and Ann and their two friends talking about children, the one outdoor concert they had time to go to last month (Bad Company reunion), and KnitFest, the annual gathering of yarn lovers in Springfield Plaza. Cheeto is panting, walking between our lawn chairs. When we stop talking about human subjects the conversation turns to the dog: "You know what he did the other day? He barked every time Kramer was on *Seinfeld,* so we call him Kramer when we watch TV!"

After an entire day of watching the dog prance around, calling him, petting him, saying *Oh ho ho, down, Cheeto, down, Cheeto,* after a day of patiently listening to stories about how it has allergies and wasn't getting along with my brother's dog, blah blah, I ask (because I feel guilty that I am acting snotty), *How come you named your dog Cheeto?*

"Well, actually, it's name is Chi, as in the center of the self in the Buddha religion, you know?" Jenn says, clinking her big tumbler of Crystal Light. "But we just started calling him Cheeto."

"Dave, can I put Amanda-Jennifer in your room?" Mark says. Dave nods, and Mark picks up his baby and carries her up the deck steps, into the porch, and she is all smiles, looking at me with her little grinning teeth as she is carried up by her dad, and she keeps looking until the wall blocks the view, held by strong familiar arms, into a dark hall, into a landscape of quiet dark carpets and air-conditioning, her mind having no need to stay up late like me and find someone's mouth to put her tongue in.

We go to the Fennings for dinner—my parents' family friends—their house smelling plastic and air-freshened yet personal, like a used mint Band-Aid. Christmas cards with pictures in holly frames. Hanging baskets and thimble collections. Mr. and Mrs. Fenning in madras shirts and pleated peach pants. Son Ken Fenning is married now and lives in Texas, and "How are you, Mike?" *Fine.* "How is New York?" *It's fine.* "Ken's daughter Ashley is so big now, and he has his second one coming." *I can't believe it, wow, that's great.*

Oh, I'm fine. My crotch is throbbing, but I am fine.

Just ten or so hours ago I went home with Eric once again. We met at the Wonder Bar and wordlessly walked to his place. We stripped fast and screwed on the bed in the curtained-off closet space Eric sleeps in. On the other side was the living room with its street-found coffee table, old couch whiskered by cat claws, blaring TV, and roommate Blaze (yes, Blaze), passed out with the remote in his hand. The phone rang, and it was Eric's boyfriend. Eric talked to George about being a go-go boy, and then they got into a fight, Eric whispering inscrutably into the phone while I lay on the twin mattress. I pretended to be preoccupied and I looked off at the wall like it was the most fascinating wall I had ever seen. I am supposed to be "cool" about all this. George and Eric have been great, golden boyfriends for an award-winning year. Everyone respects them for that. They have stormy emotional fights, make out in public, and when they don't go out and they stay home to watch videos, everyone strangely seems to know. Eric and I are supposed to be having a "Casual" relationship, which means I can't have any strong opinions and we can't quite love each other. "Casual" is supposed to be a vacation from all law. "Casual" is supposed to be fun.

At dinner with my mother and dad at the Fennings', we sit at a dark-stained dining room table with a little harvest cornhusk doll centerpiece. "What a lovely centerpiece!" my mom says.

"I got it at KnitFest last year!" Mrs. Fenning says.

Eric was drunk and I was tired, but I wanted him so badly it pissed me off, and I pressed into him to crush him closer.

"Ken's an operations manager at Bowers Technologies. . . . He went on a white-water rafting trip with the company last summer—that's when his wife Shari was pregnant, so she couldn't go."

Right. . . . I pulled down his pants with my feet and stuck my dick into his underwear.

"But he had a great time. He said that they slept in tents every night by the river."

Wow, that's amazing. Really? His face wrinkles when he comes. I left that night because he wanted me out of there. He said he wanted to go get some cigarettes, but I know he wanted me out of there.

"Yes. He said the canyons were so beautiful. All these nice reds and oranges." A memory of his smell and his warm body holds on to me like a gymnasium, a heartbreaking, sad gymnasium, and I pause and wait for all signals to pass, and then they do pass and I am there with my family and the Fennings eating boneless chicken with lemon-dill seasoning.

Finally, after an eon of time, the earth dies and is reborn and we leave. We get in the car, which has just been washed so it has that airy, vinyl fume to it, and we drive past the Cineplex Odeon and Houlihan's and Borders and Carpet Emporium, then another plaza, then another plaza, people walking to and from their parked cars, jingling their key chains jammed with glycerine glittersticks and plastic-encased cat photos. My parents want to go to a big Summer Blowout Sale at Today's Man in Springfield Plaza. What a lark—next door is CVS, still red-hot with my crab trail.

"Don't you want to come in? You need to get a suit sometime."

No, I'll wait here, I'll wait in the car. . . .

"All right. . . ."

And that's where I am right now. Through the window my parents are lit under a banner. SUMMER BLOWOUT SALE!!!! it says. My dad is looking at a jacket, my mom is picking over the 20% Off pile. They are still married and still in love. I think my brother is in love with his wife, too. They all have this calm glaze over themselves. They don't jerk their heads around quickly, they plan vacations months in advance, they stand silently next to each other, satisfied with each other's familiar genitals. God listen to me—It's not as if I have a better life plan. They are in love. I'm not.

Either they are all in love, or they have all treated themselves with another kind of A-200 removal system, irradiating themselves with serums and syrups that strip them of any of my hungry desires for vodka and crotches and Manhattan. Everything is removed. Then, barren, they have children and obligate themselves to each other until they have no choice but to love. Love Love Love! You get in a relationship and your body becomes softer and pudgily parental and you turn off your brain and buy houses and think Quentin Tarantino is "edgy." Love is nothing but a dark sister of

Casual. Love and Casual—both of them cackle when they have you in their spindly hands. Nothing isn't imprisoning.

What if I had stayed home and never moved away? Would I have been able to turn myself off and just smile and work at the Continental Reserve Bank with my paisley tie and light-gray oxford shirt? Would I have found a nice guy who would call me back, or whom I would call back? Would I be satisfied with one person, some day-manager of a video store, picking me up in his Honda? Would I let one person satisfy me?

. . . what should we do tonight? . . . why don't we go get a video and go to TCBY and then play Pictionary and then make Fudge Jumbles and watch the Thursday night lineup?

Yes, yes of course! He will be a sober man with a strong back and knuckles. Deeply religious and slightly neoconservative. Loyal to his friends, farm, and home-microbrewing kit. An Abdomenizer guy who smiles. And everyone in happyland will sing songs and celebrate our bond because suburban Springfield is such a close-knit community with such long-standing traditions. The Shell gas station will place two garden gnomes dressed in groom tuxedos in the median of the intersection. The Price Club will cater a huge banquet of barbecue meatballs and bags of frozen Parmesan cheese! Little moussed-up Walkman girls with their Pocahontas backpacks will giggle as they pass us, and on Sunday everyone will gather at the Springfield towne centre with their streamers and tambourines, dancing and laughing in concentric ethnic circles, and the townspeople will gently shove my handsome hubbie and me into the center of a skipping circle and give us dandelion chains and anoint us with the holy fluoridic water they carry from kitchen faucets. That's right, O ye olde Springfield Plaza, where everyone is supportive and long lives love.

You know what would really happen? I would be the same single, eye-strained searcher here that I am in New York—going out every night, hanging out at stupid bars and clubs, except here I would go to Chi-Chi's and Rumors, the Holiday Inn bar and lounge on Interstate 95. The same choreography with just a different backdrop of mint green and Budweiser table trees. I would sit on a stool in my polo shirt, leaning over the puffy brown rim of the bar, listening to a Heart cover band, making eyes at some guy named Sandy with a tiny butt who would end up being the cashier at Cosmetics Plus and who would be boring beyond words but I wouldn't care because I would balloon him up in my brain as my last chance at love as I have a habit of doing—thinking Sandy Tinybutt was the answer to my long search, and then I would have sex with him and eventually drift away from him like always always always.

I would be just as lost as I am now, probably—plowing through the damaged, polluted world for gratification. I would have tried everything to fall in love, as the grimy, crabby city version of me has tried. Was it inevitable? What has happened to me? How did I get to this nit-nested point?

Here I am, sitting in the car, waiting for my parents as they rummage through clothes for future Christmas presents. They are smiling and calm under the Blowout Sale, but I am suddenly flooded. The memories shower down like a hailstorm. I am in a carpeted car in a smooth plaza parking lot, eyes drying from the air-conditioner blowing on high, raining with memory, trying to see through the shower. I am some mad genealogist, retracing how I came to be here. This is my summer, this is my life.

Steve Austin

I swear, I swear, I stick the needles, cross the hearts, and hope the deaths, and swear my very first memory is that I am three and I have my eyes closed and I'm dreaming I am making out with Steve Austin, the Six Million Dollar Man.

Mr. Austin and I covered all the bases. In my dreams I remain a little boy and he is a grown man, my first man. He runs toward me in slow motion, furry furrowed brow, golden graham-cracker skin, hazel hazel face, unzipping his orange jumpsuit, exposing his brawn, him and his hairy torso on top of me and my hairless pigeon-breast rib cage. I dive my face into his armpit and chomp. Then I climb up onto his back and press my pelvis into him like a chimp. I think this is the first time I feel aroused. I remember pressing my penis into my mattress and feeling completely satisfied with the soft, puffy power of blankets and bedsheets, discovering the pleasure in pressure, and I remember my mother or father coming in, seeing me getting off. He or she tells me to go to sleep.

I watch *The Six Million Dollar Man* with my family right after eating "Pass the Old El Paso" taco meat, right before I have to go to bed in my little footsie Dr. Denton's. Steve's big body with its machinery underneath. Steve's amazing strength. Steve's blue bionic eyes. And that kinky chain-jangling noise Steve makes when he performs inhuman maneuvers. Steve is different from the others, *Jonny Quest*'s Race Bannon or Aquaman or Scooby Doo's faggily neckscarved, Mystery Machine–driving Fred. My animated boyfriends are easier to absorb into my hungry little body. Saturday morning I bump my butt down the carpeted stairs and watch TV until eleven, and then run to the kitchen and eat Boo Berry and Cap'n Crunch and Froot Loops, feeding on the crispy colors like pieces of cartoons.

But Steve Austin is not crunchy. He is a man and I want him inside me. Bill Tyner has the Steve Austin and Jaime Sommers dolls. If you pry out the detachable robot-control panels embedded in Steve's arm and legs, he will look weaker, sympathetic, in need of care.

Poor Steve without his machinery. I'll take care of you.

Bill and I build a fort in the Tyner backyard. It's spring. Mr. Tyner carries his cut lawn grass to the compost, Robbie Walters washes his Camaro, Mrs. Pennington scrubs out her kitchen trash can with Top Job, Bill runs inside to get his insulin shot, and I am left alone with our Matchbox cars, in the branches, with Steve. I look to see if anyone is around, pick him up, and slip my finger under his shirt. I unsnap his flimsy snaps, touch his soft and giving plastic back, and finger the Mattel braille on his butt. Then, quickly, I put his head into my mouth and suck.

There are lots of men after Steve. *Buck Rogers*'s Gil Gerard, M*A*S*H's Hunnicutt, *Battlestar Galactica*'s Starbuck, Starsky, Hutch, Bo, Luke, Mr. Roarke, Adam West, Carmine, Epstein, Mr. Kotter, Schneider, Greg Evigan, Gunga Din, Manimal, Jan-Michael Vincent, Jon-Erik Hexum, Johnny Weissmuller, Lyle Waggoner, that tall handsome guy from Manhattan Transfer, the *Riptide* guys, anyone from Sha Na Na, and those moody kids in swimming suits with the wet, penisy Flipper gliding between their legs.

But Steve is the first, my first. I dream of him and hump my bed. I dream of him quietly appearing in the house, slipping past my parents' and brother's rooms, his well-oiled gears smoothly moving, his intricate pistons pumping, reaching my door, sliding into my room, walking toward me, past my Fisher-Price figurines and their farms and parking lots, past the stacks of *Highlights for Children* and *Crickets*, past the Free to Be You and Me and Dumb Ditties and Hungry Hungry Hippos, and Trouble and Sorry! and Mousetrap and Hi Ho! Cherry-O, past the Micronauts and paper Muppet hand puppets and red toy hammers and pegs, and Hot Wheels and Etch A Sketch and Honeyhill Bunch and Adventure People and Fuzzy Pumper Barber Shop, past the Nerf, over the Toughskins and tiddlywinks and Frisbees and Twister and Toss Across and Sit 'n Spin, past the Connect Four and Legos and Lester and Kerplop and Gnip Gnop, and Don't Break the Ice and Don't Spill the Beans, past the soldiers and Mr. Yuck stickers, he's coming with his rough beard, he's coming his breathing, his collarbone, he's coming his wide hands, to me, to me to me.

*T*he beginning of this summer in New York and I am loaded with liberal amounts of brightness. People step confidently onto curbs like catalog models, wet hair and smiling Saturday-daytime faces. Because the summer has started and there is so much promise and long light. There are sandals and street fairs and Gay Pride in June, which is cheesy with its pink triangles and rainbow flags, but at the same time inspirational.

There are glints off the storefronts and the streets steam in rain and we squeeze seventies and eighties secondhand clothes over ourselves and then the *New York Times* will write another article about "East Village retro chic," and we mock it but secretly feel affirmed. Everyone outside wears their 1971 polyester shirts and high-school snowflake pullover sweaters and tan ninth-grade-year-book-photo corduroys. And I have met Eric. He is the beginning of summer to me.

Two nights ago, Benny and Stephen (Benny's boyfriend) and I went out to Bingo night at the Wonder Bar and I wore my green hip-huggers, yellow OP shirt from seventh grade, and family hand-me-down ski sweater, and met this guy and slept with him.

Ian. He wears an open shirt with swirly psychedelic designs, torn, faded Kris Kristofferson jeans, sandals, and a Bakelite bolero tie. He is half Thai, so he is dark and beautiful with his black shiny hair and airbrushed skin. He's a dancer, so it's hard to tell if he is coked up or high on life. Every one of his movements is an expression using a flowing series of muscles.

I love the Wonder Bar. It has red walls with kitschy nostalgic objects nailed and tacked to them: Vegas casino memorabilia, Mardi Gras beads, Barbie posters, and Candy Land game boards, with lava lamps on gold-painted sconces in every corner, Chinese lanterns, ratty hassocks from someone's basement. I love this slopped, murky style. I can't imagine a day when I will be tired of it.

Bingo is hosted by the stately, articulate drag queen Dido. Dido never remembers my name. I don't register with drag queens—they never single me out. It's the same vibe I used to get from my teachers. I look like I know my place. Everybody else always got called on because the teachers would look in my terrified eyes and see that I had done all the reading.

Every time someone walks through the door, Dido announces their arrival as if we are at an ambassadorial function in thirties' London. "The first couple of Sixth Street, Benny and Stephen!" Dido says. "And some ho."

While Dido calls out bingo numbers—"G43," "B11"—Ian pips around the room in dance postures, bouncing like an uncatchable dragonfly.

"Announcing the entrance of go-go boy, blow-job-queen Eric!" Dido says into the microphone.

Eric is this gorgeous go-go boy who dances at Freon on weekends. This is the first time I see Eric physically, at eye level, in the flesh. I'd seen him almost weekly since I moved here, dancing at Freon or on the semiglossy Freon flyer, exposing his butt cheeks. He is one of those guys too beautiful to look at because you know you have no chance whatsoever with him. I suppress my desire to whip around and look, and Ian swerves in front of me.

Wow, what great movements.

"What?" Ian screams to me.

You moved toward the bar very gracefully.

"Slip a dollar in Eric's stained underwear and he'll get on his knees before you can say 'high-risk group,'" Dido says. Everyone laughs.

"I'm sorry—what?" Ian says.

You move. You are graceful. You are very graceful.

"I guess perhaps it's because I am a dancer," Ian says, surging into a scholarly British tone and then, returning to America, he says, "I just got a gig dancing with Plenum, this very well respected dance company, and I'm dancing in the Pride Parade!"

That's great! I say, and quickly turn as Eric walks by. He has light-brown, curly Alexander the Great hair that is frosted with blond, as if he were lightly dusted with a fire extinguisher, and this evolved body on which everything rests beautifully and symmetrically in a way that is only given to plants and insects.

Later I wait in line for the bathroom, talking to a tall, friendly guy named John. John is very talkative, which I like, and he looks like a Berenstain Bear, which I also weirdly like. Eric comes up to us—apparently they are friends—and I feel a little gust in my lungs because Eric is so beautiful, and then John sort of becomes beautiful, too, like a nearby moon orbiting Eric's earth.

"Wow, I love your sweater," Eric says of my ski sweater with bright orange stripes down the sleeves.

Thanks, it's an authentic hand-me-down from my brother.

"Wow," Eric says.

"That's completely rare these days," says John. "You never see something not bought from a vintage store."

That isn't really expensive and hiked up in price, I say, and John nods.

"As it attains a higher price than what it was originally marked in the seventies, which brings it right back to the evil nineties," John says.

"My boyfriend has something a lot like that in green," Eric says. Eric, of course, mentions his boyfriend in the third sentence he utters. He must have to do this all the time to create some sort of protection gate so that he can shield away every human being in the world from hitting on him.

Suddenly Ian is in front of me again. I can't remember what I say or what he says next but we talk long enough so that we go to the bathroom together and kiss in the tiny toilet. "Let's play sword fight!" he says, and we pee at the same time and cross streams with our light-saber urine weapons. When we come out of the bathroom the bar is almost empty. Eric and John are gone; Benny is busy talking to some short black-haired boy with lines shaved in his eyebrows.

I take a shower at Ian's place. He has a beautiful uniform of muscle like fine fur, like his skin is expensive. We have sex in his big dark room—the computer humming and his stereo with those little lethal hanging speakers whispering This Mortal Coil. His parents are definitely rich.

We have great sex and do those things that signify the sex is good, like looking deeply into each other's pupils in the dim underdoor light and holding each other all night. He tells me about his beautiful mother and her four marriages and I really listen. I hold his face and he talks and then we kiss. We exchange numbers on a sheet of green lined paper he pulls out of his bag. But I am not going to call him, because I think I overly outpoured myself to Martin, the guy I met last week who never called me back after I called him three times. Benny advises me not to call and to act cool.

Benny has a lot of ideas. I always forget that I dated Benny in college. It lasted, I think, two weeks. Or four years. I have college in a mental lead box of unrecognizable transcripts, notes in sleepy handwriting, bluebooks, and unclear emotions. I can't even remember fooling around with Benny. Whatever attraction I had for him is as loose as lint in my memory. Benny's face is cute, but not for me—plain and clean, he barely has to shave, with his part-Cuban black spiny hair, clumpy like porcupine quills, and that natural cowlick in front rising off his smiling face. He is always smiling. If I didn't know him I would vote him Most Friendly on a high school yearbook page, but I do know him and that smile has everything to do with all the machinations in the brain behind it—all his plans to have sex and get in people's pants. He is the horniest person I know.

Benny is definitely cute, with his tiny nose and naturally olive skin, but he isn't someone who has been beautiful his whole life, treated with reverence and delicate hands by adults, never once feeling awkward with an overbite. He is not someone like that. He had to work just as hard as I did in childhood. He has as many stories as I do about being a sissy or monkey in the middle or the queer that is smeared in Smear the Queer. And now, like me and many other guys we know, he has worked very hard to excise that and remake himself. Now he can have sex and feel the possibility that guys may like him back.

I, too, can have sex now—I am not sixteen any longer. My desire is equal to its possibility. If I sometimes still my mind and try to perceive this freedom, it roars with all the openness of the Western plains. Or better yet, it must be like what the Chisholms felt as they crossed the West in their Conestoga wagons. But I mean when the Chisholms were happy and pioneering and breathing in the mountain air, saying things like "Giddyup!" or "The Lord has given us this great land, Sarah, and we go forth into thy hills of glory." Before they froze to death and ate each other.

Benny is a nymphomaniac Chisholm. Benny's view of the world involves the idea that every guy is willing to have sex because of a huge internal horniness, but that you have to coax this horniness out in rituals. Usually these rituals involve pinching the nipple of a tight-shirted stranger or sticking a hand down into the underwear of its wearer. His advice to me is more tactical.

When I got home Sunday afternoon from Ian's, I smelled burning bacon and found Benny in the narrow kitchen, spilling onions onto the Astroturf carpet, making omelettes for him and his boyfriend Stephen (whom he is always cheating on) (but they seem good together). I leaned on the sink, rearranged our Michelangelo's accessorized *David* refrigerator magnet, and told them about last night. Benny gave me some bullshit philosophy about the biological trappings of love—"Well, genetically, we are made up of masculine-based DNA," Benny said, because he took advanced biology in college. "Our very makeup of amino acids expends male-based energy. It is directed toward other male expenditures, so our male energy is out of balance, so we are always horny and pushing out our intensity. You may have overpowered the relationship by not taking into account what Foucault calls the 'reciprocality of conduct.' With Martin you might have sent out too much energy and sort of immobilized him, not letting him send out energy." *Right right,* I say. "Now you should try to let Ian use *his* male energy." *Right right.* "Play hard to get!" *Right.*

Right. I hate the "Play hard to get!" meme we live with. I am not good at it. I feel like it is the result of bureaucracy. Generations and generations of people pretending to be cool and aloof until it's cultural, a piled-up century of crossed wires and cover-ups and missed phone calls and people alone. All these overregulated procedures and amendments around the clear, original feeling of love, until it seems completely normal always to appear uninterested, expressionless, even if you burn for his body inside. It's kind of why models are so popular.

I want to cut through all this red tape and receipts! I want to rip off all of my retro clothes and wrap my legs around someone in public! I want to call and call and call!

There are a few people who seem above all contortions, who rise above society and sit there. Like Eric. Warm sunsets and open plains. Silent, whistling, prickling tumbleweeds.

Bathroom

I remember my houses like arms. A low, wet house with pushy, excreting oaks around it. A beige stucco house at the tip of a cactus-dotted cul-de-sac, lined with waist-high windows and constantly cooked by the sun. A geometric model home on the corner of a suburban grid with a three-tier slate patio and curtain-covered bay windows.

My family moves through three houses—from Virginia to Las Vegas and back to Virginia, and then I just make one move, to New York after college, so I am not one of those annoying people you meet in college who lists all the places he has lived: "I was brought up an army brat? And we were always moving? So I've never become sedate or settled into a place, you know?"

But the bathroom never moves in my mind. It sits there, bright tiles and Formica, with the clucking vent fan and spots of sprayed toothpaste on the mirror. The bathroom, where you pull down your pants and touch your naughty nonnies. The bathroom, seductive yet lemon fresh, beckoning yet sickening, my comrade my nemesis. The bathroom, the tiled terrorland with its pubic truths. The bathroom where my brother picks the lock when I'm peeing and pours a bucket of ice water on me; where I jerk off in silent innumerousnesses; where I take my sheets after wetting the bed and try to wash them in the sink without waking anybody up and then go back to my room and sob in my soggy sandwich bed; where I accidentally walk in on our German senior-citizen exchange student, Frau Freund, who doesn't lock the door for some reason. "Please! Please! Please!" she says and I stare at her fishily minnowed, see-through, veiny body.

The bathroom is bright, maroon, and reflective, lit with huge bulbs lining the mirror. Orange, yellow, beige floor tiles, bunched-up light-brown bath towel, tan cabinet, red toilet lid. I am burning in the sacred bathroom. I have pinworms and I am four years old.

My mother is behind me applying something, and I am inflamed. All I remember is how the treatment of it burned, and this blurry scene of me standing, pants down, by the toilet, and my mom applying ointment, or sticking a suppository up me, or something.

Pinworms are night creatures. The only way you can check for them is to turn out all the lights and shine a flashlight right on the butt of the afflicted, and there they will be, scurrying away from the light. My mother was a registered nurse before she married my father, and she is always full of fun facts like this. When I cough she calmly asks, "Is your sputum green?" and every time I have a really rough digestive moment she yells from downstairs while doing the dishes, "Don't flush the toilet so I can look at your stool!"

Most kids get pinworms from playing in the dirt, my mom says. I ate dirt in the backyard all the time, pinching it between my cheek and gum like chewing tobacco, yee-haw. "Some poor children just live with it," Mom said, steering the station wagon through the Springfield drive-thru bank line.

This pinworm moment summons a series of kiddie epiphanies. The comprehension of suppositories, my first acknowledgment of function and form, my first bodily negotiation with a man-made object. The comprehension of the word "suppository," knowing it, understanding its meaning. But then I think it disintegrates in my head, like when something painful loses its bee-sting precision in memory. The comprehension of the word "pinworms," but that, too, mutates and I begin associating it with the perceptible earthworms caught on sidewalks in the rain, with the rough feel of cheap toilet paper, and even with pinwheels, spinning and sparking on a dark pole in the yard on the Fourth of July.

For a time I think that my parents are impostors and that they are sent to study or kill me, I'm not sure, and I think the bathroom mirror could be two-way, and my impostor parents could be spying on me. They study me in the bathroom, my every gerbilly move. I enter and leave looking straight into the mirror with a scowl, knowing someone is behind the glass and, defiant, I say, "Hi! I know you're there!" Then, when I am done humiliating myself in front of Them, I turn to leave and sharply bark, "Bye!" to the mirror again, marching out, going down to dinner, where my family, the puppets of the Abductors, sits. There they are: Mom, Dad, Mark, munching away, solids macerating in their swallowing puppet mouths. At my place is a lightly breaded pork chop with peas and a still, full glass of poisoned milk.

My family members are robot pawns of a whole secret system sent to observe me. Any moment I could be abducted and I will finally see the real people behind them—the suited, scientific officials studying me with their beady aspirin eyes behind two-way mirrors clutching guns and suppositories.

The Suppository Syndicate.

These SS men are behind all mirrors, lipless, observing me. I hear them calling my name when I am alone. They make the house move, they control the air, they live in the vents. They are everywhere: behind mirrors, in the turned-off TV, whirring in the blender and garage-door opener. Green vampire suppository men under all couches at night. Top-hatted, pill-shaped SS men at the end of the hall. Tiny carping suppository men that appear in my hand when I dream, squealing and hopping until I close my hand over them, cracking their suppository spines and squishing them like mud between my fingers.

My only escape from this two-floor Colonial Habitrail is my

room. Incredibly, despite their power, they cannot observe me in my room. With my door closed and the shades drawn, I baffle their panoptic plans. Sometimes I will be far, far away from this safe space, down in our rec room basement, and I will stop playing with my various toy piles and the house will be silent and evil, and I know They are making it that way. I know they are finally mobilizing their kidnap coup, and I have only a few seconds. Calmly, pretending nothing is wrong, I stop making the Cookie Monster rape the Rock 'em Sock 'em Robots and I place them down and, with a fake smile, saunter up the basement stairs, and then, at the top, I take a breath and sprint. I run past the kitchen before they wriggle through the backs of the cabinets, past the hallway closet before they creep through the parted winter coats, up the stairs before they unlatch the hatches and rise up out of them, down the carpeted hall before they bust through loose seams in the walls, and I get to my room, and I slam the door, and I sit there, listening, waiting for their sighs of disappointment, for the shuffles of their black shoes, for some sound, and they retreat back to their places, slinking, receding into the bathroom glass.

I'm at this corporate coffee bar on my thirty-minute lunch break. Spindly-legged stools and Portishead. I have an assignment temping at the American Liver Association all summer. Data entry in a cubicle in the middle of the office with walls too low to pick your nose, 8:15 A.M. to 5 P.M. Monday through Friday. Someone kill me, now.

There is this girl who sits in the next cubicle, Gina, who is fucking hilarious. She has a curvy body, really big boobs, a streaked dye job with copper tints, and this sneery mouth with lip liner and sepia lipstick smeared on it. She commutes from Ridgefield, New Jersey, but goes out every night, even more than me. She keeps Vivarin in her desk drawer. Just working there a week and already we have become fast friends. She tells me about her boyfriend and I tell her about how I just met John and his cute friend Eric at Bingo before I went home with Ian, that little shit who never called me.

Last weekend was Gay Pride, and I spent it on Ecstasy, howling, walking around in the gold boot-cut jeans I got at the Salvation Army for three dollars and a blue tank top, and John was wearing a terry-cloth beach shirt and army pants. He slipped his hand into mine when we were crushed in a crowd, and we watched the fireworks together, my arms around him. He's so cute and wide-bodied—a little taller than me—I am not really feeling hugely crazy about him, but maybe that is my problem. I'm impatient and grabby. I should let things flower and bloom into a corsage of love as if I am a serene, organic farmer, softly tilling his land, humming Shawn Colvin songs.

Today I told Gina about John, and she interrupted me. "Oh my God, it's like Costas that I'm seeing—he's Greek and I don't really like him but he's *so* goddamn *good* in bed, but he's so dumb he thought that Boston was a state! Ha ha ha ha! Can you believe it?" she said, and just then as I was laughing our boss Joyce walked up to us and reprimanded me.

"Okay now, Michael? I'm just going to mention that I feel you are not respecting the job requirements." My face burned with shame. Gina was not reprimanded.

When Joyce turned to Gina, she just sat up straight, picked up the phone, and said, "Yes, hello! American Liver Association! How can I be of help to you?" Joyce stopped hovering and walked into her office, and instantly my phone rang. *Hello?* "It's me!" *Gina?*

"Doiy. Me and Elise, the person who was you before you, used to do this all the time. It looks as if we're talking to people and doing work! So have you had sex with this guy?"

No!

Why not?

I don't know. We just didn't. I want to let things develop naturally. I think he's cute though. He's tall, and has curly hair and is kind of smart. He has this totally hot-as-shit friend Eric.

"Costas has a really hot friend too—this guy Stavros is so so so *hot*."

Uh-huh.

"Yeah, and one time I caught him looking at me on Costas's birthday. We went to Lord Stanley's, this really nice bar with all this dark wood around, and Stavros kept looking at me and buying me drinks."

Eric's really nice and has an amazing body. He's—

"So is Stavros! He has these huge arms—they're like as big as my waist! But I like Costas's body better because he's sort of well-proportioned."

She told me all about Costas—his body, his car, his cherished grandfather's cufflinks, weekly hair trim, big dick. I listened for a really long time, so I felt like it was okay to ask how to deal with John. "Just ask him out on a specific dating activity," Gina said abruptly, and then started telling me about the sex-slathered weekend she had in Atlantic City, even though Costas is an asshole and she hates him.

I asked Benny what to do last night and he did the same thing he always does. He sat with Stephen next to him and looked at me with this winning grin, and said, "That's too bad about John/Ian/Martin/fill-in-the-blank," and then stretched his hand out to Stephen's weirder, bonier hand and grinned some more, so that I comprehend that he is in a relationship and I am not. He's been going out with Stephen for about three months now.

Stephen sleeps over almost every night. He's a window dresser, but you cannot call him that. You have to call him a "visual merchandiser." He swoops into our place after draping forms (mannequins: also a bad word with Stephen) and starts cleaning every surface of our apartment with jittering vigor. One time he took a rag to our front door buzzer, clearing out the caked dust that had collected over the years in the plastic intercom. Another time I heard a squeaking noise, and, ready for a rat, walked into the bathroom, only to find Stephen scraping the lichenlike crud on the bathtub with a plastic spoon. "It's the only thing that works!" he said. He did that for two nights, and it made these awful screeching noises that made my teeth itch.

He becomes very angry and curt when he cleans. You have to leave him alone, because if you enter his radius of attention he would notice the dirtiness in you.

We've spent three months like this: Stephen comes to our place after work, cleans something, rearranges the furniture, and then slowly his eyes redden and he ebbs into sleep. Benny comes home and makes curried vegetables. We get ready for bed and then Benny wiggles his eyebrows and says, "Well, have a good night, Mike! I know we will." And I have to coo conspiringly. In the morning he comes out smiling the expensive-dinner smile of sex and says something like, "Did you hear us? Oh my God, how awful." Then Benny comments about how great Stephen's body is and how he is virtually odorless. But they are in love, so they have all the right in the world to oppress me, don't they? A single gay guy has about as much privilege as a smoker.

Gina at least likes to create energy in me—she made me call John right there in the office, and I did, and now John and I are going to see some Generation Y, gross-out, comedy-ensemble film tomorrow night.

Creamers

In my first home, in Virginia, sisters Debbie and Dana Creamer and I play together from ages 5 to 10, a designated age range like that of a Milton Bradley game. Near the end of our play partnership, before I move away, before Debbie and Dana start spotting in their terry-cloth shorts, the girls and I play Office, The Floor Is Made of Hot Lava, Sticks! (in which we tie scarves to dead branches and wave them around), and numerous horror-story dramatizations in the dark, scaring the shit out of each other.

The ghost stories are always the same, with frothy, climactic endings that lurch your stomach like a free-fall machine.

My brother Mark, though, can scare me with one simple sentence, at any time, day or night.

"You know what?" he says to me when I am brushing my teeth. *What?* I gurgle.

"Abraham Lincoln's head is floating in your closet."

He says this and walks down the hall to his room. *Shut up!* I say, too late, shakily, while the image of President Lincoln, yellowed and wrinkled, with his frowning mouth and daguerreotype eyes, begins to collect in my head. I spit out my toothpaste and walk slowly out of the bathroom and into my room. I turn out the lights and leap into bed and look at the opposite wall, panning the room, the striped soldier wallpaper, the desk with *Far-Out Facts* magazines and Magic 8-Ball and Etch A Sketch on it, to the closet, with its overpainted white slats and red knobs. I wait for it to move. I close my eyes and wait for it to move in darkness.

I lie on my back and bring my hands into prayer and ask God

(who is also, in a way, Lincoln's head) to please make it stay behind the door, where the head is perfectly welcome to float over the stack of board games and jigsaw puzzles.

Dear God, please keep Abraham Lincoln's head in the closet. Amen.

This happens for a long, long time, at least a year, every night. During the day I forget how tearful I am at night. My cold mattress of terror seems to slip my mind until I lie in it again, and then it slowly chills me.

Debbie and Dana and I also play Store, and I sell potions I make from very, very fine red dirt that I put in little acorn tops. Girls get to have very decorative, fairylike merchandise, with their little displays of pinecones and stones and dandelion heads on two-by-fours. I decide to become a girl for Store so I can have the license to own a persnickety girl store.

I ask to be called Nellie.

"What's for sale, Nellie?"

Well, let me tell you, miss! We have sassafras leaves, precious pebbles, and red dust!

I sell a lot of product one day and run home for dinner, very proud. I run with my arms up to my shoulders, and I am giggling. My brother sees me from his window and screams down to me, "Stop running like a girl!" and after just one single reprimand, I understand what he means. In one evolutionary movement I transform from girl to boy, bringing my arms down to my sides, curling my hands into fists—and I begin to run like a guy.

Debbie and Dana come over and we go down to the furnished basement and play Studio 54. We tape huge sheets of tinfoil over the bicentennial posters, flip the light switch on and off for that strobe effect, and stylishly sit in beanbag chairs on the shaggy rec room rug. Debbie is Liza, Dana is Bianca. I always have to be Halston. We'd lean over to one another and talk lightly in each other's ears and laugh and laugh and laugh—ah HAHAHA-HAHA!—then we'd crush up SweeTarts on a Holly Hobbie hand mirror and snort them.

Debbie and Dana have a little pond in their backyard that Mr. Creamer made. It is thick with algae. If we sit there and stare at it long enough, a salamander will appear, and it will wriggle and push through the muck, making the gooey sound of a body bending in a sticky substance.

The Creamers' house smells like sickness, as if every surface was just wiped clean of medical waste, leaving a thick, fake-floral scent. A house made of diaper aisles. Debbie and Dana have a brother who lives in a converted attached side shed. He wears a bib and has blue puffy eyes like a baby bird's. A generator chuffs humidified air into his white shed room and expels warm air out onto the brown grass below it. The brother spends most of the time inside, smashing together large Lego toys in the doorway of his shed room, wheezing. The Creamer girls ignore him and I do, too, except one time Mrs. Creamer brings him outside with a helmet on and a white jumpsuit that covers all his limbs. He ventilates through a crude mouth hole, his huge, strawberry, inside-out lips drooling. "Don't stare at him!" Debbie yells to me, and I look away.

The Creamers are Lutherans. Debbie and Dana have a huge book of Bible drawings, each page another vast pastel landscape with tiny robed peasants marveling at miracles. Everyone wears robes in pinks and salmons and light blues. The trees are fecund with plump green leaves. The ground looks gooey and orange like Circus Peanuts, and there is always a well-placed, strange, big gray rock somewhere for Jesus to sit upon.

Mr. Creamer is a tall man with long, long legs that are seventy-five percent thigh—they jiggle when he moves. He jogs constantly, because this is when America is in love with jogging, and he wears a red, white, and blue one-piece jogging suit. He jogs down the street and past the school, to the pool and back, his chest moving like loose, leathery breasts through his jog suit, which becomes see-through with sweat. Many times, especially after school, Mr. Creamer just stands in the open garage in his jogging suit. *Hi Mr. Creamer!* I say, and he waves back, adjusting the elastic of his pants.

"Hi, Mike!" he says. "Come on up here, come help me put together this birdhouse!" *I can't,* I say, which is true because it's dinnertime.

Once Mrs. Creamer stands outside our school and hands out little Jesus comic books like *You Are Naughty and You Are Going to Hell!* I bring one home and my mom rips it out of my hands. "Oh God! This is trash!" she says, and she throws it into the trash can. Her reaction is so allergic and fast and I do not believe her. For a rare moment, I doubt her taste. I sneak out to the garage and peer into the bin to find it. The little devil points at kids smoking and kissing and says they are going to Hell. Hell itself is badly drawn—there are stick figures with dots for eyes and little downturned comma mouths, crooked stalks in shaky flames.

• • •

Downstairs in their rec room, Debbie Creamer pulls up her shorts. "My dad says you can come to Bible school with us on Sunday." She gives me an invitation to Bible school. I bring home the rectangular card with a teddy bear in the corner. In bubbly letters it says, "We want you to come!" My mom looks at it pleasantly with wet dish-washing hands. She goes to the phone and calls Mrs. Creamer. "Lucy? Hi, this is Kay. Hi, how are you . . . ?" They talk on the phone and she gets off and she looks excited. My mother has never taken me to church, and I can't really comprehend why, only that she doesn't really seem to get along with the Creamer parents. Still, she will occasionally say, "I wish you knew more about religion," in a repentant voice. Now, on the phone, she seems perked up. Here is a perfect opportunity for a quick, free Bible brushup for me. All her guilt, all the stubborn grease of worry and concern that she may be accidentally raising me as a hippie, is lifted away. Her face is alive, her grin is real.

On Sunday, the Creamers and I pile into their large RV, and Debbie and Dana and I play magnet Parcheesi on the oval table in the rear. Their brother sits in a bunk by the bathroom, wheezing every ten seconds, and right when you have forgotten about his last watery gasp, he wheezes again. Mrs. Creamer, plugged into the front padded pas-senger seat, turns her head and looks at him with her big sleep-deprived eyes, and lolls her head back around to the road.

The minister at the Bible school is well liked by everyone and a hero to all children. "Don't stare at his hand. He lost three fingers saving a puppy from the train tracks, so don't stare at it," Debbie snaps as we walk up to him. All the kids gather around him and he enfolds them in his long arms in a spontaneous, saintly tableau. He has on a red-and-blue-checked lumberjack shirt. I look at his hand, and his thumb and index and ring fingers are pudgy stumps that move like chopped schnauzer tails.

We file into his small chapel and sit in his pews. It reminds me of the school cafeteria—if it were suddenly made sacred—with the overabundance of plastic chairs stacked in the aisles, the brown linoleum floors, the gummy storm windows locked with levers. The minister welcomes us. He is filled with joy to see us. "Guess who else is filled with joy? It's Jesus," he says. "He is so happy to see you are here," he says, and I feel Jesus sweeping around our bodies in his pastel pink robe, with his smooth brown hair and beard, smiling. Jesus is among us.

The whole day is mega-booked with Bible. We sing in a chorus, we play Jesus games, we get Jesus workbooks, we watch a filmstrip about Creation. We rush around from room to room like a Disney World ride, as if there is another tour of kids right behind us, so I become completely dependent on the Lutherans to get me around the cinder block maze of the church and its annexes.

We quickly pass by the cafeteria, and I see that some volunteer mothers are setting up a little snack table for us. I frantically scan the spread as we dash past the doorway to Bible class. In Bible class we learn all sorts of things, but they immediately move out of my mind because I am just thinking about Ronald McDonald fruit punch and those delicious cookies some mother made—frosting spackled between two graham crackers. I love those cookies. They always taste woody and finely aged.

After snacks the minister disappears. The cafeteria doors open and they lead us into the sun. Mr. Creamer is standing outside, leaning on the passenger door of the RV, the engine running, the blue brother rocking himself in the window. Engines are always whirring and huffing when he is around, I observe. We walk closer. I also observe that Mr. Creamer looks very annoyed that he has to keep driving us around, and for a few seconds I can comprehend the weariness of adults.

Mr. Creamer is normally very nice and his cheer is everlasting. He dares us to do things. "Hey, Mike, I dare you to try to reach that branch! I dare you to run and dive through my legs!" We play in his pile of cut grass, and he comes out with Freez-Pops when we jump through his hissing sprinklers. On Saturdays he makes Kraft Macaroni & Cheese and calls us in, and we each have a place set up for us with the napkin folded in triangles and Fritos sprinkled on the side of the bright orange glutinous mass of macaroni. We squish through it and it makes a smacky noise that reminds me of salamanders in mud.

Mr. Creamer hovers around us for a while and then slips out to the garage. He goes and plays with tools in the garage, sometimes whistling—in his weenie outfit, moving wrenches around, turning on the table saw, arranging bolts and nuts into their clacky plastic shelves.

I never go into his garage. Not because I don't want to, but because I always feel like I should get home and do my homework. I am not curious.

One time I am over at the Creamers' to find Debbie and Dana, and Mr. Creamer says, "Hi, Mike, no, Debbie and Dana are at gymnastics. Why don't you go in the backyard and wait for them?"

I sit in the backyard and Mr. Creamer closes the sliding glass door behind me and I have my back to him behind the window. It is a very bright, cloudless day, and the cicadas are clicking in intervals. When I turn around, Mr. Creamer is just standing there, his figure obscured in the shadowed gloom of the family room.

The Creamer girls finally come home and we all go to the backyard and we are playing Store and I am Nellie, and Debbie says very sternly, "Nellie, Nellie, come here." She grabs my hand and takes me to the corner craw of their house. "Let's show each other our parts," she says, and she pulls down my pants and looks at my wiener. She pulls down her pants and I see her vagina. She spreads it open and it is pink and I think of being in the cold, caged shopping-cart seat when my mom takes me shopping and pushes me past rows of meat in the huge refrigerated supermarket.

"I'm going to peeeeeeeeee!" Debbie squeals, and then it gurgles out and she stands there hopping and spreading out her fingers. She screams and screams and then, inside the sound of the screams, I hear a larger, low, gravelly second voice. "Debbie," it says. "Debbie," it says, and then I smell a tobacco-tinted breath, and with that breath comes an arm that reaches behind me and grabs my shoulder, and turns me toward its attached face.

Mr. Creamer bends in very close to me, his ashtray mouth full of corncob teeth. "Michael . . . I don't want you ever, ever doing that again, do you understand?"

I nod. *Yes.*

7 wear the gas-station-attendant pants and that ski sweater again because it has John's smell of wallet interiors and one cigarette. My brother used to wear it on our family ski trips. I don't remember what I wore on those trips except for my red snow pants, because I would always have to go to the bathroom when we were on the slopes and I looked down at them often while I made them warm.

I slept with John last night. We never got to the movie theater. We rented *Leaving Las Vegas* and didn't watch it—just reenacted it by drinking two forty-ounce malt liquors in Tompkins Square Park. I asked how Eric was doing and John's eyes flared. We talked about Eric for a while—I could tell John has a huge, juicy crush on him that he has been trying to dehydrate into the smaller, prune-size emotion of fellowship. He always brings him into the conversation: "Eric? Oh, Eric's cool. He's doing great. Eric's doing great. He and George had their year anniversary and it's great, I guess." He stopped there, but his mouth seemed on the edge of enunciating "But Eric deserves better." He kept mentioning Eric's name in this strange boldfaced way. "**Eric** just bought the new Saint Etienne album and really likes it," or "One time I was hanging out with **Eric** and I was telling **Eric** how tired I was."

I sat there and nodded while he spoke. "That's funny. Because **Eric** says 'Right' a lot, like you do."

Really?

"Yeah. **Eric** says it's sort of this dead-air filler. You both do it a lot."

Right.

"See?"

Ha.

I didn't really care that John was trying to reanimate me as a Frankenstein Eric. I didn't care at all, because I was already far away, falling for Eric myself. We are so much alike, I thought, Eric and I. We talk the same way. As John talked, I fantasized about Eric and me sitting in the grass, our knees brushing, and our clipped "Right"s filling the air, making perfect sense to each other.

I asked John back to my place. We lay in bed after wiping up our seed with my Cancún beach towel. After wiping up Eric with my Cancún beach towel.

3:30 P.M. at work. My head has started nodding in palsied rolls and I become a drooling gum ball of exhaustion. I went to the corporate coffee bar to sit for thirty minutes and make the day end. A woman walked in, helped by her friend, a man of the same age, fifty to sixty. She had a very bad involuntary Katharine Hepburn head shake and was blind. He read to her the overly stylized coffee menu. "Pumpkin blend, cappuccino, mochaccino, mocha java, hazelnut, African jungle nut," and she broke in, sweetly requesting "Hazelnut," her head joggling.

Her friend said, "Don't you want to hear the rest?"

"No, no thank you," she said. "Hazelnut sounds wonderful." He helped her reach for the cup and eased her around to the door; she shuffled forward in a long purple jacket with the sleeves rolled up, shoes matched in purple—someone who thinks positively and would say, "I just start every day with a smile!" She seemed so satisfied when she placed her order. Or at least she put on a good show of satisfaction.

I am like her, grinning through everything. I noticed after a night with John that my face hurt. Ever since I graduated from college I have this behavior around guys that I can't seem to shake—a pleasant, smiling giddiness. I don't remember exactly when I got that emergency smile, but now I can't shake it. This grin is a tight cover over anything too expressive or sudden that might erupt in me. Uncontrollable emotions do not shoot out of my face—they bubble and simmer, like a casserole in a conventional oven, a fuming fumarole, a little smoky volcano.

Hi, I'm Mike, hi, I am fine! This is fine! No, it's fine you blew me off! No, it's fine I called you six times and you never called me back! No, it's fine you are paying me only ten dollars an hour with no benefits! I'll be your temp! Fine!

Other people are allowed to scowl. Gina will come in every morning, her knee-length navy skirt stretched tightly over the bell of her hips, her hair meticulously held in place by tortoiseshell combs, her face screwed up into a scribble. "I am not a morning person," she says, and then sits at her desk with her maple nut scone, calls her mother, and yells at her for offering to darn her snagged sweaters: "You'll just put dorky patches all over them, Mother, no!" I can't believe what she gets away with. She even glares when Joyce tells her to refill the copier or that she misspelled "cirrhosis" in *LWQ* (the *Liver Wellness Quarterly*). Her face stays scowled until four, when she'll call her friends and plan to meet them at Taco Tuesdays or Schnapps Shots Night. She'll laugh loudly and fill up the office with "No! Really? Get out!" and neither Joyce nor anyone else will tell her to be quiet, because we are all so grateful for a break from her crabby daytime face. Gina lets everything out in front of everyone. I feel like I pollute when I show too much mood, so I smile, even when I ache inside.

Mom does that, too. Me, my mother, the blind woman, smiling in default. My mom in her quilted blue velour zip-up bathrobe, sweetly smiling, getting along with everyone, forgetfully appeasing difficult moments at department store counters and Giant supermarket checkout lines with the anesthetic of grinning. Like that time I was twelve and we went to Utah to go skiing and my dad made Mark and me get up at 6 A.M. so that we could be on the slopes by 7 A.M. on the dot—a strange middle-class simulation of a farm family hoeing the fields in the mornin'. Every day that week we would ski until our knee joints hurt and I would have to endure Mark telling me I ski like a girl, flicking me on the head, and Dad giving me constant pointers on how to lean forward and plant my poles because I probably swished my hips around too much. Then we would go back to the condo and my mom would be at the stove, pretty and fresh, calmly making spaghetti, and I would fall into the sofa. She would rest her cool, understanding hand on my forehead, I would fall alseep, and then it would start all over again.

Then one morning the Bangles were going to be on the *Today* show. I loved the Bangles. (It was when *Different Light* came out, when their hair was ratty and up in crocodile clips, but before "Walk Like an Egyptian," their stupidest single, catapulted them into larger, less interesting fame.) We were eating breakfast in our little wood-paneled and skylight-slatted ski chalet, and Dad made us hurry up and grab our skis right at the commercial break before the Bangles were going to be on, and I lingered a little, waiting, holding my skis, goggles on my head, until Dad yelled from down-stairs, outside the pine A-frame condo, "MIKE!! Hurry up!" and I had to go just as the Bangles were being introduced by Bryant Gumbel. I tried to look unfazed about it, but my face slowly red-dened. Then Mom looked at me, put down the Tupperware she was drying, and came over to me with her hands in her bathrobe's patchy yellow front pockets. My mom, who had an enviable day of shopping for Hopi Indian jewelry and fudge ahead of her, who must have known I was gay, was full of sympathy and said, "I'm sorry you can't watch the Bangles, I know how you like them. . . . I'll watch them for you and tell you what they say, okay?" And my thirteen-, fourteen-, oh God maybe even fifteen-year-old mouth got all tear-filled and I just grinned and said *That's okay* . . . and I left.

The uncomfortably scary thing is that John reminded me of my mother this morning. We woke up and went to Prana, that plain organic food store on First Avenue, and I was buying my stupid food for my awful job, describing strangely detailed parts of my past, like being carsick in Las Vegas, my childhood ear infections, and my senior thesis in college, because I couldn't believe that John had made it this far into the next day with me. I dropped the 79-cent cup of Brown Cow Groovy Guava Yogurt and it plopped on the ground, cracking its plastic side and leaking cultured ooze. I picked it up and I was suddenly overcome with the idea that it would be bad to admit I dropped it, so when we went up to the reg-ister I just, weirdly, lied, and said, *I found this on the floor,* and then just stared blankly as the hemp-dressed cashier girl asked Leela, the other cashier, if she wanted it because it is an organic food store and we are all supposed to feel horrible if anything goes to waste. John and I had to stand there, in a painful lingering lie, waiting for them to just fucking throw the goddamn tub away, and finally we were able to slip out while all the store people and customers peered at us because they knew that I was lying. I was thinking as we left that John stood by me like Nixon's Haldeman, calmly efficient, and we walked toward the subway and I felt so much for him, and I wanted to kiss him so much, and we walked to the corner of First and 1st where we were going to part, and I looked at him and the block's storefronts eased by his head and he grinned that grin, that blanketing lie of a grin, and I bet we will not talk again.

Dancer Guys

Annie comes. All the girls from the neighborhood, the Creamers among them, fill their little lungs with *Annie*-mania. Every female child auditions for the role of Little Orphan Annie in her red dress and curly red wig. In the TV ads, Annie screeches to an audience, blinded by stage lights. On quiet summer nights when houses are filtered with screens, I can hear Debbie and Dana's girl-child wails drifting through the paved streets of our suburb as they vie to be the next little orphan. No one really cares a smidge when you're in an orphanage—it's a hard-knock life.

Satisfied with being Nellie, I interestingly have no desire to portray this female role. In fact, Annie kind of scares me. Her hair looks like a wig, yet it also looks real and cemented to her head. Her dress is so bright and flawless; she is clean and professional and has never known doubt. "I am a child!" she seems to say through her grin, strangely androgynous like Peter Pan. She looks like she hides something adult under her clothes, something secretive, something she shows no one. Whatever it is that Annie and Peter Pan have between their happy little legs, you know it is prematurely hairy and that it smells.

It is a strange time because Debbie and Dana have become consumed with making it in showbiz. Their eyes fill with ambition and they never stop smiling. They practice their shaky loud vibrato voices everywhere, especially when we walk home from school. We pass Katawchuk Creek: "We are crossing the rivahhh!" Debbie sings. We walk up Heandy Hill Road: "We're gonna make it after all!" Dana wails. "Ev'rything has its place and ev'rything is coming up roses!"

Would you please shut up? I say.

"No!" they sing.

God, just shut up! I say.

"You can never stop the power of song!" they scream over the rush-hour traffic. They are on either side of me singing in high, high pitches, and it makes my stomach feel sour and my head hurt.

My mom wipes the counter with a damp rag and says for me to drink a glass of water. It was one of her quicker decisions, because there has been a spate of newscasts on local television about child migraines. We go to a doctor who wears a tie with Bugs Bunny on it and he sticks his cold ear otoscope in my ear and it feels so good. Nothing is wrong.

• • •

It is also the height of the "I♥NY" campaign and on TV they show all these overexuberant Broadway weirdos dancing around a fake New York street, and that's what I believe: New York is a colossal big red heart with the Statue of Liberty on one of the lobes and a bunch of faggy guys in sequins with bubble butts like boobs doing Bob Fosse jazz-hand routines.

"I♥NY! I♥NY!"

They are like nothing I have ever seen before, these guys. I'm not talking about chesty, wedge-haired soap opera guys or bright-eyed, thin-wristed musical men with their warbling voices and rag-time clothes. I mean dancer men. Flaggy, faggy dancer men who are hot and wear headbands and/or rainbow flamenco sleeves, and I can tell they have naughty needs, and that those naughty needs veer very near to my own naughty needs.

Dancer men are sex. I haven't had sex education in school yet, but I can't wait because I know they must have a whole workbook on these guys. They gyre around and melt to the floor and explode out of dry ice in the amazing shimmering colors of cars or guitars. You always see them unified, earnest, behind some big sensation like Cher, thrashing their lubricated arms around as if they were the flittering reflections off her sequined gown, or pulling up their satin jumpsuits and wriggling their genitals into position before taking their places behind Dionne Warwick for the *Solid Gold* Top 10 Countdown.

I stare at those dancer men with needful eyes, their needful eyes matching mine. Those dancer men make me feel very delicate behind my ribs. I suppose one reason I'm not hopping on the *Annie* train is that I am obsessed with them.

I want to be one and practice with towels. I swoop them around and splay them out in fan-shaped displays. I smear Vaseline on my lips and it looks like lip gloss. I glide to the floor and climb out of invisible cages and swirling smoke like a cartoon blue feline.

Dancer men frighten me with their leotard liberty. They seem so brave and unashamed. I am too afraid to heave out all my longings like that—to be an effeminate pixie freak with huge, overwrought emotions. I want to join a troupe or get involved in the Afterschool Kids Chorus musical theater or Dance Alive!, but I have an older brother who monitors my every effeminate gesture and I don't have the guts to stand up for myself, so I just play soccer instead, running like a boy.

I take trombone because I really want to play flute but the flute is a feminine instrument. No one else ever tells me that there are feminine and masculine instruments, no one ever yells at me that the flute is a sissy stick. . . . I can just sense this traveling through the stuffy elementary school air.

I sit in my room practicing arpeggios and the chromatic scale, yanking the trombone slide, lubed up with Pond's Cold Cream, up and down, up and down. I am not good. My lessons are with Mr. Reer in a tiny room at school with white corkboard walls. We sit side by side in small chairs made for lower grades. Mr. Reer is young and hidden-handsome. He wears thick black glasses and has a skinny boy-body he drowns under big, ironed, button-down beige shirts. He is having a love affair with this instrument and always tries to bring me along on his magic journey into the wonderful, elastic, versatile world of the trombone: "The trombone was invented by blah-blah to exactly re-create the human voice," he says. "The trombone is considered an indispensable instrument in every symphonic blah-blah band," he says. He keeps singing to me before all the chipper, sunny sonatas he makes me play—"Ta ta ta teee TEEE TEEE ta ta!" And when I play, he earnestly says, "Open your throat, Mike! You need fuller sound!" I ask him what he means exactly. "Just let your throat open when you play. Just open your throat." I try to open my throat, but I really have no idea how to open one. I sit up tight-butted and hold my arm out from my side gracefully, like a dancer.

Grace Jones is a guest on *American Bandstand,* and she has these two backup dancers, one blond, one black-haired, in sheer space suits. I hungrily study the screen for the backup dancers. I don't even look at Grace Jones. She is just an angular, annoying column in my way. They dance on the edges of the TV screen behind her, but you can see only parts of them: half a torso, an arm, a thigh, and sometimes their determined, proud, smooth faces adorned with headbands and dramatic slashes of purple blush. Near the end of the song, they show the black-haired dancer crouching, looking up at her. Then his huge, clear eyes focus on me, and his irises and eyes and eyelids and mouth and nose and body rush into me and I try very hard to reach my mind into that studio he stands in. I've got big, *BIG* dreams, he says to me; I am burning with dreams and I want you with me, he says.

"Look at that fairy," my brother says behind me, and I have a battery surge inside.

very day is the same. We all come in to the bright light of American Liver—our computers humming, our copiers buzzing, electricity already coursing through the walls, holding Starbucks bags with muffins and grandes. We deeply breathe in the thick, reconstituted staff air. We take off our little foam-stained coffee lids and someone says, "Oh my God, I need some caffeine! I need my coffee fix! I need my sugar fix!" Someone says they didn't get enough sleep last night, someone counts down the days to our three-day weekend in September, someone says, "Mike, the copier's jammed again!" someone says, "Did you see *Seinfeld*? It was so funny! Ha-ha! Ha-ha! Ha-ha!" I've been here six weeks, 8:15 A.M. to 5 P.M., and I already think I have seen Joyce and Gina and the rest of the Liver gang more than I have seen my father my entire life.

I feel a bit different this week because Joyce has gone on vacation. Gina and I have been doing nothing except talking on the phone and writing letters. Joyce went to Disney World with her kids, but Gina and I think she's a lesbian, the last closeted lesbian in this city, with her passable dark suits and shoulder pads and Madeleine Albright scarf accents. Her corner office is dark. Sometimes I go in there, use her fancy pens, and feel a small sensation of rebellion.

Gina and I went out last night after work to have multicolored daiquiris. We went to the Big Apple Eatery, this "I♥NY" theme restaurant with a huge wall of taxi memorabilia and barrels of frozen drinks. Gina arranged for this gay guy Jerald to meet us there. "He's so, so great! He's so nice and just like you!" she said, and just as I met him and said hi he snapped his fingers above his head because suddenly "Supermodel" by RuPaul came on. He swiveled his neck around and said, "Girl, they turn it out here! Furreal! Work!" Then he seriously started vogueing in the bar, all these middle-management men in their cheap suits glaring at him. When "I Will Survive" played, Jerald sang along really loudly, screeching the falsetto part. He is a good voguer, though.

I left sort of early, and walked east toward my apartment. Everything was closing, tired assistant managers ratcheting down the gates of storefronts, Sixth Avenue clogged with taxis and wealthier commuters in very clean Jeeps with tinted windows. I waited under dirty scaffolding for a Walk signal with a bloated, drunk investment banker and an old, insane woman in too many sweaters ranting about how the fruit is too ripe, the fruit is too ripe. Behind her bottles of cleaners glared out of the Rite Aid window. It's such a sad Taco Tuesday to me.

There is nothing that creates a faster feeling of sadness than when someone sets you up with a person who is brilliantly incompatible. Jerald vogued and I felt lumpy, unlucky, and anointed with doom. Out there, in the vast earth full of loud, wrong people, is the one person whom I should be with. He leans against the fake mahogany of some distant theme bar, somewhere in Mexico City or Sydney or Reykjavík, standing with a Wild-n-Fruity daiquiri in his hand, filled with doom, too, and we will never meet.

But Jerald is much more truthful to himself than wacky me in my secondhand clothes. He is also more truthful than those "straight-acting" gay guys in boots and baseball hats that you see across the Wonder Bar, holding their beers like blacksmiths and posing like lumberjacks until Madonna flashes onto the video monitor and suddenly all of them squeal and start lip-synching. Jerald is one of those guys who uses the word "diva" a lot, but I had the same chiffony longings as Jerald did when I was a child. I guess so does every other gay guy in America, and we all aren't as brave as Jerald. I just warped and conditioned those longings into whatever bizarre hybrid of masculinity I exhibit. I think I am being honest, but maybe I am denying a more true inner drag persona and the fact that Jerald grosses me out is just an internal-femme-phobia. I know that this all sounds so college-gender-studies-department.

I kept walking and looking through the grates of closed storefronts, thinking Jerald is so much more authentic than me and that it's all my fault I don't like him. I am another freak in the world, diverting my desires. Like John, who is in love with Eric and has to dumb down his emotions and just be friends with him. And that is why he can't call me, because he is too involved already. Eric doesn't divert anything. His beauty is as simple as a geometric shape and he is in a relationship. It's so easy for people who are clearly gorgeous—perfect, pretty polygons. Eric and his boyfriend, or those model couples like Esther Cañadas and Mark Vanderloo who frown their padded pillow lips when they get in fights in front of restaurants and quickly make up, clutching each other in floppy cashmere V-neck sweaters. I can't believe I am thinking so much about Eric, and I have said a total of three sentences to him, and why is everything so out of balance—why can't I like the correct guy? I walked east and stopped to look at the chrome bell of an Urban Outfitters' display case to see if I didn't look too upset, yet still attractively despondent enough to go out. Then I went to the Wonder Bar with Benny and we got pretty drunk, and then I met Rod and went home with him.

At work today Gina came in and said she got really really drunk with Jerald and went home and slept for thirty minutes. "You didn't like Jerald, did you?" she said. Before I could answer she ran to the bathroom and puked because she was so hungover. She couldn't do anything but hold her forehead in her hands the rest of the day, so I was able to tell her all about Rod without her interrupting me.

Rod made me wait down on the street because he didn't have his key. He had to jump up onto the fire escape of his building and scale the black metalwork to the sixth floor, break into his own apartment through the window, and then come back down to get me. I've met Rod twice in the past and he's worn the same pants both times—huge extra-wide pants that come down stiffly in columns. Each time I meet him I pretend I haven't met him, because he doesn't remember meeting me because we are being casual, and casual means you are waterproof and no one's face soaks into you.

He looked like a costume of a storybook tree in those pants. Benny calls the pants "chicken-dancer pants" because that's what those speedy techno kids look like when they dance—dancing chickens.

Rod has embraced the stylings of drum-'n'-bass electronic music—this spacey, shiny sort of look—with his bowl-shaped haircut tapering into Hasidic curls at the temples and Gore-Tex wardrobe and absolute statements about pop music, like "I don't listen to anything but instrumental music—all other music seems a-*poc*-ryphal." It's five in the morning and the rats scurry through the trash behind me. Rod came through the door and opened it for me.

Rats have damaged tails, I said.

"What?"

Nothing, I said, but I always felt that those scaly tails of rats look like chapped skin in need of moisturizing. If you could just smooth a little Wondra on them. I watched them tumble over one another and I said, *Hello.* I said to Rod, *There are a lot of rats here on Ludlow Street, many more than at my place above Houston on Sixth Street.* I thought it would be an efficient way to inject the location of where I live.

"Love rats."

Oh God, you're not some sort of PETA animal fanatic, are you? I said.

"Totally," he said, jumping the steps three at a time. "You shouldn't kill anything. We are all connected."

I walked up the steps conservatively, because I got the sense I was supposed to seem shocked and shy around him, and I heard him get to his floor while I passed dirty doors and two landings, each one smelling like an eggs Benedict mixture of pee and mayonnaise.

He lives in one oblong room, the shower planted in the kitchen like an appliance. To the left, a curtain partially hid a deep closet-like space, piled with wood scraps, plastic tubing, Christmas lights, corrugated cardboard, and, below, a running toilet. *That's a waste of water,* I said, and he ignored me. To the right, past the kitchen, piles of books and magazines lined the lower part of the walls the same way Grandpa Joe stacked his *National Geographics* in his bomb shelter. Tacked above the mess are small bits of paper with spontaneous-looking scribbles on them. I could make out only a few of the words, like "imaging the apparatus" or "lack autonomy." They were his only decoration. I thought of how he may be an insane pack-rat person who collects balls of fiber and thinks a computer in Belgium is tattooing bar codes on people's foreheads. I thought maybe later he'd strangle me. "Totally *go* for it!!" Benny had said at the Wonder Bar.

I toured the apartment, darting my head around at dramatic angles, as if I were introducing my character to the audience in a one-act play.

"What are you doing?"

I'm pretending I'm in a one-act play, and this is the first scene, so it's very important I establish my foreignness to the space, I said.

"Oh, aren't you the ironic one?" he said, which made me flush again. "Does this mean you'll never say anything real all night?"

That comment immediately seeded the notion within me that I was lying, and I cannot say "I'm not lying" without smiling and looking like I am lying. He was smart and confusing me and I became more attracted to him. He plopped down into a beanbag chair. Ten well-sculpted little spaceships were on the floor at his feet, made of bluish clear plastic, a central orb with red wires ringing them. I could make out tiny motors deep inside.

So, when are you going to go to Mars? I asked, sitting below him, leaning on the beanbag. He started running his fingers through my hair, softly, as if he were appraising a doll head, but he stopped suddenly when I asked this.

"How did you know I wanted to go to Mars? I love Mars! Do you know how cool that planet is? And how close we are technologically to actually be able to inhabit it? The landscape of Mars is practically like the desert in the Southwest—pretty much like Las Vegas."

We started talking at the Wonder Bar because we were both looking at a framed poster of Caesars Palace hanging on the wall. I once lived in Las Vegas. I was about to tell this to Rod.

"Hey! Wanna see something so horrible?" Rod jumped up and ran to a pile of magazines that would have looked like someone's recycling if we were outside. He pulled out one—I couldn't catch the name of it, but I gathered it was some sort of science digest for environmentally concerned readers. He flipped for a while and turned to a page about salamanders.

"Amphibians are dying. All of them everywhere, and nobody really knows why."

But you do, right? He slightly ignored my sniping.

"Well, some people, cool people, believe it's because of pollution. Amphibians live in the interface—the top of the water and the wet ground. They are a key transitional organism. And if they are dying it means a whole lot about our ecosystem. The sick thing is that scientists have discovered that all the bleaches and detergents we carelessly dump into the waterways have an element within them that mimics estrogen. So you have these freaky mutations: salamanders with doubled ovaries or these weird, useless tripled genitals."

I hate salamanders! I said. *I used to go play with them and then go in and eat Kraft Macaroni and Cheese and it was the same sound!* I said. Rod barely responded. *I guess you believe people are also feeling the effects,* I said. Rod pressed down his curls with his palm. While he talked, I slipped next to him in the beanbag chair.

"Oh my God, yes. Look at any talk show. At least once a week there will be some show about some couple that can't have kids, because his sperm count was feeble or she was barren, and they bring on some doctor to talk about the latest advances in artificial insemination. Some scientists have found whole species of birds whose behavior has completely changed. Male birds are so uninterested in sex that female birds have had to nest with each other to compensate for the males' frigidity."

I scanned myself for something to say. I came up with this: *What about people and dating and stuff? Maybe, like, like people are becoming more frigid because of the poisonous ecosystems. Maybe, because of shampoo and dishwashing liquid and Woolite, people are just becoming more and more assholey or something and can't seem to get together and date properly.* I got up and stretched onto his mattress like an earthworm. His mattress was thin and uncomfortable. *I have this unexplainable lump in my left breast. Maybe that is a big ball of Fab, collecting in my breast and mutating.*

He came over and plopped on top of me, knocking the air out of me a little. When I was in college and I read *The Origin of Species,* I thought for a while that maybe homosexuality was some sort of depopulating mutation within humans, a built-in, naturally selected deterrent to heterosexual sex. I mentioned this theory to Rod.

"It's totally plausible," he said, and I figured out right then that his face is perfectly two-dimensional. His nose cut his face into two reliefs; his eyes set out far apart from each other on two planes, bisected like insects or fish. His face came to me, and I expected it to divide and pass by either side of my head because it is so symmetrical, a smooth hallway.

He is one of the strangest-looking people I've ever seen. So, so cute, but strange—almost alien, or like some royal line of blue-bloods who, after hundreds and hundreds of years of intermarriage, live with pronounced features. Rod stood up at the edge of the mattress, bending down from this diving-board position toward me. He is very lean and white and has all his clothes off and hovers there and I push my face into his pelvis.

Benny and I sat at Paradise Muffin Company last Monday. I had a mushroom "warmie"—they stuff dough full of pesto and mush-rooms and brown it into a tit shape and place it under an amber lamp so it is constantly warm. Benny had a fudge bundt. I cannot stop thinking about Benny's fudge bundt while Rod and I have sex. "The way I see it, we have a few years left," Benny said. "We are twenty-seven and we have until thirty-five and then we will have to become interested in fetishes and tit clamps." Andrea, Benny's boss, came in this afternoon with a guy—they work in her apart-ment. Andrea's forty-five and is a dominatrix. Benny is her recep-tionist and does her bookkeeping. "If you find love hang on to it," she said to Benny once, "or you will be like me." "And then she went in her bedroom with the guy and went to work." Benny said, "All I could hear were clinking sounds. Little hooks clinking into other hooks, and chainlinks tinkling. Clink! Clink! Clink! Clink! Clink!" Benny kept saying, "Clink! Clink!" *Shut up, that is so scary,* I said, but he just kept on saying it: "Clink, clink, clink."

Rod came, then I came, then we went to sleep for a few hours, and we curled around each other on the mattress.

"Have you heard of Manuel De Landa?" I shrugged. "He pretty

much believes things are controlled by density. Density, density, density."

I sat there naked. This was very much like a new kind of pornographic educational cable show. *Mr. Gay Wizard.*

"Like, if you pour water down a slide, it flows evenly, right? Until you add more and more water and soon rivulets and little whirlpools form." He appropriately whirled his arms, the muscles working visibly under his thin, thin skin.

"The turbulent flow possesses an extremely intricate molecular organization. That's density—a natural process of self-organization, order spontaneously emerging out of deep, massive chaos. Now, De Landa is trying to apply that self-organizing theory to inert, nonorganic material like machinery, man-made things."

Rod talked in sudden articulate spurts, leaving me small windows to try either to ask questions or to find some way to comment and look smart. I tried very hard to stay on my toes, even though I was dead tired. But Rod is the first guy I have made out with in a long time who talks more than me. Usually, on any other person's flaky, dirty mattress it would be me spouting out a theory, trying to keep away the dead air, but Rod is very talkative.

So, what does he have to say about the turbulence of our stupid lives? Anything? I asked Rod, still slightly drunk, and drunk with fatigue, and kind of happy with my delivery.

"Actually, he doesn't even think our lives are as interesting as the things we've created, like computers and tanks and missiles. He believes the artificial intelligence created in warfare is completely playing out these natural self-organizing principles."

God, that is so creepy, I said. We sat there for a while, silent. I was only thinking about how good he looks after sex, with his hair rubbed free from its gel, his heavy lids even heavier, his cliff-bridge nose, and I thought about whether or not I seemed stupid to him, and I tried to focus back in on what he was saying.

"And there's lots of stuff written about the behavioral impact of crowding and everything—like about the crammed Japanese population—but who cares about us, when our machines have already gone ahead and detached themselves from our control and are now self-organizing?"

Right, I said. The one thing I was trying to imagine was my little computer game Merlin with its self-organizing mind. *Remember Merlin?* I ask Rod, and he shakes his head no. *It was this little plastic red phone-shaped toy with a keypad that played six different games.*

It was the most convincing game I have ever had in my life. It was one in a generation of little futurismo space toys that were the capitalist products of a seventies abstract aesthetic: Simon, Pong, Galactic Man. The High finally merged with the Low and made Merlin. *The games were . . . It's really hard to remember. Oh God! I can't remember! Tic-Tac-Toe was the first. Then Memory, which was a rip-off of Simon, then Roulette Roulette Roulette! It was Roulette! Which I never played. Then . . . Name That Tune, and then this musical composition program where you could play your own songs, and then this Flash Zap game.* Oh God, I thought there was so much potential in that thing. You never got bored with it, not because the games were interesting, but because you had the option to switch from one game to the next. *What a fool I was for Merlin! I was Merlin's slave! It had enmeshed me in its greedy lust for higher evolution, and now look at it! I enabled Merlin to become the Internet!*

I went on like this for a while. I thought it was brilliant, but Rod was silent until I mentioned outer space in my tirade. He lifted his lean arms. Rod talked wildly about Las Vegas as the city of the new millennium.

"When we build our space stations on Mars, they won't be light and small and white and compact and curvy like everybody thinks. They will be like the big casinos—huge and tall and lit and electric and rotating."

He told me, his slitty blue eyes glassing over, that the Luxor, the Egyptian pyramid hotel-casino, has a light shooting out of the top of it that is the strongest light in the world and that it will be the first thing that aliens will see when they land. They will land in Las Vegas. He went on and on about how amazing Las Vegas is, how it's the city of the future because it's entirely built for leisure and entertainment. I nodded and listened to him and gave him looks of agreement but I barely saw the casinos when I lived there. It's against the law for minors even to watch gambling take place, so I was always having to walk quickly past the big game rooms in the hotels. Even the slot machines in the supermarkets were off-limits. Bored guards would shoo me away if I came near them. "Don't stare at them!" they would yell to me, and I looked away.

I wanted to tell him I actually did care about crowds. Not animals. Not artificial life. I don't care about anything but people. I don't care about fluid or molecules or little, wet, earnest-eyed salamanders. All I want to hear about is who likes who, what embarrassing thing happened to whatever friend of mine, which stars are doing drugs or are gay. Just people. People people people. I was about to let this slip out when a mouse scrambled up onto the comforter, scurried around in a circle, and then darted off into a dark crack between books.

"Oh, they always do that in the morning," Rod said.

God, that is so creepy, I said. We sat there for a while, silent.

Within the next half hour we began to detach. We peppered our conversations with "I'm so tired," "What time is it?" and "I've got so much work to do." The glow of early morning reminded us that we both had very well organized, tight schedules that included a volatile, fragile female friend who would go crazy if we were late to meet her. We exchanged numbers, and he kissed me goodbye with animation. I went home at 6:30 A.M., showered, and got ready for work, replacing my smoky slut gear with Banana Republic khaki pleated slacks, a poly-cotton oxford shirt, and a paisley tie— sexless, shapeless, tidy. I sat on my hand-me-down red comforter with wet hair. I detected the faint whoosh of plumbing in the building, and on the sidewalks the clomping of shoes, and felt all the people in the city waking and moving.

Here we are in big New York City, living in density on top of one another. I imagine there are completely loony complexities organizing around us all the time. With the right devices—Geiger counters, metal detectors, fibrillation pads—I bet I could scientifically measure how much more complicated my emotional life is here in a dense city than in some clear, airy rural landscape. I wanted to quickly call Rod and tell him this and prove that I can synthesize subject matter, but I didn't call until the next day. I left an empty, chipper message that he never returned.

Orgy

We are a military family and live in Las Vegas for one formative year, but then move back to the bland unenchanting load zone of Springfield, Virginia, where no one shows their boobs and where every median is lined with azaleas.

In Las Vegas we live in a *Knots Landing*–like cul-de-sac next to the highway ribbed with billboards, and we have a basketball court and a pool and a water softener, a tube-shaped machine that hums like a refrigerator. No one in my family knows what it does exactly. It filters salt either into or out of your drinking water, but then why does everyone want soft water so badly . . . ?

What *is* soft water?

Everyone around us is divorced. Constant traffic of separated parents visiting or dropping off their children. One time a girl I don't know is kidnapped by her father a few blocks away from me. On my way to William E. Ferron Elementary School I see this girl Natalie who I really want to be friends with because she seems well-known or something. I try to bring up something serious to start talking to her.

"Did you hear about the girl who was kidnapped?"

"Yes," she says. "That was me."

My mother finds freedom in her rootless Las Vegas days. She decorates every room into a contempo, Southwestern tepee place. She waters cacti until they look plump and waxy like apples. Our whole house is covered with Native American rugs and horsehair sculptures and cactuses and kachina dolls, grass-cloth wallpaper in salmon and rust colors, and a cute miniature papoose door-knocker. But in Las Vegas everyone coopts Native American culture. This is before traffic and overbuilding, before the MGM Grand Hotel fire, before the Strip is enclosed in a bubble, before *Showgirls*, and before Las Vegas cleans up and focuses on family entertainment and casinos drip with kiddie attractions.

My mom and dad go to casino shows and bring back brochures and programs and leave them on the kitchen table. The next morning, I eat cereal and stare at pictures of Wayne Newton or Robert Goulet or Rip Taylor, flitting his flippy hands in the air filled with his confetti and frills. On the inside, there is always a shot of a topless showgirl, with her huge boobs and peacock headdress.

My family takes walks on the Strip almost every weekend. We go up the tall, tall Dune casino in a glass elevator, climbing soundlessly up the side of the skyscraper, higher and higher above the blimming lights in grids. I stand close to my dad and we stare at the daylight light. "Wow! Neato!" he says, hands patting my shoulders. He smells like the offices he comes from.

The television is very different here. They advertise casino shows and something called *Boylesque* that I cannot quite get my mind around. Also, there are lots of commercials for carpet. The Carpet Barn, CarpetMania, Rug Room, All Carpets. During every commercial break, there is an ad for Gus Dupre's Buffet at Caesars Palace. "Come to my boofay," he says on the TV ads. "It's an orgy of food!"

All my questions about how real television is are answered when we actually go to Gus Dupre's Buffet. My dad drives us there almost every Sunday. It's in one casino's tiered showroom, deep in the back of its gambling hall. I am extremely afraid I will be arrested for looking at all the adults lustily gambling. I walk behind Mom and Dad as if I have blinders on, never stopping, but taking in as much information as I can with peripheral vision. I hear the fresh tinkle of coins and perceive only a smear of lights that it may come from, imagining their source: plastic chips in edible colors, dealers shuffling wildly, cherries and lemons spinning in slot machines, clinking showers of quarters pouring out of their mouths, and sweaty gin drinks.

The buffet is huge. We sit in a curved booth and walk down and fill our oval plates from trays of log-shaped omelettes and massive platters of pineapple wheels and tumbling grapes and perfectly pinafored cold cuts. Chefs carve giant slabs of beef that glow under red lights, or create fruit-filled crepes to order, swooping their arms into stainless steel buffet troughs for glutinous scoops of blueberry and cherry filling. My parents even let me drink the mimosas. I actually learn the word "mimosa." It becomes one of the large words I know that I am proud I know, like "biodegradable" or "liquidation sale." I dip my plastic cup into a fountain of champagne. Every Sunday I gorge myself until I have to hold my stomach in the station wagon, exhausted and sick with food. "Mike's drunk! Mike's drunk!" my brother says.

There are several huge, barren lots in our neighborhood—big squares of trashed, worked-over desert. One near our house takes up a whole block, and kids converge there, speeding around on this muddy, dipping trail with their dirt bikes. Kids disappear there, abducted by freaked-out hippies who feed them angel dust and LSD and turn them into feral hippie children. I go there often, always cautiously, with my friend Wade Gregory. I go there with my fate in mind—thinking that I may very well never return.

Wade is tall and has a crew cut with golden hair bristling on his crown. Wade has all the Heart albums and wins ribbons in sports like soccer and sometimes wears shin pads casually, like bracelets. If tougher, messy-mouthed, and scabby Dirt Bike Kids are around, Wade will throw something at me and move away a credible distance and I must pretend to myself to be satisfied playing alone.

Dirt Bike Kids are the kids who like to yell and bleed. They kick the sides of cars as they whizz by on their Huffy bikes. They can throw things far and bash in lizard's heads with their canvas high-tops.

Wade, who likes to blow up anthills with firecrackers, is much calmer. He is an adjunct member of the Dirt Bike Kids. If I seem scared of his explosives he will tell me to shut up, Jolly Ranchers clutched in his fists. I just put my fingers in my ears and say, *Oh well,* in my plugged-up-nose voice because in this weird natural way, I know I must act like a geek, the sissy, and I know that to achieve a convincing portrait, I must have a plugged-up-nose voice. We go to the lot to find buried *Penthouses* and *Hustlers*. We excavate parts of the lot that look like places where the hippie teenagers gathered at night—little grottos with underbrush and beer cans slanted in the sand in a Stonehenge circle. We dig and dig. Sometimes we actually find something, a worn page of some cartoon woman with monstrous breasts riding a sexually frenzied horse, or parts of photos: a thigh, a made-up face, a tongue sticking out, a drawing of a vagina that makes us giggle nervously in awe of its huge hairy capacity for horse dicks and missiles and penis cars. We also look for lizards. They dart out of their holes if you stomp on the ground. We throw cans at them or try to capture them. I catch one by its end and it detaches itself from its tail, which wriggles in my hand like a finger.

I make a time capsule and bury it next to the dirt-bike path. My mom gives me a washed-out Jif peanut butter jar and I fill it with empty Pop Rocks pouches, a Sprite bottle cap, a William E. Ferron Elementary School pencil, and an extra, detached hand from the Galactic Man Interchangeable Space Play Center. I write a paragraph about my life and draw pictures of what people in this time period wear: drawing this bearded man and beehived woman decked out in Bedazzlered pants and rainbow bathrobes.

Dear futur peopl who pick up this capsil,
It is very hard to live in this time period.
I sure hope you make alot of changes!

Our school is white, one-story, and round. Rooms are not rooms, they are "pods." Classes are not classes, but "groups," and we gather in large carpeted areas with retractable walls. The school's hallway is perfectly circular, and when I'm lost I walk in loops around and around like an ohming Hindu until my pod emerges. I spend all my time with my girlfriend Christi, who is obsessed with horses. She has a blond, bright pixie cut and blue tessellated eyes. She, though, sees herself with a chestnut coat, and a white star on her forehead and snout. When we walk through the playground she harrumphs and clomps her feet with purebred pride. I have to call her Cloudy. I am not embarrassed to walk beside her. She takes me to the least-used edges of the playground, hidden by hedges, where she has me pretend to feed her sugar cubes and carrot tops. She licks my hand and talks about getting "lathery." We are a very popular couple and we spend much of recess walking around holding hands, making appearances at the jungle gym or gravel section, stopping by the old dodgeball court to see the old dodgeball gang, still single and smacking the ball around. We have an unspoken, solid relationship until one of the tetherball kids asks us if we are going to be married. *Yes, definitely!* I hear myself say, but inside I think, *I am living a lie.*

Everyone in our neighborhood has a pool. Wade's parents, the Gregorys, are a swinger couple who live next door to us and have a pool with a Greek-ruin design: crumbling columns, naked statues without arms or noses, and water trickling out of a burst urn. You can see it outside my brother's window. My brother says that at night they have all these people over and have orgies. I didn't know what an orgy is, but I know it has something to do with a buffet table.

Mr. Gregory is part Asian and was either in Vietnam or from Vietnam. I do not know the difference. He has angry, angry hazel embers for eyes, and when I am going up to their door to ask if Wade wants to come out or to collect money for the William E. Ferron Elementary School UNICEF drive, he answers the door and never smiles. Wade asks me to sleep over and I bring my multi-detachable Galactic Man toy collection and Merlin. I walk into the foyer of the Gregorys', and Mrs. Gregory is wearing a terry-cloth minidress with an elastic stringless top that bunches over her chest. She's holding up a little round tray with one hand like a waitress. "Hello, Mike," she says, looking me over. I feel like she is a little disappointed. "Wade's in the rec room. Do you want some Nutter Butters?" she asks, bending down so that her tan orgy breasts dangle in the terry cloth. I say *Yes, thank you,* but she thinks I say no and quickly turns away with the tray.

The Gregorys' house has a long curved aquarium that traces through the house, from the front foyer up the wide, banistered stairs and along the upstairs balcony hall into Mr. and Mrs. Gregory's huge sunken bedroom. It bubbles, underlit, with orange and blue fish swimming in a colorful, Froot Loopy landscape of rocks and plastic ferns. I cannot look at it for a long period of time, because it is too much—it is a watery slot machine that is too much fun for me to behold and someone is bound to tell me to stop looking at it. The rec room is next to their bedroom. It is a large white room with toys collecting in all the corners like dirt. Wade is beating an Alfie the Talking Robot with a plastic bat. We set up his Matchbox car-racing track and pitch the cars through the plastic troughs. Wade is obsessed with his bat and tries to bat the Matchbox cars. We go down and eat mini-pizzas in front of the TV. Wade brings the bat. Wade wants Cheerios with sugar for dinner, so he gets that too.

We go back upstairs and I bring my Galactic Man backpack neatly packed with my Galactic Man Interchangeable Space Play Center—Lightbeam™ and his comrade the Silver Soldier™ and all their various space-travel equipment of ships, globes, helmets, oxygen tanks, tentacles, and guns. I have named the Lightbeam figurine Roan because I am attracted to it (I suppose I think of "Roan" as a meaningless sound close to "moan"—a sexually meaningful sound—but desire is not that explicable, then or now or ever).

Wade grabs my Galactic Man Galaxy Pack. He twirls around the Space Moth Transport Tank by its wing, then he bats it. He rolls the All-Terrain Asteroid Land Cruiser down the stairs until there are loose pieces shaking around its hollow body. I try to inject a story line into Wade's destruction. *Let's make them travel into another time where they can only float!* I say. *Let's have them get sucked into a frozen world!* I say. I am more interested in making these figurines develop interpersonal relationships so that they must rely on each other for emotional support in tough times because then I can make the male figurines hug each other. I know I am being sissyish but I can't stop myself. Wade just rips off the arms of Roan. When he does this I swallow a sadness in me and let it be.

It is late. We build a fort out of sheets that we pin low over us. Wade is stiff and is clicking the flashlight on and off. He keeps poking at Merlin, making it hiccup with bleeps while it tries to keep up with his rapid jabs. I get scared because it is very late and I have never been up past twelve as far as I can remember. I smell Wade's upchuck Cheerios breath and it heats up the air under the comforter. He pulls out his penis and says, "Let's touch peenees!" which sounds strangely childish coming from him, even though we are childish because we are children.

I touch his little piece of rubber tubing and he touches mine and then he laughs again and suggests we kiss each other and he kisses my peenee and then I go down there and kiss his peenee and then suddenly his mom comes in and says, "Go to sleep!" and I quickly jitter back into a prone position. Wade falls asleep like a narcoleptic, making me look like a hungry maniac moving away from my prey. "Go to sleep, Mike!" Mrs. Gregory says. I look at her in the doorway and she is in a bra and panties, tweezing a cigarette between the fingers of her left hand. From then on, whenever I go to the Gregorys' I am treated like a sex offender—like someone marked for life, who might explode and dive onto someone's genitals. From then on Mr. Gregory adds an annoyed mouth to his stern, staring face when he answers the door. I never sleep over there after that.

My family goes to another buffet, and I get loopy again on champagne. "Mike's drunk!" my brother says, but strangely I can tune him out. We are gliding through the streets in our plush station wagon. I am in the interchangeable trunk seat that faces the rear of the car, the waist belt digging into my stuffed stomach, the streets receding into haze. I am not sad or imagining anything. I am just full.

Say It

Hey, look what I found, it's a wand. The Silver Soldier can use it. Maybe it's a magical wand, maybe it's an invisible wand.

"Wand of invisibility."

Right. That's what I said.

"You said 'invisible wand.'"

No, I didn't.

"Yes, you did."

No, I didn't.

"Yes, you did."

You're just deaf.

"You're just retarded."

You're a hippie.

"Fuck you."

Eat me.

"Take it back."

Fuck off.

"I'll fucking spit on you."

Ow—okay I'm sorry.

"That's not enough."

Why? I said I was sorry.

"Sorry for what?"

I'm sorry I told you to fuck off. Let me go.

"What else did you call me?"

Will you at least stop leaning on my arms? The blood is running out of my hands.

"What else did you call me?"

I'm sorry I called you a hippie.

"Okay."

Your mom's a whore.

"Fuck you!"

I saw her in her bra and panties. I saw her boobs.

"You don't even know what you're talking about."

I saw them.

"You're such a little fag you have no clue what tits are."

Fuck you.

"Fuck you."

Fuck you.

"Fuck you."

I hate you.

"You little fuck. Eat the dice. Eat the dice."

Okay, okay.

"Say 'I'm a big fag.'"

Okay, okay! Fuck you!

"Say it, say it!"

Okay, okay! I'm a big fag.

"Say it again."

I'm a big fag. I'm a big fag.

*T*he American Liver Association. I live here now. I know no other home. I have become a part of the putty-colored cubicle walls. I am one with the printer hum, the framed collages of pastel triangles and circles, the soft timbre of multiple phone lines. I know Joyce's ankle-high commuter pom-pom socks, I can quickly spot misplaced Wite-Outs and stray butterfly clips in the dark carpets, I know people by the sound of their far-off footfalls, like the clomps of Clyde the night-shift janitor and the periodic klonks of his plastic bins. But most of all, I know Gina. I know her scratchy morning mood, I know the hiss of her Diet Cokes, I know her left-hand drawer of Tampax Super Plus tampons in the orange-and-blue box. I can divine the slightest change of emotions from just the sound of her exhalation or the clatter she gives to hanging up the phone. I've heard every story of her life: her absentminded, irresponsible Pisces sister Anya, her Acura, her craving for frozen yogurt, her rings, her shoes, her tears, her urinary tract infection, her golden years at cheerleader camp, where she met Tracey and Jennifer and her other friends featured in her pink soft-sculpture desk frames. Some days we barely say a word to each other, but we are comforted by each other's simple physical presence. We walk around each other silently, like two married elderly Philadelphians celebrating their ruby anniversary.

Now Gina's on vacation with Costas, and I feel a confusing gape in my side, as if someone took away my comfortable sofa throw pillows. Costas took her to Cancún, to stay in the honeymoon suite at the Tropicana. She said she was going to have to pretend to be sick and to please, please, please finish entering the names of ALA members in the Indiana area. All week I have been typing in the names of families from Bloomington.

I am nervous because I keep belching up my tequila shots from last night. Are they detectable? I bet my Liver family knows all the symptoms of cirrhosis, and just one of my alcoholic burps, drifting snakelike through this dead fluorescent office air, will be enough for them to nail me.

But I don't think these people ever go out. Rita, the systems manager (whatever that is), who's in a tucked-in Gap shirt every day, properly wearing sneakers on Casual Friday and blow-drying her hair into a long, tinted hairspray fluff: "I had such a great weekend! I walked down to the farmer's market and bought the juiciest tomatoes!" And Joyce, in her pilly poly-cotton, waist-length pink coat with big pockets at the hips and fake Hermès scarf: "Manhattan Cable is actually a better deal, if you consider the installation fee, and you get a free remote!" I just want to suck a big cock hungrily in front of them until I make a whimpery choking noise.

I went out with Adam last Thursday, this wonderful, nice, friendly, well-adjusted guy who is interested in what I have to say. He is tall and has fumbly big hands. His eyes are darkened with a strange natural eye-shadow.

Adam and I went to see a puppet show and he talked about it for so long it began to bug me. "This show really feeds me, you know? I just want to go out and create! You know?" We stood outside at intermission, all the smokers fogging up the front steps with their cigarrettes. I thought, I have to breathe in this second-hand smoke, and this secondhand conversation, where I just say "Yeah" a lot because he is so boring to me. He stood leaning against a car outside the experimental theater on Ludlow flushed and flunking, just a block away from Rod's place, and I stared at Rod's window and imagined pressing into his beautiful naked body on his filthy floor because I have such mutated requirements now of who I am attracted to that I can't truly like someone unless he doesn't fully like me back, or is far away. But facts still exist. Adam is really into puppets. I do not like Adam. Aren't puppets reason enough?

Of course that didn't stop me from giving him a blow job. Soon I said I was tired and then pretended to go home, but I just went out and did shots and started singing "Cocaine" with this fun fake-blond girl.

On Friday I was sick of waiting around in another fucking bar to talk to some guy when all it is that everyone really wants is to just have sex. That is truly all I want, especially when I am at Freon watching Eric wriggle around on a box above my head. You just crave sex after watching him. He is a human candy bar impulse buy—moving effortlessly and beautifully up there with a king-size Snickers down his white cutoffs. I crave him and then have to widen my craving to include other people.

His shift ends and he climbs down from the box, some Porky Pig muscle guy taking his place. They shake hands like tennis players. "Hey!" Eric says to me.

I have a lump in my breast! I say.

"What?" he says over the new song by Marilyn Manson.
Never mind.

Then a thin man, in baggy clothes, comes up behind him. He is
wearing a big knit hat that eclipses the stage lights. "Hey!" Eric
says, and kisses him. "Hey! This is George . . . this is . . ."

It's Mike, I say, before I even have to discover whether he
remembers my name. *Hey.* George shakes my hand and looks at me
like I am a customer service representative.

His looks are hard to understand. His clothes—warm-ups and a
long V-neck shiny shirt—are of that deejay mixmaster nylon material. They skillfully drape over his body so that you can slightly see
the musculature and know it is amazing without thinking he is
showing it off. His face is plain and square with a beauty mark
under the left eye. I bet everyone who meets him thinks they discover him because his looks register slowly. He stretches his vascu-
lar neck and presses his lips close to Eric and mutters something to
him. Eric chirps out an answer. "See you," Eric says, and the sylph
takes him away with a hand on his tailbone.

If I don't have sex tonight, someone is going to pay! I said.

"Yeah, you are," Benny said, and we laughed because we both
decided to go to Ozone, this sex club on 21st Street and Tenth
Avenue next to a post-office hub. We take a cab there and Benny
makes the driver turn up the radio because they are playing Deee-
Lite. We walk down the sex club's street, parked mail trucks lining
the curbs. The door has a red drippy biblical *O* painted on it. Men
appear from between the trucks with baggy jackets and baseball
hats and walk swiftly toward the door, down the wide block lit

with one streetlight, ducking their heads, averting their eyes like Buddhists.

"We are the world, we are the children . . ." Benny sings as we go in, and I giggle. The door is lighter in weight than I thought and bangs when it shuts. It costs ten dollars to get in and you pay through the little box-office window, and then open a heavy gray door that they electrically unlock with a buzzer, and then you enter through this cranking amusement-park turnstile into a large dark room. A handful of men sit in a section of red cushioned theater seats in rows like a DMV waiting room, watching porno projected on one wall, their breathing drowned out by the grinding sound of porno music: bad keyboards and pitter-pattering drum machines. When the turnstile cranks, everyone looks toward the door to see someone walking in, looking at the new patron's wide eyes and fresh hunger.

To the left is a bare bar. Nobody leans there. There are three bowls—one with condoms, one with pretzels, and one with Oreos. In the opposite corner is a little well-lit room lined with coin-operated lockers, all with clean orange doors reminiscent of a Scandinavian train station. A television monitor hangs from the ceiling, playing safe-sex videos of urban kids with thick Brooklyn accents listing what is risky sex. A round table and a few plastic chairs are arranged below it, with a wooden box resting on it. SUG-GESTIONS!, it says, painted in friendly purple, a supply of stubby pencils and squares of paper stocked in its side shelf.

Obviously, no one hangs out here. When we were cramming our things in our lockers, Benny sat down at the little table and pretended to be absorbed in the safe-sex information. Past the bare bar, up a few steps, is a dark hallway that runs the perimeter of the remaining two walls. This is where the men are—all behind the dry-wall. The hallway is lined with booths with creaky doors. The booths look like primitive dressing rooms in a cheap department store: darkness, no mirrors, warped, compressed wood dividing little rooms with planks to sit down on and little hooks for jackets. Here, the men file by, one by one, without expression, looking into your eyes. This frozen expressionlessness takes some getting used to, but I can do it—muteness, visual signals, no subtle codes—I can handle it. I am pretty sure I can handle this.

Men shuffle by the booths, shoulder to shoulder in moving crowds, pressing against one another. They are either very tall or very short, nothing in between, and they wear tight-fitting tank tops or T-shirts or baggy hip-hop clothes. It is important not to wear anything fashiony or European (prints, mock collars, distinct fibers) because, even though ninety percent of these men are involved in the industry, in here fashion means you are needy.

Some sit lounging in the booths and stare at you when you walk by and wait wordlessly for a guest to slip in, and then they close the door and clank the cheap latch and soon you hear sucking and spanking noises. These booths are predominantly full of gross men who look like math teachers from elementary school, my father's friends, or shapeless communications specialists from the Liver Association, so I walk by very quickly. I try to stand in one of the booths but it reminds me of standing in my cubicle at work so I have to leave.

Past these booths, in one corner, is a doorway opening onto a dark interior, as if this room swallows light at its entrance. Men approach the doorway and slip inside, disappearing into the dark. Benny and I stand outside. I've been here twice before but I've

never walked deeply inside that room—I hover around the rim
hoping that someone friendly and magnetic will motion to me, or
that I will become careless enough to pull myself through the doorway. A very muscular man with sandy blond hair walked by—*That
guy is hot* I said, and then Benny said, "See ya," and swooped
through the crowd after him. *Fuck off,* I snapped. Benny walked
ahead and disappeared into the bunches of clothes. Everyone
moved away from me because you are not supposed to talk,
because when you talk it apparently obliterates the silty construction of manliness every guy here has assumed for the night.

The most important sexual nodes here are either a cute young
face, or chests and biceps. If you don't have the face, you can create
allure by pumping up these four muscles on your body—four sig-
nifiers, four circles, four balloons, slowly bouncing around the
room. Men walk around and around here in tight shirts exhibiting
their chests and biceps, and if you are stoned enough, you can squint
your eyes and just look at the scene as a play of shapes—circles
everywhere floating in the dark.

Whatever signals they have, they are silent. Every time we come
here Benny gives me this little lecture, "Just get into it—don't feel
like you have to *explain* everything." He, of course, can pose easily.
He dips down his baseball hat, forces the natural curves of his smile
into a wide, straight line, hooks his fingertips into his pockets, and
shrugs while he locks his arms at his sides. Suddenly he is a desirable archetype. He is a wiseass, naughty truant who plays in the
creek and throws firecrackers at cats. The kid with the messy
mouth and short attention span and dirty fingernails and stringy
hair you wanted to know in elementary school.

I have problems slipping on a fetish. I cannot seem to fix on a specific portrait, and I cannot get my face centered and still so I can superimpose an expression onto it. My face twitches. My eyes dart. When I look at these steel-faced gym-pumped men, I wait and wait for their faces to lighten up and say, "Ha-ha! That's so funny!" but they never do. It's as if everyone is holding his breath. I have a problem in that I wish for the soft sides of things. When I was a kid, I looked deep into the cruddy, misshapen plastic faces of my soldiers and Galactic Man toys. They would hold their weapons and helmets and ray guns with their fixed wartime expressions, but I would look for the hint of feeling in them. I would stare at them and wait for their faces to crack and for them to sigh and say something like "I'm really really homesick" so that my life would have an emotional crescendo.

I keep seeing people I know from aboveground, like Jerald, that queeny friend of Gina's. I see him walking into the hallway, and he's in jeans, a cutoff T-shirt, and a baseball hat, looking suddenly more manly. He has a blank look on his face, his arm set, permanently flexed, holding a Budweiser like he's John Henry with his hammer. He sees me and I swear he registers my face before he quickly clomps away. His T-shirt has "World Wrestling Federation" printed on it.

I imagine Rod here, and I think of him studying the silent passing of signals, and how he would think of it as an ecosystem. All of the guys without voices, displaying their visual bumps, attracting one another without words like mating arthropods. I wonder what Rod would do in this wordless ecosystem. He could come in here in a lab coat and scrape samples of dried semen off the walls of the booths and postulate again about how the world is polluted. Here in this sweaty, stuffy, crotchy silence, men puffing out their chests is an example of mutation.

Once, long ago, in some purer, less polluted world, men were naked and hairy and friendly. "Hi, how are you?" they would say to each other. "You are cute. Do you want to fool around?" "Sure! Let's go, kind friend!" But now the world is littered with bleach bottles, soaked with pesticides. In our warped brains, we have developed mutated mating rituals that lead us into dark sweaty dens where no one talks. We are injured, clicking crickets flopping around in circles, miscommunicating. And we pay for it, too.

Suddenly I think I see Eric and my heart leaps. But he disappears into the long crowded hall of booths. I am pretty sure it was him, but I cannot be certain. He is here—is he here? Either he and his stern icicle boyfriend are fighting, or they have an open relationship.

Eric is here—Is he here? I am glowing thinking of seeing him . . . God, Eric, all my theories sputter and die around you. I wouldn't care how heterocentric it seemed, if I had you, I would take care of you. I would march off to the American Liver Association in the morning with the paper folded under my arm, whistling and starched. I'd buy you a washer-dryer and Gucci go-go pants, but you wouldn't have to go-go dance anymore because I would provide for you. Unless you really enjoyed go-go dancing, which is totally cool with me, because I would be really open-minded and accepting, too, if that's what you wanted to do. That's fine.

A tall, cute, dark guy brushed by me, looked at me, and smiled. I couldn't see him that well, but I thought I saw that he had a round, cute face, and that he was tall, wearing a loose, white, long-sleeved shirt and baggy pants and a hat with a Nike symbol. He walked farther into the crowd and slipped into the doorway of the dark room. I inched into it and pressed myself against the opening, smelling the tart sweat and mouths. I was pushed toward one wall behind two guys making out, kisses smacking, the soft sound of pants and jackets rubbing against each other. I could not discern the edges of the room. At the walls, or what seemed like the walls, there was more vigorous grunting. Someone began to breathe rapidly and orgasm. I couldn't see anyone. I searched for a Nike symbol, for the tall body of that cute guy. I felt around, hoping to use some latent Helen Keller skill to determine which one was him by touching the shoulders of men through the loose drapes of cloth. Hands from odd angles squeezed my butt and unzipped my fly and I waved them away but they came back like puppets with powerful hinging clutches. This drunk guy kept yelling this slurry sentence—"No I'm nadda drag queen!"—over and over.

Then someone came up in front of me. I found him (or I think I did) and I felt for him, but I had trouble discerning his front side from his back side because he was in these goddamn hip-hop clothes. I couldn't tell if he was facing me or turned away. So I felt a thigh and a waist and an arm, through the fabric, billowing like a loose parachute. I reached up and felt for the brim of the figure's hat, for the Nike symbol, trying to read it like braille.

Thank God someone lit a cigarette, and in that flickering second I saw the face of the figure I am touching and thank God I was grabbing the right person and I am touching his torso and he grabs my dick and jerks it and sticks his finger in my ass roughly and I wince and then, thank God, he understands that signal and isn't one of those scary, poking sex freaks and he softens and slowly unzips his pants and pulls out his dick and we jerk each other off and I come and he kisses me and there are extra hands around us patting and brushing by us like jungle foliage. We kiss among the hands and cloth and I kind of laugh because I suddenly imagined the hands were framing us with satin gloves, these jazzy hands like the hands of dancers shimmying around our bodies as we press together.

The Sensation

I am a moving rollerboy, I roll into the future.

I can hear the thumping bass of Mark's stereo down the hall. All the music he listens to has lyrics mentioning devils and bleeding and highways and hell, which really scares me. He will come up to me while I am peacefully playing with my Galactic Man Interchangeable Space Play Center and he will scream lyrics like "Kill me with a rusty knife!" or "I'm riding on a highway to hell!" and I cannot believe he thinks it is okay to say those things, because he will be so punished by God for saying them. But still he blares his music, and it vibrates the walls.

He has one album that he never listens to—Linda Ronstadt's *Living in the U.S.A.,* the only female singer in his entire collection. She isn't satanic—she is on the cover in a blue satin jacket, tight black satin shorts, and big rubber-wheeled roller skates.

I am a moving rollerboy, I represent promise and hope and the future.
I have the grainy stardust of miraculous television flying through my hair.

I love roller-skating. Some days I go to school, learn, run home, and eat dinner really quickly, and then go to the tennis court by our house, which has a smooth, debris-free skating surface that makes you feel professional and somehow more mature when you skate on it. I even wear my own little tight satin shorts which I asked my mom to get me, very carefully, when she was distracted and content making a macramé wall hanging.

Mom, is there a way you could get me some satin shorts?

"Oh, Michael, satin shorts? That's so weird . . . but all right."

I get them and slip them on and run to the bathroom and climb up on the countertop and stare at my ass in the glow of satin's Vaseline-like embrace. The satin makes my skin feel constantly cooled. There is a stray eyeliner pencil of my mom's in the cabinet. I dot the underside of my eyes with it and look in the mirror. I suddenly look much more desirable.

I am whooshing through mysterious mysts to a tingly soundtrack.

I am zinging through the air. I am aerodynamic. I am sexy. I am curvaceously sexy.

One day I decide to wear them without any underwear. They make me feel sheer and elegant and sexy and weird. They make me walk differently—I can feel the balls of my femur bones swinging in my lubricated pelvis sockets. My little piddle-poo is lumped up there, like I am some sort of child-porn go-go boy. Or just someone from Germany. I roll and roll and roll and skate and skate and skate. God, I love these shorts. They are so satiny. They make me feel something and I call it "The Sensation."

I roll around and around the edge of the court all through dusk, rolling and rolling, skating and skating. That smoothness, that forward rolling, that gliding, plastic feeling of rolling on rubber wheels—

I am a moving rollerboy, I roll into the future.

I have the grainy stardust of miraculous television flying through my hair.

I am whooshing through mysterious mysts to a tingly soundtrack.

I am zinging through the air. I am aerodynamic. I am sexy. I am curvaceously sexy.

I am of undefined sexuality and can fly.

I know that when I am older I will be part of a supportive, joyous, New York roller-disco crowd, joining hands and gliding along the smooth, smooth surface of adult landscapes. I know that this freedom I am feeling is a slat of light leading to that superstar city world.

"Ha-ha! You look like a little gaywad!" My brother Mark catches me dancing in front of the long mirror in my satin shorts in Mom's walk-in closet. And then we wrestle on the floor, and we do that thing where you pretend to have a knife in your hand and have it pointed toward the other guy and you make that suspense tambourine music: *Da na ss-ss, Da na ss-ss, Da na ss-ss.* And then Mark pins me down, and instead of the usual spit torture he throws some pennies in my face, and one gets in my mouth and I swallow it. When I tell my mother what happened, her jute macramé potholder project falls out of her hands.

"Oh, Michael. Why did you swallow a penny¿!"

• • •

Like a Trojan woman banging her gourds at the horror of war, my mother dramatically begins to clean. She slams down vacuum-cleaner heads and jugs of Tide with an emotional fury. She vacuums the creases in the clay coil table lamp and brushes out the crumbs in the Santa Fe sofa. She runs over every surface, including my face, with a damp cloth.

"I can't believe this, Michael! When you go to the bathroom, I want you to call me. Do you understand?"

Yes, I say.

But I know what she is really thinking about. The water softener. She believes the water softener coats everything in salt and corrodes the pipes, and my mother is always freaking out about the water's salt content, especially now, because this is the time when America is obsessed with salt. All the network newscasters are yammering about sodium, cancer, and the SALT II treaty. This is a moment of heightened sodium awareness and Mom is always afraid the pipes are going to burst because of the world's salt leaks. In her imagination, the combo of salt and copper has apocalyptic, atomic properties—a corrosive ball of radioactive ash.

Every day for a week when I go to the bathroom, I have to yell for my mother—*"Mom!"*—and she comes in with a Popsicle stick and a paper towel. She fishes my poo out of the toilet, lays it on the towel, and squishes through it to find the penny. She rolls up the sleeves of her quilted Color Me Beautiful bathrobe and maniacally rummages through my poo for *seven days.* I have to stand there and watch her do her archaeological dig. It makes the salamander-smacky macaroni-and-cheese noise. It is so disgusting.

"I don't know why I am doing this," she says.

Seven days! For those seven days, I augment my nighttime prayer by asking God to grant that the penny passes soon. It becomes very scripted and I say it very fast and exhausted, as if I am punching a clock when I leap into bed.

Dear God, please keep Abraham Lincoln's head in the closet and please let the penny come out tomorrow.

By the seventh day Mom is filled with this crazy motherly fury that has never before been so acute. She is squishing through my waste, and I hear her murmur. She sees it, the penny, and digging through the shit, her body-wave hair disheveled, her turquoise earrings and Shawnee tribe bracelets rattling, she grabs for it, holds the dingy penny in her fingers, and says, "Here. Is. Your. Penny." The salmon-colored towel racks, Pueblo light fixtures, and Hopi sunset wallpaper surround her in warm hues. I see the corroded penny, then her hand, her bathrobed arm, her crisis face.

7 meet this painter guy at Flamingo East, a lounge. Everyone is wild about lounges. Lounges, where people can lounge! Lounges, where people can do Ecstasy and talk to one another and grind their jaws, which is what the painter and I are doing when we meet, and he tells me he is a painter, and I am *so* interested. "I'm a painter and I use the color red. Nobody uses red really. And I mean a deep, deep red, and I can just stare at it when I brush it on a canvas and it is so intense." It is humid and 2 A.M. He wears jeans with a wallet chain, a white T-shirt, a baseball hat pulled so far down over his eyes he has to tip up his head to see. I am wearing my dad's madras pants and glasses and blue polypropylene or whatever shirt.

Then Eric walks in. I watch him slither his veiny body through the crowd holding his drink up and smiling. I try not to focus on him, testing to see if he will say hello. I am a fourteen-year-old girl.

"What's up?" he asks. He gives off his fluorescent glow.

I am totally on Ecstasy, I say, flushing.

"Eric! We're leaving!" this sneering drag queen calls from across the room.

"All right! Hold your horses!" Eric chuckles (he is so good-natured to everyone!) as he grabs the back of my neck. "Have fun, sexy," he says, and kisses the bare bone below my ear, and then he walks off with trails in the air behind him. You would think that I would feel a kind of small death after he leaves, but the good thing about this drug is that it equalizes your clutching hunger and you gush for anyone. So I turn around and there is the painter guy. *Hi,* I say, and look into his dilated eyes.

Okay, his story is that he is a painter and kind of will not stop talking about it, but it's not necessarily that annoying because it makes sense when you find out he is twenty-nine and was in the foreign service for four years. He grew up in Maine and went to the University of Minnesota and lived in Seattle on this isolated hill that you had to get to by a gondola and sometimes he would be trapped there for weeks because there was too much wind and he would just sculpt and eat aloe and yucca. Then he moved to New York three months ago. . . . He's a painter and has an interview with Alex Lichter, who was Calder's secret lover for ten years and apparently did all his work for him late in life, like Dorothy Wordsworth or something (I didn't even know that Calder was gay!). His name, get this, is Jack Flex. He has a beautiful face and an amazing body and a huge, huge beautiful dick.

We are sitting on a lounge couch, twisting our legs around each other like praying mantises, the painter and I, and suddenly Ian sits beside me. Ian is also tripping, fancy that. The painter is busy looking at the colors of the lampshades, but he keeps one hand kneading my leg. Ian and I are overbrimming with Ecstasy-induced affection. Ian looks into my eyes and says, "You know, I know we never call each other but . . . remember when we hung out and we were talking about *Farinelli?*"

Uh-huh, I say. I don't remember, though. I remember playing sword-fight with our pee streams, but not that. *Farinelli,* I vaguely remember, is a movie about a magnetic eunuch opera singer that

Benny and Stephen and I went to see when I was the third wheel on one of their romantic brunchy Sundays. The film, I remember, had a soft, glossy look to it, and the guy was gorgeous. For a couple of weeks all the magazines had gray box sidebar articles about "eunuch chic."

"Well, you are my Farinelli," Ian said.

I smile. Ian then rises from the couch significantly and walks off. The painter and I sit there feeling each other's muscles and tissue and skeletons, and then after a couple of hours we both rise and he puts on my jacket for me and zips it up and we move through the boneless people, as soft as lounge couches, nothing has any hardness to it, and we walk to my place, he is holding me from the back and keeps stopping us so he can mash his hard-on into my ass. We walk up the stairs and the dog downstairs is locked out and sleeping in the hall again and the stairwell smells like dog. Jack stops me on the stairs and lifts me up and presses me into the prickly plaster wall and I have my legs around his waist and we are kissing and breathing so hard I am making a kind of huffing noise, and the dog is barking. *Arf*—Jack is pushing his fingers through my jeans up into my butthole. *Arf*—I grab his pelvis and it curves up and into my ass with his big hard-on. *Arf*—He pushes his tongue down my throat and it's a long, long tongue. *Arf*—Ian said, "You are my Farinelli." You're my Farinelli? You are my castrated opera star? Get Ian out of your head, Mike, Jack is here, and he is pinning me against the wall and the muscles in his stomach are crunched and hard for you, he is pressing and spitting and licking you for you—*arf arf arf.* God, I want him so badly, and we go into my room, and he wants to fuck me. I thought I would want to, too, but then I thought we could wait until the next time because he definitely likes me—I can feel it. What am I thinking? This isn't some procedural mating ritual, this is sex, so I should have it. I don't care. He is on top of me and I don't care.

I feel like we're these variables that are fitting together or something . . .

"What do you mean?"

I feel like this is historic.

"Historic."

I feel very present right now. Like I am going to remember this, well, like, you know when you know you are going to remember something?

"I don't know."

Like when your eyes are working very in sync with your brain and you definitely are going to remember the moment.

What are you going to remember?

Me on top of you and your face where it is right now looking at me.

[Pause]

"How do you want to get off?"

What do you mean? How do I want to get off? Like, what do I like to do?

"Yeah."

What do you want to do?

"I asked you."

You want, um, to screw me? Right?

"Yeah."

I would. That would be cool. But . . .

"Come on."

But I don't have anything . . .

"I do."

But I don't have any lube.

"I do. Come on."

Afterward I felt wideness slowly narrow. He got up and went into the bathroom. When he came out I heard Benny opening his bedroom door and whispering hello. "I'm Benny!" he said gleefully. Benny drilled Jack with questions. I heard Benny's smile as he asked Jack what his paintings were like. I heard Benny explaining how bacteria proliferates by the use of autoinducers. I heard Jack answering in short, gruff responses. I had this jinxy fantasy of hearing Jack's distant voice talking to Benny in the coming days, since we'll be dating exclusively, and I would be sleeping and he would come back in here and shake his head and say, "Benny's hitting on me again. Benny is such a weirdo. I only like you," and curl around me and exhale into my neck, hot breath, hot breath.

"Are you gonna come to my studio tomorrow?" he'd ask. "Of course." And after getting something done in my life really efficiently I would go to his studio space out in Brooklyn in the cavernous warehouse he renovated with the dance company he shares it with and I would walk in and say hi to the dancers who have pretentious names because they're from San Francisco—"Hi, Onyx, hi, Logos!" "Hi, Mike, Jack's in his studio as always," they'd say, and the three of us would do a little fun dance improvisation as I walked across the floor to the freight elevator in the back—"Ha-ha, see you guys" I'd say while laughing and then the elevator grate would close and I'd go up three floors to Jack's studio space. The elevator doors would open, light would be streaming through huge skylights, playing off the flapping wings of the family of white doves that strangely have made their home on one sill. Jack would be way over on the other side of the studio and walk toward me, wiping his hands with a turpentine-soaked rag. He would have a little bit of spackling or gesso or whatever on his cheek and he'd say, "I just finished a piece," and then I would walk up to it, my shoes klonking on the floor, and I would look at the huge canvas and find it breathtaking. "It's, oh my God, so beautiful" I would say, and then I would think of something very smart to say about it, and I would hold him from behind and I'd rest my chin on his shoulder and we would stand there looking at his creation.

Jack came back in and said he had to go soon. *Cool,* I said. I walked him to the door, and Benny was standing there in a towel, just out of the shower, and said, "Bye, Jack! Great to meet you!" and he somehow rested his hand on Jack's stomach while he said good-bye. I looked at this hand planted significantly on Jack's stomach like the U.S. flag on the moon. Later, after Jack left, I sat feeling the crispiness of my hangover skin and the strange dilation of my penetrated asshole.

We used a condom. In the brochure-driven AIDS-paranoia world, though, a dick near a butt means you are dead. . . . God, what a fuck I am. It's so difficult to keep sex beautiful. I mean, the memory of it. The act is a surf of skin and meaninglessness—I float there kissing. It's after the fine flotation that I start casting significance onto sex. At work, on the subway, in bed the next night alone, I stiffen and remember. If this was 1979 it would just be anal sex, nothing else, just a stupid entrance into my ass, but now sex becomes exponentially more significant the further from the moment it gets. Sex acts can become historic events like a bridge bombing or an aerial attack: "I had anal sex on December 17th, 1994: Here is my commemorative coin to mark the auspicious occasion!" I even *told* Jack I thought the sex was historic. Because I can't seem to let sex be simply what it is—sex. I tried to make our screw some major plateau of man.

Benny came into my room. "So! What's up? How did it go with Jack?"

I don't know—I can't tell what's up—we had really good sex, but then he left, but I guess we'll just talk later on.

He put a wet, squeaky-clean arm around me. "Oh. I'm sorry if I've been flirting too much or something. Maybe he's not into being tied down, and he wants less-committed sex."

I became very tired after he said that.

Bed

My mom's name is Kay. She's a petite, pretty blond woman with a nervous face, delicately wrinkled like run hosiery. She used to be a model in the fifties and there are pictures all over my grandparents' retirement ranch home in Arizona of her on runways in white gloves. She smells exactly as you would expect—contained pot-pourri breezes and baby-powder elbows.

My dad's name is Walter. He was in the military, still has his dog tags, and has a natural cowlick that gives his combed, grown crew cut a boyish hedge. He is strong, busy, laughs loudly, and has a hard paunch and Popeye forearms. He doesn't need glasses, jogs every morning, and trumpets out "Jesus H. Christ" when he's mad. He smells as you would expect, too—airplane fuselages, chalky deter-gent, and the faint ashtray gusts of offices.

Their bed is huge, whooshing with air. It's lower to the floor than my bed, more contemporary, always made and smooth. It has no smell. I hear nothing when the door closes and they go to sleep. Their sleep seems solid and fitless, the darkness under their door vast.

Mark's bed is strong and made of a high-tech white material. It is also low, wide, but smells of Mark. I cannot place the odor—not tube socks, not the papery crotch of magazines, not saliva, not benzoyl peroxide. Something else.

My bed is old and long, springy and warped. My dad got it from my uncle. My cousin slept in it until he went off to college and was killed by a drunk driver. It is made of thin dark wood, with a big headboard that has tiny *x*'s scratched into it from my cousin's restless, dead fingernails.

From the ages of five to thirteen, a picture is taken of me blowing out the candles on every birthday. And every year, somehow, the flame in the photograph superimposes onto my head. I wear my Incredible Hulk T-shirts and tight satin shorts and the flames consume my head . . . for nine years—from a small flaming five-year-old to a thirteen-year-old forest fire. I grow up in fear that I will be engulfed in flames at any second, so I lie there in the hand-me-down deathbed in my little flammable flannels, praying to an asbestos god for wet, wet asbestos dreams.

I have very graphic sexual dreams of liquidity: me nudging into a body of anonymous men with thick waists and wide backs that I climb on like jungle gyms. They all smile and say things like "Having a good time?" or "Hey there, horsey!"

They change into flat roads of skin, torqued and enwrapping me. Their bodies melt into viscous globs and then so does mine, but we are still breathing with desire for one another, and I tingle with need for their formless bodies. I marvel at the strange fact that the need for the body is still there, but the body is botched and carnified into taffy. Then I wake up and have to put on my rugby shirt and jeans and walk to school, carrying my trombone, feeling falsely knocked up and full of empty desire.

My dreams have networks with all-star lineups. I live in the skin-enwrapping arms of a different man every night. Captain Kirk or Steve Austin or Robert Conrad in his tight *Wild Wild West* trousers—it doesn't matter anymore. If he is a man and he has been on TV, he has been in me. I go to sleep like an exhausted whore in a whore-house, lying there, waiting for another hairy humper in my bed.

What I absorb during the day will rub up to me at night. If you are shirtless, on TV, you are eaten by me and I will chew you like cud in sleep.

It is warm and spring and my family is out in the pool playing water basketball in back of our Las Vegas home. I am in the air-conditioned upstairs, and I can hear their splashy actions at a distant, faint volume. I walk into my parents' room, by the vast and quiet quilt of their bed, and into the bathroom, huge with its semi-opaque sliding shower door. Tampon box and scattered whiskers. A breeze and my brother's laugh gusts through the thin window. A magazine is open on the floor next to the toilet, the page open to a broad-shouldered, hairy Marlboro Man. I feel a turn in my stomach. I look around the silent, dustless bathroom, lean down, and kiss the Marlboro Man on the mouth.

We moved back to Springfield that November.

*G*ina came back from Cancún with a tan and a strange, sober knowledge of relationships. She says she and Costas worked through a lot. I try to imagine them having serious talks while they sit on magenta beach towels with foot-long daiquiris. She is deep in self-analysis now. She isn't drinking coffee or eating dairy. She is reading *Should You Leave?*, *Breaking the Rules,* and other self-help books stacked on her desk and neatly arranged by size. "I was in a constant state of opposition to him. But I really learned to trust him, especially when we were parasailing. I was expending too much female energy and not allowing Costas to use his male-based energy. We worked through a lot," she says, shrugging her composed, secure shoulders.

"I don't know—I pushed Costas away and maybe you subconsciously are attracted to Jerald, but in your conscious body you try to complicate things. Maybe you are avoiding honesty as you think you are pursuing it." It's true. I am now unconfrontational and afraid. Maybe I am attracted to Jerald and I am so completely screwed up it feels like repulsion.

Gina relays her dreams frequently. We were printing out envelopes and she explained how last night "I was Queen of Coney Island and stood in the bumper-car area and my mother came up and said she was a prostitute and then I was suddenly petting a penguin and the white center of its stomach came out and turned into a bar of soap. I also keep having these sex dreams involving people I don't know. They come into my bedroom, which in my dreams is a pink palace, and they ravage me."

Oh my God, I said, *I used to have those all the time when I was a kid. Once I had this dream that I was having sex with this glob of flesh, just a big ball of skin.*

"Gross!" she said. She scraped her long fingernails along the corners of her mouth. She's always really paranoid about her lipstick collecting there.

We were like these piles of horniness.

"What are you talking about?"

She looked at me then and said (I can't believe she said this), "You know, I hate to be such a bitch, but you have really been filling your speech with too many self-references. You have talking about yourself a little too much lately. Maybe you are avoiding letting other people in."

I paused in front of the laser jet. I just said, *Oh my God, I'm sorry, I don't mean to be so self-obsessed,* but secretly I was thinking about all the bullshit I have had to listen to the past two months about her and her Greek studbag Costas: "He's so hot! I hate him! I think he's the one!" As if I had nothing better to do than just be another Jerald queeny turtlenecked fag friend of hers. Workweek after workweek I have pretended to be animated and interested while she talked about her peanut-head straight boyfriend. I gave her advice, I analyzed her wardrobe with her, I asked her about his kissing style and dick size and would say *Woooo!* when he called her at work.

When I told her about how I saw Jerald in the sex club, she just said, "Well, Jerald is dating someone now."

But I saw him there!

"Well, you said it was dark, maybe you thought you saw him. Jerald isn't that slutty." And I said, *Oh, come on, Gina, it's not like you aren't a whore too,* but that really offended her.

"Fuck off!" she said, and she walked away. I wanted to shoot her. Why are women so freaked out about sex? I'm sorry—I know it's different for women. I had enough feminist assistant professors in college to learn about the looming overarching theme of rape in our patriarchal society, but I feel women should all stop being so nervous and own up to their sluttiness instead of giving in to the whoredom myth that society casts on them. Then again, I have noticed recently gay guys doing this just as fervently. When I go out to a bar, the first thing someone will say to me is "Wow, I haven't been out in a long time," or "Yeah, I don't really drink so much anymore," and then later on you will see them at a sex club and their faces will twitch with recognition and they will walk on burning their eyes into the eyes of other guys. Benny is right. Gay guys never want to expose the underground volcano of desire they have fuming inside, but it is there.

MAkOS

In sixth grade, students in the Springfield, Virginia, school system are required to take the four-section science-health requirement "Man: A kourse Of Study," unhumorously nicknamed "MAkOS" on all the stickers, folders, filmstrips, textbooks, and worksheets.

In MAkOS, we study the habitats of four creatures: the salmon, the herring gull, the baboon, and the Eskimo, one each quarter. We learn about their traits, instincts, and habits, but now I remember only one thing about each organism: the salmon swims upstream to spawn and then dies, the herring gull regurgitates its food to feed its young, baboons exist in close-knit packs and have no single mother after birth, and Eskimo families live tightly together in their igloos. We are supposed to see that there is a consistent, common thread among all living things: that we are born, we reproduce, we die. The teachers set up a little MAkOS workstation in the central "Learning Pod" connecting all the classrooms. It has colorful posters and "Fun Sheets" hanging by thumbtacks in kooky cocked slants. The MAkOS workstation has a "Wonder Box" on the little round MAkOS table. For extra credit you can pick a "Wonder Thought" and sit and think about the question ("Try to imagine YOU are a herring gull—where do you go to feed YOUR young in the winter?"). The Wonder Box is stocked with stubby pencils and squares of paper for you to write down your wonders, but all you really have to do is sit there and stare for five minutes to get extra credit. Otherwise the grades of MAkOS are based on four final projects— one for each creature.

I have somehow conned my mother into doing my final projects for me for the first two sections. Trying to be firm with me, she occasionally suggests I start thinking about my MAkOS final project a month in advance. I always procrastinate until she angrily whips something up, with me looking on, trying to be innocently repentant, as if I were learning a vast amount about fish or birds by observing her. She cooks salmon cakes for the first section and I bring them to school on a gigantic shallow tray covered in tinfoil. She makes a herring gull pillow stuffed with cotton balls with

Magic Marker eyes and feathers for the second section. "I am not giving you any help on your baboon assignment, do you hear me?" she snaps, roughly handing me the stuffed gull.

Troy Tumfeld, my round, oily friend, never does a project, and teachers give him F's, but he knows how to work the system. He buffers his fail status by racking up extra-credit points: changing the bulletin-board paper, scanning Woody Guthrie lyrics, and sitting in front of the Wonder Box—tiny, undetectable, easy efforts that transform his F's into C's. No one pays attention to him.

My MAkOS teacher, Mrs. Moore, doesn't like me. I think it's because I am quiet, frightened, dutiful, and unpopular. There are many teachers in sixth grade who, like Mrs. Moore, love only the popular kids. Mrs. Moore's bright, fake face is a simple mocking mouthpiece of the Board of Ed.–approved curriculum, and behind her quiz grades and lesson plans and extra credits is the popularity hierarchy—a much more complex, insidious, impenetrable grading system, with levels and rewards, that in sixth grade is taking shape like an unknown virus, a hierarchy that Mrs. Moore secretly encourages with her smile.

Mrs. Moore's face visibly lifts when Tasha Bartok, a pretty, blond, well-dressed girl being groomed for future homecoming courts and luminous lunch tables, asks a question. And if the sporty, soccer-playing Derrick Graham burps loudly in class, she admonishes him with a tiny detectable grin. Mrs. Moore is very top-heavy and wears tight shirts to show off her ample apple-shaped frame. We call her Moore the Whore because big breasts mean you are a slut.

For all of sixth grade, people like Tasha Bartok and Derrick Graham are integrated into my life as if we were sewn together. I know everything about them from 8 A.M. to 4:30 P.M. I see their coats and book bags and Toughskins tags. I can deduce their home-life through clues like what lunches they eat, or the cycle of repeated wearings of outfits. I can tell when they are tired. If they are suddenly sick I feel a little lost. We are a platoon.

There are other kids you see in the halls and in the other pod classrooms when they retract the walls for rare group projects and rarer assemblies. These are kids whose names you know, but who never sit in the same classes as you—you just pass by them at recess or in the bus lines. You see them over and over and over, year after year, growing and looking at you with their little, helpless, safety-conscious, patrolled eyes and you watch each other zoologically. People like Cassie Sales, Meegan Cook, or skinny, big-eyed Jeff Wrenn, whom I always see in lunch lines. I know things about them: Cassie is very proficient in language arts, Meegan likes Smurfs, Jeff Wrenn made a successful and huge diorama of the Cave Life of Cro-Magnon Man that was talked about for weeks. And sometimes, when there is a fire drill or an assembly and the entire school of five hundred is seated and arranged by class and grade, you can look over the ocean of Garanimals and gabbling heads and marvel. You can breathe deep and take it all in. There are a million stories in this school. I am but one.

Dan Gordon, a "burnout," also gets special treatment from our MAkOS teacher, even though he is more delinquent-popular than a member of a cliquish inner circle. Dan Gordon has unbrushed teeth, greasy, long, bowl-cut hair, and far-apart slitty eyes, and he wears a Judas Priest baseball shirt every day. His real age is a mystery—it's been said that he was held back three times. With his dark peach-fuzz mustache and a body odor smelling vaguely like

Mike Albo

Campbell's soup, he seems like a different, wilder species. He sleeps in class, skips class, walks the halls with a cruel face making comments about anyone who is unpopular. "Pick 'em up, you little fag," he says to me, kicking the books out of my hands in the hall. I always have at least six books in my hands that I carry in a sliding, precarious stack. Book carrying is just one example of the many enforced social behaviors of the popularity hierarchy. There are two ways to hold your books:

#1. In front of you, stacked, like a feminine, flustered librarian;

#2. At your side, gripping the stack firmly and propped on the hip, like a masculine miner.

When I try to hold my books in the second position, someone like Dan Gordon kicks them out of my hands and they tumble to the hallway floor, so I must carry them in the feminine first manner, enforcing their visual divisions, keeping me down in my school serf role.

I know it's part of some social experiment of Mrs. Moore's when she has Dan Gordon sit next to me for the baboon section of MAkOS. Our light-brown Formica-toped desks are pressed together, he sits with his legs wide apart, taking up legroom, he slouches back and I sit upright, hyperconscious of the seam between our desks. I have never felt a border more.

Dan Gordon brushes into class minutes after the bell, a waft of smoke, beer, and leather Camaro interiors following him, holding his two worn, thin, lightweight books at his hip. I am afraid to look at him. Mrs. Moore is showing a film from the *Mutual of Omaha's Wild Kingdom* Classroom Series in which Marlin Perkins and his sidekick Jim trailed a pack of baboons. They observe the baboons as they hunt an injured antelope and whoop across the yellow, flat,

104

African landscape. In an example of the cruel jungle, the youngest baboon is killed in a sudden chase and attack by cheetahs. As the baboon lets out its last breath, Mrs. Moore gasps and turns away from the screen.

I sit stiff, thinking Dan Gordon will detach Mrs. Moore's girlie squeamishiness and float it like a laughable mask through the air and attach it to me. That is what happens to butts of jokes like me—a large general essence of joking or laughing or happiness could be rerouted and refracted into a hot beam onto me. I must be careful never to get too confident or happy—I've got to stay on my toes.

Dan Gordon doesn't bother me in class when he needs to copy off me and to repeat the homework assignments that he never writes down and never completes. In fact, he doesn't tease me at all. He's actually quiet in class. He looms beside me like a burnout memorial.

He does tease Tasha Bartok constantly, until finally she raises her hand and asks to be moved. Dan says, "Why shouldn't she sit in front of me? She's carrying my child!"

"Shut up—that's a lie!" Tasha cries. Mrs. Moore releases a nervy laugh, telling Dan to go out into the hall. She gets confused when the gentry clashes. A few days later, or a week or so (I can't remember), Dan is not in class anymore. From then on, Troy and I call Tasha "Mother of the Baboons" behind her back.

I lie to my mom and tell her I'll finish my baboon final project for MAkOS, but the cold, hard reality is undeniable: I once again wait until the night before. At eleven o'clock that night, I remember Mrs. Moore's soft spot for the baby baboon. I decide to write a poem about its sad death.

The Littlest Baboon

In their green world,
the baboons peacefully play
on the majestic African plain

But the jungle is not always green
It can be red with brutality
And one sunset,

the baboons danced in their
close-knit pack
and suddenly a cheetah attacks

ripping through the family
and dragging off the pulsing carcass
of their precious baby

Its head barely attached, dangling by a strip of skin
to its little mangled dead bloody body.
And so the littlest baboon
Sadly waved goodbye.

The next day, after Darcy Springler presents her presentation of bamboo vegetation, I stand up in front of the waist-high blackboard and read my poem. I look up at the last line and see Mrs. Moore's eyes tear up.

It's near the beginning of spring, the first warm day, the buds are blooming, the custodians are repainting the blacktop, the distant sounds of lawn mowers come and go through the hinged windows, and we start the Eskimo section of MAkOS. We are shown filmstrips of Idee Magmak and his wife Kinyook, depicting how they live hand to mouth, eat whale parts, rely on the capricious tundra for survival.

Troy is in the Red Group, so I spend lunch alone, which doesn't bother me because I just roller-skate instead of talking to anyone. At lunch, I eat quickly and go to the repaved parking lot, which fumes of tar and has that smooth, glissading skating surface. I roll around and around the edge of the court all through lunchtime.

I am skating during lunch in the parking lot, sweating in my corduroys and breathing in asphalt fumes, and a rock flies by me. I stop and look around, but don't see anything. Another rock flies right by my eye. I look up again and see Dan Gordon walking toward me. He throws another rock at me, this one hitting my arm. Next to him is a girl my age I have never seen before. She is in purple pleated pants and a white T-shirt with lace around the collar. Her eyeliner eyes hover behind long, brown, thin bangs. Her stomach is unnaturally fat—perfectly, centrally round. She is pregnant. She looks at me with an absent expression and I immediately think she is "on something," even though I have never really seen someone "on drugs" before. I only know those legends about hippies on acid trips who have gone crazy from drugs, who have tangled hair and wild, glowing eyes and live in your backyard late in the night. I begin to quickly take off my skates and put on my shoes so I can run. Dan Gordon glowers at me with his shoulders pushed back. He looks like he is posing as a bully, taxidermed and fake, and not really seriously tough. He blocks the opening to the tennis court. "Hey, you little fairy."

I am gray and bloodless and sick with fear. I react the way I always do in these situations, as if I were possessed by some sort of British ambassador.

Why are you doing this to me? I say, with this weird sense of propriety.

"Fuck off!" Dan Gordon says. "Fuck you! I'm gonna fuck you up!"

Just leave me alone, I say.

"No. I'm gonna fuck you over," he says. "Do you know what it's like to be fucked?" I look at the girl because she is a girl and not as naturally malicious. But she steps up next to him with this bitter, foul expression on her face, the muscles of her mouth withering into a dramatic cry.

She lifts a hand, and points at herself. "It hurts. It really hurts."

I don't make a move. I think I would spook them if I did. This is the closest I have ever been to him besides sitting next to him in MAkOS, but I am always staring ahead, so this is definitely the longest I have stared at a burnout. Dan is oily. The oil shines under his nostrils, and thickens his peach fuzz. I am so afraid of him, but I am so drawn to Dan and his wife, and I look at them with concern. I think I can help them or still befriend them, or train them like animals to like me by somehow signaling correctly. I think maybe I would be the one, thin, twittery boy who would, like Jane Goodall, be able to coexist with them.

Later on, in junior high, when the burnouts are at the peak of their power, and I hear about Drew Groves getting it on with two girls out by the baseball field, or Alisa DuShaw getting an abortion, or Tammy Brownside swallowing Andrew Schwertzer's cum, or even later on in high school, when the burnouts do burn out, I know I have missed my chance at communicating with them. In the parking lot, the teachers come out and yell at Dan Gordon to get off the school grounds, and someone gently pulls me back through the blue school doors. Now I just remember to remember them— because they are important, because I feel fear, and because they make me meek.

7 am at the corporate coffee bar by my temp job. The radio just played the Go-Go's. "It's an eighties flashback favorite!" the deejay said. I can't believe that the radio is making me relive things already as nostalgic flashbacks and I haven't even lived a full life yet.

Now they're playing some awful tinny dance music with a screeching diva over a three-note repeat that has been behind every damn song since Technotronic in 1989. Tight-shirted muscle queens love this music: someone screeching "Take me high-yah!" or "Deep deep deeper love!" going on and on and on, never a change, never a conclusion, never a quiet moment when somebody just hums softly and relaxes. Why is everyone screaming so much? Since when did this become official gay music? Nothing depresses me more than the notion of gay consumerism—of gay people considered as just another demographic bloc. There was a time when gay people felt new, I guess, when we were just carving out our identities as a certain segment in society. When we were angry that we had no positive "representations" in entertainment. When we fought to be worthy of having our special symbols and T-shirts and television shows. But then we got those things and became boring. We got blond highlights and became *E! Entertainment* news anchors. Everyone becomes boring. It is a physical law. That is what I believe.

• • •

Maybe I am becoming boring, too, with my limited teenage obsessions with all my manufactured Mr. Wrongs: Martin, Ian, John, Rod, Adam, Jack. Jack. I don't even know his phone number and I've made him a little caricature. Jack is a sellable dippy Top 40 song to me—burning and broadcasted and doomed to slip down the charts after it reaches its highest mark, but I bought him. He is a hummable chorus. He came in, penetrated me with his penis power chords, and then fizzled.

But then there is Eric. . . . Eric always there, Eric dancing and winking at me, making special guest appearances. I can feel Eric sliding up the charts. Now, though, I've been seeing him more and more. I see him all the time at the Wonder Bar. He stops on his way to George, who stands in the corner with a grim face and his baseball hat pulled low over his eyes. Eric and I talk about how great the summer is and how the smoke is hurting our eyes. George looks at us and I am suddenly juiced up with congeniality and wave and I say, *Hiya George! How are you!* He holds up one hand flatly. Eric goes toward him. The beautiful, sweet, unattainable Eric, the crossover hit, the hot new single, the bubbling-under remix.

I'm sitting on a wiry stool in a coffee bar. Two strange, chubby twins are sitting next to me, with red curly hair, sitting silently playing chess. They look and dress exactly the same, pacified with their mirror bodies. Five kids come in, all students, all about twenty or so, and they wear wide-legged pants and droopy shirts. They have thin wrists, and the two girls wear tiny underwear tops. They are all talking loudly, with their skinniness and snaps and fake bitchiness and eye-rolling, and they have jokes involving catchphrases from summer blockbuster movies, and they have on T-shirts of bands that play music exactly like older bands that play music but with brighter graphics. The boys are effeminate and talk about the *VH1 Fashion Awards.* One of the guys glowers at his friend—"Get your fucking jacket off the table! God!" They freak me out because their energy is so misdirected into dramas about jackets and television, and I recognize that and they don't.

Years will pass and they will do the exact same shit I have done, and then they will sit in coffee bars writing in their hot diary about their dumb sexual encounters and then look at the mass of men they have tried to connect with and feel older. These kids are all looking at fashion magazines and wearing Calvin Klein underwear. A *Vanity Fair* lies on the table with an article about "The New Hollywood"; next to it is a *Maxim* magazine with the headline "The New Punk." The new jazz, the new cocktail generation, new faces, new looks for spring.

I hate the fake world. I hate the hairless-beauty youth culture being hoisted up around me. I can feel myself moving out of my demographic. I am perched on the end of the MTV generation. Next comes the twenty-eight-to-thirty-five demographic, which is built on envy and lust for youth. We will have to look at new posters and magazines and underwear billboards and the people will be younger than us and we will have to long for them and the youth they have.

Why am I preparing for age like a congenital disease? I even have visions of it. I can look at my friends and see them as old. The skin pulls down over the terrain of their faces, and their Lite-Brite eyes tuck into their sockets, and their flesh hangs like wet fabric and I become sad. I see them under the commanding tent of their skin, trying to burn with intensity and youth, but they can't do it.

I am ready to be old now. I am beginning to feel that all these halfway experiences at trying to be in love are part of a process of reverse osmosis in my system to secrete any strong glandular feelings of love or desire into other parts of my body until I am denseless and all I feel is a dull aching longing.

I am so dried up I can't tell a story. I have no more energy for anyone. . . . Gina today was updating me on Jerald's love life. He and the guy he met broke up and he was really sad for one day and then he started dating someone new who is really rich and named Pryor and who is taking him to Greece to stay in a house on white cliffs that belongs to his best friend, Sigourney Weaver. Apparently he has had no problem at all finding the man of his dreams. I guess being a split personality who switches from butch to snap queen is seductive.

Gina shook her head while we were walking back to the office with our afternoon grande coffees. "He went out with this guy for four weeks and they were so, so in love. But then Jerald said he thought that the guy was pushing and pulling him around emotionally," she said, "and he had to break up with him because he was just like, 'I finally have the emotional maturity to have a relationship and you're doing this to me.' And now he's going out with Pryor, who is *so* much cooler. Jerald wants to take it slow so he is just going to go to Greece for a week, but I was like, 'Jerald! Carpe diem! He really likes you!' But he's still feeling a little edgy about Pablo because Pablo was Latino and really passionate and wouldn't leave his side unless he was going to go weight lifting." We walked into the waxy lobby, and Gina chopped at the air with one hand.

"But I was like, 'Whatever, Jerald. Do whatever you want. Take it slow or don't.' He's so weird because Pablo was like his first relationship and he's twenty-seven!" she says with shock.

I tried to laugh and say *Uh-huh* after she said that. I may be paranoid, but there was this moment of silence after she said that where I bet she realized she was talking to me, Mr. Nonrelationship Man. It's like when you are describing someone and you say, "She had blond hair and she was really fat," and then you realize with this obvious, flushed, seat-belt-jerking reaction that the person you are talking to *is* fat and you feel horrible. I bet that is what she felt.

I stood there and softly said *Oh my God,* but I floated in my false inflection of shock because here I am, never having had a relationship that went beyond four weeks and I am the fat, fat age of twenty-eight.

The closest, most recent time I have witnessed love was when Stephen told Benny he loved him. It was in Midtown last week—I was there. Even though Benny goes to the Ozone and has sex and flirts with every man that I talk to, it was very touching in its thirty seconds. We were walking away from a Korean restaurant, through this blowzy plaza with its leafless trees covered with lights, a flat cement fountain, underlit and constant, and Stephen put his arms around Benny, gave him a flower he picked from an azalea bush in the skimpy gated garden, and they lagged back a little, and I heard him say, "I love you," and I was suddenly embarrassed to be overhearing this. I had to wait for them at the street and they turned to me with their exfoliated, just-kissed faces, and Benny pretended he was surprised to see me. "Oh! Mike! Well, hello!" and I was forced to be crabby and neutered, like a stodgy old aunt with nothing to do.

But they just broke up. Stephen discovered he had crabs two days ago. I came home from work and Stephen was naked, spreading A-200 lice-removal serum all over his lightly haired body, yelling loudly to Benny.

"Oh God, who else did you sleep with?" he would say, and then Benny would quietly name another person, then Stephen would ask again. I walked to my room, lunging through the hallway where Benny crookedly stood, and closed the door politely, but I could hear everything. I had to go to the bathroom very badly and I didn't want to disturb their fight, so I had to pee in a Tower Records bag I had on the floor. I could have kicked myself, because I was crinkling the bag closed when Benny mentioned a name that sounded like Jack, but I wasn't sure.

Benny, I remember, started begging, then squealing, and then his squeal melted into a cry in one long vocal note. Stephen rinsed himself and left. Benny cried all night. In my room I cried, too. I understood that they were love objects for each other and it made me sad. It's almost an aesthetic reaction—no, I mean it's an abstraction. I can see them as an abstract version of a relationship—two dissecting circles tensely disconnecting. It is an arrangement of sadness. Two objects and a third object, me, angled against them, forming a triangle. I can get sad at basic shapes now. I am going crazy.

Since that night Benny has become very ideological and defensive about cheating on Stephen. This Saturday while we walked around buying records, he kept trying to explain himself.

"Sometimes I feel like it is my job to challenge everyone's sexual hang-ups, you know? It's like I am here to flirt with everybody and eroticize everything." It sounded so patriotic coming from him. Benny the great, grabbing pioneer. Benny the Brave, a lusty explorer like Lewis and Clark.

I'm not so innocent. Stephen and Benny always had very loud sex. I would walk by Benny's room on the way back from the bathroom as his door closed and hear them titter over whispered personal jokes. In forty-five minutes, at the end of their Cocteau Twins CD, I would hear grunts and squeaks, and I would quietly pad out into the hall, where I could clearly hear them mashing and smacking their torsos together, the rustle of sheets, the corky noise of the cheap wood of the futon frame, the vacuum suction of dicks getting sucked, the popping out of penises from mouths. I hated it but one time I masturbated to it. I stood there alighted on the balls of my feet, jerking off in a strange, fidgeting balancing act on the hardwood floor. I got to know the sound of the floor settling and was able to schedule my creaks to match it and the central air.

Maybe I jerked off more than once.

Hornito

My one friend, Troy Tumfeld, I've known since we were hardworking MAkOS partners. He sat next to me after Dan Gordon was kicked out of school. He is going through puberty early and is pear-shaped and has shameful early hair on his stomach. He is awkwardly tall with blond sheepdog hair. He is more loyal than Wade was back in Las Vegas, because Troy is invisible—no one knows him at school, and, like the neighbors of serial killers say on the news, there is nothing interesting to say about him. He does nothing extracurricular except watch TV and drink cans and cans of Crush. He has an amazing ability to never direct attention to himself: Teachers never call on him, Eric McNight never calls him a fag, he is never pelted with spitty Creamsicle tops on his way home. I try to sop up Troy's invisibility, but I never get that infection. I just stand there in school with my flittering eyelids—a visible, shiny sissy boy. I have a magnetic, headshot attraction for teasing. Troy and I sit next to each other in one class, social studies, and Eric McNight sits behind us. "Hey, Liberace, want a flower?" he will say to me, and Troy will be there in an antimatter universe, untouched, next to me.

Maybe it's because his parents are divorced. That always gives someone an edge, a wise-eye, wry expression to the face. His parents are divorced, but live blocks from each other. In the summer we go to his mom's basement apartment because she has a pool nearby. I sleep over at Troy's almost every Saturday, coming straight from a soccer game, grass-stained and head-bruised. Troy has a TV in his room, with full Tier III cable, a Betamax VCR, remote controls, and an Atari game center with Pong.

Troy's mother has a moussy Goldie Hawn long, loose perm and wears little terry-cloth tube tops without bras. She works at Hair Pair and then goes out to Chi Chi's Mexican restaurant until 4 A.M., so we have the place to ourselves and watch cable every night and then make beds in Troy's room out of the sofa cushions that smell as if they have been basted in a sauce of Hungry-Man TV dinners and cigarettes. Troy's room is pungent, with its Doritos dust, sour-smelling tube socks, and his crusty orthodontic nighttime headgear hanging on the bedpost.

In the morning his mother will come in and whine, "Baaaaybeeee, could you pleeease clean your dishes up? I'm not your maid, baby." She then goes back to her bedroom and there will be some thick-framed man with a receding hairline sitting up in bed with a big bear bare chest, and she shuts the door, and a waft of their oniony fucking breezes into my face. If I was smart I would creep to the bathroom by her bedroom at night to hear them screw, but I haven't really figured out exactly when it is that people have sex yet.

Troy has a laminated porno magazine he rescued from the neighbor's trash that has a man with a mustache coming pearly thick semen all over the face of a woman with lip-glossed lips. One time I go over there and we set up to play a Dungeons and Dragons game, The Lost Island of Scylla. Troy's character is Zor, a seventh-level ranger with wizard powers. Zor is a warrior, but also extremely agile. Mine is Taran the Snake Man. He is a wizard fighter and he's got four arms, a cloak of scintillating colors, and a magic Wand of Teleportation. Taran just bought an invisible ring with the gold he got when he killed the Gelatinous Cube. "Did you bring your three-sided dice?" Troy asks. *Yup, and my four-sided, eight-sided, twelve-sided . . . and twenty-sided,* I say. Troy pulls out the porn and we look at it, sitting Indian-style across from each other and we both have hard-ons. Suddenly the corners of Troy's eyes constrict involuntarily and I look at him and he is huffing, and suddenly his lower body curves inward like a dog shitting and his pelvis twitches in his shorts about five times, very slightly—one, two, three, four, five—and then we pretend nothing happened and go on playing Dungeons and Dragons, rolling twelve-sided dice for charisma points.

Since those pressured, stressful MAkOS days, I have made a concerted effort to finish my projects. It's those extra little touches that get you the grade. I color-code my map of Africa, align my multiples of nine, and include illustrations in my reports on Molly Pitcher and Crispus Attucks. I have become especially good at science projects—I construct my three-paneled backdrop crisply and write procedures and conclusions in big neat black Magic Marker letters. I win two Sleepy Hollow Science Fairs at school. One year my project is the Polarity of Light, and I demonstrate how light travels in waves with lenses from polarized sunglasses. The next year I make a hornito, which is a low oven-shaped mound of volcanic origin. Hornitos sometimes emit smoke or vapor from their sides and summit and can be found in many Latin American countries. I create a hornito in a huge terrarium, using a hot plate and burying it under an intricate layered pile of lime, gravel, mulch, and peat. It sits there and steams and fills the whole gym with this boggy raw smoke.

Mrs. Shaw, my science teacher, has a square head, and a clubfoot, and loves to see us learn. We are always having to come up and touch things or trace long words in the air with our fingers. She gives me an A for my hornito; "I'd love to see it erupt!" she writes on my notebook, with a smily face. I read my presentation on the hornito in front of the class, holding three-by-five index cards. Jeff Wrenn raises his hand. "Um, Mrs. Shaw? Hornitos are actually called solfataras and aren't found in Latin American countries."

They are too I read it! I say, burning in front of the class, looking around, lost, guilty, frightened, naked. Then Mrs. Shaw smiled, said thank you to me, gently pushed me to my seat, and pulled down the sleek, shiny topological map of the world. The day went on and I began to worry about other things, like scary teenagers smoking, nuclear war, and soccer practice.

My dad makes me play soccer for nine seasons. I have never, ever wanted, ever, to play soccer. I wanted to be in the Boy Scouts, mostly because I liked their little pockety, patch-covered suits and the fact that all the boys stood together being buddy-buddy, putting their arms around one another. My mother didn't want me to join because one time she was driving home and passed by a group of Webelos and she waved and the troop mooned her. So I have to play soccer.

I am on the Hornets from fifth grade to ninth grade. Team pictures curl in their cardboard stands on the family-room shelves—all these lanky adolescents with nylon-mesh tank-top jerseys on and serious expressions, hands behind them, flexing their shoulders to look broader, and me, on the end or squatting in the first row, with my layered cut-by-my-mom hair tufted out in all directions, smiling with a strange, awakened, open mouth.

I am not good. I can't run fast, can't dribble, can't kick the ball in any direction. "Albo! You suck!" all the kids yell, using my last name for that tough cadet effect. "Albo bites!" they say. "Shitty Albo!" they say, or simply, "Albo's a fag." Once a week, another kid on the team realizes that my name sounds like "elbow" and/or "Alpo," and in a rush of creativity, his eyes widening, a smile of delight lifting his face, I have to hear it all through practice: "Elbow! Alpo! Elbow! Alpo! Alpo elbow!"

"We're all important on this team," gruff, paunchy coach, Mr. Tingle says when the kids get too unified in teasing me. "Even Elbow. I don't know how, but he is." And then everyone laughs and looks at me and my face wobbles between tearful and smiling and I push out air from my stomach and stabilize my face and laugh, too. They make me left fullback, and I stand on the side of the field praying the ball will never come, making wishes by blowing on the dandelion tufts.

I have a very blurry misty idea of what I really want to do—

blurry because it is a girlie thing and I am not allowed to think girlie thoughts so it fogs in my head. I want to play hand-clap games. Sometimes when I am walking home from school I see girls in front yards, sitting Indian-style, in their supportive, quilty-girl community, making dandelion chains and doing hand-clap songs like "Miss Susie Had a Steamboat" and "ABC My Mother Takes LSD" and "Ms. Mary Mack, Mack, Mack," and I walk by them, with my trombone, longing to sit with them and sing.

Then I go to soccer practice and I stand there in the left fullback position and look off at the dissipating jet streaks in the blue suburb sky singing songs to myself. I slightly clap my hands in formation on my thighs. The ball comes sailing through the air and smacks me on the side of my skull, and then flies far off into the goal. "That's right!" Mr. Tingle yells from the sidelines. "Use Elbow's head!"

The mothers make a banner for the Saturday scrimmages, with the team name—The Hornets—and the names of all the team members under it in juicy bubble letters with little filmy wings made of mosquito netting. I stare at my name, cocked at the top of the banner, and think about how undeservingly equal it looks next to the Jims and Daves and Johns. And I look at Derrick's name, the blond, flossy, tight-chested halfback whose sweat would string his bowl-cut hair into lengthy wet tassels. During warm-up, when we have to run three laps around the flat, treeless field of William Howells Lake Park, Derrick will kick me in the ass, and one time, I swear, his hard, cold cleated toe felt like it entered my anus.

But there is no erotic story about Derrick. We don't bond like an unlikely ragtag pair. He never puts his arm around me, or tosses the ball at me and says, "You're okay, Albo." He never kisses me behind the lime liner shed. He never pulls down his shorts and shows me his blossoming manhood. He is cruel, he laughs at me with everyone else, he ignores me until the ball comes rolling toward me, and he will say, "Albo! Albo! Over here!" and I will always be surprised at the sound of his voice knowing and vocalizing my name and the ball will come, hit me in the head or face, and go.

I have never understood balls—how to manipulate them or care about them. And after practice I go home winded and close my eyes and see them—balls—on nightmarish trajectories toward me. I fill myself with panic, imagining those round, contingent, cruel capsules—baseballs, tennis balls, volleyballs, footballs, Ping-Pong balls, pachinko balls, softballs, squash balls, croquet balls, hockey pucks, billiard balls, badminton shuttles, balls. Balls. Balls that smell like fresh air and pumping lungs and leather and mowed lawns— rolling toward me, speeding with kinetic energy, full of probability and emotionless direction, coming after me, coming up to me because they know I can't control them. Derrick floats through the air with his balls, lofting and controlling them. I can't conquer nature like that. I like small weeds and anthills and quiet sparrow chirps and the play of light on the electrical towers.

After warm-up, we stretch and do push-ups, and run around the field, then take off our sweatpants and play Shirts against Skins for two hours. I am not one of those boys naturally born with a boyish, slopy, Genet frame and I pray I will be a Shirt and not a Skin. I do actually pray. At night I kneel by my bed, mimicking a position I've seen in a Norman Rockwell painting or a ceramic figurine of a chubby-cheeked boy in a little blue union suit with his little hairless heinie peeking out of the seat, and I put my hands up to my head and pray to God, *Please do not make me a Skin next week.* And, miraculously, with God's help, I do not ever have to be a Skin.

The Skins are always the more athletic boys, anyway. When Skins were younger they were Dirt Bike Kids. Skins stand there in perfect soccer formation, forwards, halfbacks, fullbacks, goalie, in tight shorts and stiff tube socks. They have chests that are little miniatures of what's to come, with their even-placed caves and curves and collarbones. They jump for the ball and concentrate and say "Go" with easy, natural, ambitious voices. When the ball comes toward me, and one of the guys approaches me, I try to look as if I am concentrating on the ball by getting right up to my adversary, and we have the ball between us, close together, grunting, and I feel the kid's hard breath blast, and put my face in the space between our chests, whiffing the boy's damp clavicle.

Afterward we go back to the locker room and all the sweatpants are in a pile. Sometimes we just wear each other's sweats, and I can tell who the owner is, each sweaty prepubescent. Mack's air-freshener dandelion dander, Rod's dog pee and meatballs, Wywy's family-room carpet and plastic extension cords. Derrick's odor surrounds me especially. Yum. It smells so clean. Ivory Soap and young milk-shake necks.

I play on the Hornets for five seasons. My dad coaches for two seasons and I get worse, always scrambling around on the field, missing the ball, tripping over my legs. I am addled by him telling me with fervor to do things from the sidelines, how to stand, where to move, and telling other boys to kick and run harder. His attention is suddenly so specific. I stare at him, trying to work through the levels of our relationship. He is my dad. He is my coach. He is my dad and my coach—and then the ball sails by.

Games begin—a blur of effort by all the boys around me, yelps and goals and frantic faces—and the games end. We line up and walk down the midline, slapping one another's hands, saying "Good game, good game, good game" over and over, trying to look as if we don't mean it. Everyone walks to their station wagons. The moms and dads say, "Thanks, Walt! Thanks, Walter!" as they carry away their big coolers that slosh with loose ice.

*T*oday Benny and I sat in the Wonder Bar, which is a block from my apartment, cackling and stoned. We slumped in the secondhand velvet sofas, and Benny pointed out this tall man by the phone. He had on a red race-car-driver pullover striped with silver reflective tape and tight black vinyl pants, flaps and straps hanging from the legs. In bright orange letters, the word "ON" was spelled out on his belt buckle, but I realized later I was reading it wrong and the word was "NO."

We agreed that he was beautiful: long, black, curly hair, white, blotchless skin, and a lean, lanky frame. "He looks Polish or French or something," Benny said, "or Eastern European, maybe? But slightly Japanese."

We stared at him aggressively and then he broke through our gaze and walked over and sat down. His name was Miles. He introduced himself as if he were at a church dance, but with his legs apart and hair in his face.

We talked about astrology. He's an Aquarius. He has huge hands and holds them out, heavily, cutting the air in a manly manner, like a morph of surfer and father. Then he looked at us and told us what we were in past lives: "You were a ruler of some kind, in the ruling class in Greece," he said to Benny. He told me I look as if I had been a Roman soldier. Benny laughed. He told me that I had a young soul. He also said he thinks he's been around the earth "as a soul" for a long, long time, and that since this is true, he feels more at ease, more resigned to life and its blows. His voice as he explained this was rough, as if his throat were sausage-smoked.

He seems psychic because he is quiet. He talks in low, low tones, and in circles, like a sage would: "I don't know if it's really true or not, but I do feel like there's an extension, that this life is a stage of an evolution of my soul—I feel kinda old—I think I'm getting close to that last life when I don't need to be reborn again." He reminds me of those conversations I had in high school about the universe and endlessness and what does it all mean. Miles stands and shows me his pants—he made them—and then prepares to go. We live on the same street and I say *Oh, how weird—we live on the same street,* so we walk home together. *I have a lump in my left breast,* I say. "Uh-huh," he says, like it was a boring everyday fact.

I didn't tell him, but I had seen him twice before. Once, he was walking on the south end of Tompkins Square Park with a short woman. Miles, in the middle of summer, was wearing a skintight tank top, a bright blue vinyl shirt with the sleeves sliced off. *Oh, Mr. Hip,* I whispered to Benny as we passed him. The other time was at Hippiechix, where they play funk and classic rock ironically and the drag-queen hostesses pass out pot brownies. Miles was wearing another tight vinyl outfit, this one hot pink, pink sunglasses, and a huge fake-fur pink muff on his head. "Don't You Want Somebody to Love" was playing, and I completely remember he went out to the middle of the floor of the bar and started dancing by himself. He spread out his arms and swiped them around with stiff, violent movements, and people around him ducked. Then he crouched, lifted his arm straight into the air, making robotic motions, like the Tin Man just after being oiled.

"What is up with that guy?" I remember Benny saying, sneering as he chomped on a brownie.

Miles grew up in Hell's Kitchen. It's so much more legitimate and grounding for him to say that than me. I moved here with everyone else and we all live in tiny expensive apartments and got temp jobs and try to become stars. Miles has had a hard life that people secretly wish they had. We do drugs, have risky sex to catch up, and then go back to the suburbs with suitcases of laundry and see our parents and think about people like Miles: the city urchins, the garbage-pail kids, the authentic squatters, the scrubs, those people who don't have to talk about themselves in blabbery conversations because their lives speak for them.

He lived most of his life on 49th Street, with his parents and an older brother and a younger sister. His parents were tailors with a store on Broadway until he was a preteen, and then they opened Aunt Ettie's Tailors on Long Island. He told me this in bed, sheets draped over our pelvises as if we were complying with FCC regulations, so I tried to provide bad banter, like we were on a prime-time soap opera. Miles, though, doesn't understand how to perform his life.

Is your mom's name Ettie? I asked.

"No," he said. Silence.

Whose name is Ettie, then?

"I don't know. I'll have to ask."

Okay, Miles is weird. Benny says to me that he is scary, but he is so beautiful. I look at him and the feeling of his beauty clouds me until I am unclear. He doesn't care about details. Miles tells me things in short mutterings and without wanting a reaction. Everything he says just lays on his lap or on me or on the floor like dirty clothes. And I can pay attention to it all because he is so beautiful, and he sits and stares off at a window and the stage is set for me to stare.

Benny and I are drinking beer and Miles calls. I tell him to come over and in an hour he knocks on the door. This is what he wears, from the inside to the out and from the feet to the head:

Two unmatched shoes, a glittered gold boot on the left, a white-and-black bowling shoe on the right. Black tights with a loose belt made of laminated Monopoly money. A Renaissance-patterned minidress with flowing sleeves. A black vinyl vest with the comedy-tragedy theater masks pinned to the lapel like a brooch. Two different gloves: A black lace "Lucky Star"–Madonna glove on the left hand, and a thick leopard-print glove on the right. A big puffy soft-sculptured bright-green clock around his neck, hanging low, a long leather coat striped red and black, with sheep's wool glued on its shoulder and back like lashes from a whip. Black lipstick, purple glitter eye-shadow, his hair teased into two vertical nests, a huge hard hat covered with blue-and-black-spotted fur that flops down the sides like dog ears from a *Banana Splits* character, and red-and-white soft-sculpture spikes tied to the top like a pith helmet.

I am very tense. I hate myself for being superficial. Benny pretended to be comfortable and cheery, and then the next day he calls everybody and tells them what Miles wore, razzing me for months. The next day I ask Miles why he wore that outfit. "I don't know. That's what I do. You've got to understand that. I have to stand out." Miles doesn't want to be casual. He asks me if I think about him all the time. He sits me on his folded, cruddy comforter that he sleeps on and looks at me like a painting. He decided some-how that I am irreplaceable.

Miles's apartment is tiny; the kitchen counter is at the foot of his bed. He lives alone, on 6th Street. Clothes, boas, capes, fabric, hang on every wall, and his paintings are stacked behind a big shelf of sound equipment and a keyboard. Miles's paintings are colorful, adolescent, and spacey, like colored-in, fleshy drawings of the flying-saucer wars boys draw in the margins of their math spirals. A lot of his paintings were destroyed last year: "This guy I was going out with set my studio on fire." There is an amazing picture of Miles as a kid on his fridge. He is standing in front of a cin-derblock wall, painted an institutional beige, scratching his chest under his red-and-blue shirt, his hair in a stringy mop top, his eyes perfectly, artfully skeptical and wise.

I'm trying to be one of those people who has a relationship and when you see them they smugly say, "Oh, I don't go out that much anymore." But I still go to the Wonder Bar every night, so I am not doing too well. I saw Eric there yesterday. *How are you?* I said.

"I'm fine," he said, trailing off. Something was wrong, and it had to be his relationship. *How's George?* I said. "He's okay. . . . It's hard, you know. He can be a real asshole. I love him. But he can be a real asshole."

Yeah, I know what you mean. Miles is really weird, too, I said. If I was going to be dating Miles I might as well use him as a seductive decoy duck. Eric just looked at me and nodded without reaction, and didn't ask who Miles was. I don't know if he ever really absorbs facts about me. He went on to talk about George for a long time. George comes from a tough family full of trauma. George's brother shot him in the throat with a BB gun when he was twelve and it sometimes hurts for him to talk. George was a merchant marine and was once literally shipwrecked. George has a huge penis, which sometimes aches and hurts him like his throat does. "It's just so weird, but I love him," Eric said with the trails falling from the words again. "It's a beautiful thing, what we have." I felt scorched when he said that. He kept talking in a melancholy series of self-help sentences: "It's so codependent. George and I had . . . have a real depending relationship. He needs someone who is always there." Eric seems so honest, and I feel complicated. I am sad for him, sad for myself, happy to see him, captivated, cotton-mouthed, nervous, grotesquely starstruck, containing myself from touching him, and swimming in elaborate, toxic seasonings next to Eric's fresh, rare, red meat.

"This is such a cliché," he says.

No no no no, I say.

"But I want to . . . you know . . . discover me, so I can be stronger and more self . . . that I love myself and that is hopefully all that matters."

No, totally. That is so right. You should, I say, and I never mention Miles again because I want to be part of the strong, alone world so I can be there when Eric comes into it.

We are in his bathroom in his tub. Miles is starting to get the idea that I want details. He sits up. "So. Um. Do you want to hear about Nicole?" Nicole is Miles's best friend. They are devoted to each other. She kicked a guy in the balls once for making fun of the way he dances. She and he are the only remaining members of their band, What We Call Corn. She is short and has shoulder-length brown hair and a perfect little-featured face and pursed lips like a silent-movie beauty. She is apparently psychic, too. She speaks exactly like him, stressing odd words with gloom. All his friends do that. They waver from articulate to autistic in time-lapse motion, like they try to make you believe you are tripping on a heavy dose of mushrooms.

He pulls out the What We Call Corn CD. "This is the only one I have. We lost the master." The song is good, but I can't judge things anymore. I think anything is good. Nicole yelps the same lines over and over in the song—"I am a superhero / I've got a superego / I am a superhero / I've got a superego" over and over, repeating, repeating, and then I realize the CD is skipping. "Oh, no," Miles says softly, mouth down in a frown, and then, at the perfectly, bathetically timed moment, he says, "I was supposed to be a superstar but something keeps going wrong."

Nicole's birthday party in Williamsburg. Miles and I go in his friend Blake's Rambler. Blake is driving. He is thirty-five, fair, slightly wrinkled, and quiet, too. I get in his car and nobody introduces me to his wife Theresa, a messy Asian woman in a long black coat. They make me nervous and I introduce myself. None of them talk. The car's roof upholstery has been ripped off, leaving crumbly orange sponge above our heads.

"Don't touch it—it will fall on your hair and look like dandruff," Blake finally says. He's been working on a film for three years, his first full-length feature, about a band, drugs, and people trying to become famous in the East Village. "Basically it's about people that he knows," Miles says, and he, Nicole, and Theresa all play roles in the film. It's called *For the Longest Time.*

At the party Nicole meets Benny. We are having a fun conversation—trying to predict when we will suddenly get potbellies and become old, down to the month it will happen. Benny believes it will be when he is thirty-three in February. Nicole says nothing, and then turns to Benny and says, "God hates you." Benny turns to me, laughing and terrified. "Wow! You sure got me!" He glares at me because none of us ever say anything conclusive about anyone, and we are vulnerable putty to psychics and their cruel absolutes. "That Nicole girl is a bitch!" Benny whispers to me later.

On our last night together Miles and I ride the N or R uptown to see Luscious Jackson in Central Park. We're going to his friends' party first. He looks toned down—wearing a modified zoot suit made of wrinkled black rayon. His black hair is combed back, vampirelike. I start telling him about pollution and about how we are all mutated by detergents and cannot be capable of natural relationships.

"They found . . . there was a white buffalo that was born . . . and in Indian legend—"

American Indian? Native American?

"Yeah. In Indian legend a white buffalo means Earth's revenge. The Earth is purging."

That freaks me out, I say.

"Nicole wrote a song about it. The lyrics go: 'White Buffalo, White Buffalo, God's tough love.'"

The train is accelerating out of the 8th Street station, the pillars and people flashing past fast, and he turns and asks me if I believe in true love, and I say *No,* then I say *Yes,* then I say *I don't know,* then I say *I hope I do.* We're silent for a while. "Do you think of me as some oddity in your life?" Miles asks loudly. Everyone on the subway darts looks up at us and then they quickly bury their faces in their magazines. He yells even louder that I have been stringing him along. *How?* I ask. *What did I do?* I ask. He's right, but I have to pretend I don't know what he's talking about because of the subway audience. I want to like him but I am always so tired when we talk. I understand, finally, that I will never like anyone who has had an interesting life. The doors open, thank God, to our stop. I tell him I can't date him exclusively and he calls me a fake loser.

"You don't understand anything. You're stupid and you pretend to be interested in things. You're a fake loser." Then he walks away. I look around and laugh because I am immediately humiliated with the commuters on the platform. I stand there and cross my arms, and it seems like such a superficial thing to do. Everything does— the way I sit, my fake grubby retro clothes, my hair, my hands resting in the lap of my fake legs. I tried to have a relationship, but discovered that I am a bratty, pointless Pinocchio.

Oh my God, he called me a fake loser, I tell Stephen on the phone. *Oh my God, he called me a fake loser,* I tell Gina and Lea and Victor and John and Jim and Tony. *Oh my God, he called me a fake loser,* I tell Benny.

But wow, I think I had dated Miles for almost a week. That's a record . . . almost the course of a large wax candle. *Wow,* I say to Benny. *I had a relationship that lasted longer than a week. How historic.*

"You know, I didn't want to tell you this when you were seeing him," Benny says, "but Miles was flirting with me when he was sleeping over here. He would smile at me on his way to the bathroom." *Right,* I say. Now that Benny is single, he's even more of a horny whore—always, always placing himself right in the craw.

But Benny reads Eastern religion now. He listens to the teachings of an Eastern philosophy professor on these tapes he bought called *The Yoga of Love.* Now he explains his insatiability with scholarly seriousness—"Love is the unity of samsara and nirvana, nirvana meaning 'to live in the eternal now,' and samsara meaning 'memory,'" Benny says when we are drinking Bloody Mary specials at the Wonder Bar. "I am too pressed into my personality to be able to allow other personalities the ideal conditions," he says, "and I am too involved in life. The male echo of myself has captivated me." I was freaked out by that line. "I smother love with myself," he says.

That freaks me out.

"Oh God, who cares, right? Do you want another Bloody Mary?"

SuperTV

My first orgasm is fresh and innocent yes. I issue it forth from scrambled television pornography. I am in seventh grade in my soccer sweatpants on a mottled orange-and-yellow mohair blanket. Every Saturday at 2 A.M. SuperTV, the coded pay station, shows porno. It is warped and negative but clear enough sometimes for a good shot of a dark penis in a glowing white vagina. I try to make out the enclosure and determine the corners of the room and which are the women with blurry white smiles and which are the men, pumping and fucking. I have become very adept at decoding a human from the negative space around him. I look for Harry Reems's mustache or Marilyn Chambers's wide smile or the comforting, recognizable tit fuck. Occasionally, black cum shoots across two white-tipped boobs for a half second, and then the image stretches into swirly lines of erotic putty. I mash my crotch into the blanket, squeeze my thighs in, and soon my eyelids purse and I am completely involuntary.

I stroke in front of the TV every night—making no noise, industriously, quietly. I am watching TV. I am watching TV. I am watching TV.

I'm watching TV. I sneak downstairs and watch *Saturday Night Live* and everyone's wearing knee-high boots, cowl-neck sweaters, and rust colors. Rust, rust and dusty blue. I never understood that. All their jokes are about how dirty and disgusting and crime-ridden New York is, which is puzzling because I thought that New York was clean and well painted.

I'm watching TV. My parents watch movies starring gabby, worried-faced women with layered hair and hairy men with tits like Elliott Gould and Richard Dreyfuss. It is always raining and they seem very frustrated, holding hot dogs in their hands with black slightly frayed fingerless gloves on, yelling at each other so you can see bits of wet bun in the sides of their mouths. "Honk! Honk! Get outta my way!" "The radiator's leakin' again!" "Whaddaya want for nothin'?!" "I love ya, Debra, an' I don't care if the whole woild hears it." It's easy to imagine the hairy guys giving all the women pearl necklaces like Harry Reems does to Marilyn Chambers, all the time, backstage, upstairs, possibly in the bathroom when the camera isn't rolling.

I'm watching TV. I am beginning to see that the city has a dark side. People steal hubcaps and do angel dust like on *CHiPs*. That took place in L.A., I know, but it's on television, and television is the city. Not a metaphor or simulacrum or whatever—it is it. The place where people have late mornings and disco nights. The place where people live in huge, strangely wet *Flashdance* lofts—a motorcycle parked in the middle of the floor with a camisole draped over the handlebars.

My family finally gets Tier I cable, thirty-eight viewable channels at my disposal—I flip through the channels, searching for men, for torsos of men in open shirts, or unbuttoned shirts, or (praise the Lord in the sky) no shirts. I look for Michael Landon, a potential swimming scene, old jungle movies, telethons with dancers, former football greats clinging to the old days by wearing their old jerseys that are too tight for them, blimpy-ribbed men from fifties westerns, a lightly dressed *Password Plus* guest, even Schneider from *One Day at a Time*. I sit there glazed like duck sauce to the small screen, in my happy privileged home, late for soccer practice, thinking about that time in *Fame* when Coco had to take off her blouse for that spooky artsy photographer, and she does it, peering at him with hate and ambition, unbuttoning each button, sobbing, biting her lips. And I think, *God, I can't wait to be exploited like Coco.*

*T*elevision is so true. It's like I learned in college when all I did was watch *Melrose Place* in the dorm suite with Keerstin and Il-Sook and we screamed with laughter about how stupid it is that the cast always goes to the same place—Shooters. Then you move to the city and you have no money and you work nine million hours a day and all you want to do is find a place close by your apartment so you can try to fall in love, or get so drunk you crawl home and you realize television is so true. Wonder Bar, Freon, and this coffee place—my backdrops.

I am crap tired. I made the mistake last night of going home with this freak of nature. I walked out of the Wonder Bar at 4 A.M. after their margarita special, drunk as a sponge, full of tequila and Benny's coke, and as I was walking down 6th Street I saw this big orange-colored man. He had a jacket unzipped, showing off his muscle frame and camouflage pants and a strange Jheri-Curl mohawk toupee that shook on his head as he walked, but oh no, I didn't let that stop me. *Hi, how are you,* I say. "M'name's Eddie," he says, yanking at his trousers.

We went to his place on 14th Street. "You work at the hardware store?" he asked.

No, I work for a nonprofit organization. I looked at him while we walked into his building. His body was shaped like an inverted pear, with desperate, football-pad muscles piled upon his shoulders. His face, in the unforgiving hallway overhead light, seemed impacted with implants. His cheeks and chin jutted out over skin that looked tired of being tightened. I stopped looking because I was afraid I would see scars tucked into his fake hairline.

We walked into his apartment. "I didn't know you were a gay boy," he said, while he opened the door to his small, mint-green one-room apartment with a lacquered bookcase and gold lamé throw pillows on a velveteen comforter, and pictures of him in gilded frames holding up nieces. "You like art 'n' stuff?" he asked. *I guess.*

"I'm a straight guy," he said, placing his keys on a neat stack of leatherbound books and *Martha Stewart Living* magazines, taking off his jacket, placing it neatly on one of his gargoyle Bed Bath & Beyond coat hooks.

"Why don't you put on some music while I take a dump?" he said, and pointed to his tall CD rack—Streisand, Garland, Vaughan, Estefan in every notch. "Here're the girls!" he said gruffly.

I stood there not moving. I tried not to take in too many details while he lightly ran the faucet. "Phew!" he said on his way out, coming over to me, taking a gunslinging wide stance and looking me over. "Yer a hot little gay boy."

I have a lump in my left breast.

"Really?" he said, uninterested. "What are you, an artist or something?" he asked, grabbing my head and pushing it into his chest. "Ah can't believe Ah'm a-doin' this with a gay boy. You like this? You like suckin' on my nips?" he said. I didn't say anything. I suddenly flushed with fear. I forgot to put a new cartridge in the printer. Gina was printing out the *Liver Wellness Quarterly* labels and the script started fading and she asked me as she rushed out to change the cartridge and I didn't. Gina is so helpless with the printer and I have to do everything there. I seem to be the only one who knows how to dig paper out of the copier and get that sooty thick ink all over my hands, the only one who knows how to jimmy the fax spool so it eases out properly. This means I would have to go to work early.

"You like suckin' on my nips?" Eddie said again, so I just said *Yeah*. It came out as an exhale, but he didn't even hear me, he just kept talking, filling his apartment with his booming Confederate flag accent, reverberating off the *Arena* magazines and petunia planters and Armani Exchange underwear: "Ooh, baby, suck on my nips, ooh, suck them, suck them, yeah."

His dick never got hard. When he was kneeling before me, I looked down at his scalp at what may have been surgically planted plugs. I tried very hard to figure out if he really, really believed that I thought he was straight or if this role-playing thing was supposed to be this shared illusion, and, if that was the case, then why was it alluring? What is so attractive about a lie? And then I came.

Slater

Mark is not my brother. He is from Opposite Land, sent here to kill me. He is a Dirt Bike Kid, a Skin, he wears Adidas and jeans with ease. He has a broken nose and droopy eyes that give him an air of drugged criminality, which justifies everything he does. He apparently broke his nose when he fell off his unicycle, which he spins around on in the driveway all the time. I think this is a lie—I think he broke his nose in some stranger, dark way that involves a car or a girl with a lot of makeup on. He has been getting into trouble lately and he gets C's in school.

Last month, right before I was going to bed one night, the door-bell rang and my mom answered the door and there was a police officer, his big, blue bulletproof body with Mark standing in front of him. Mark was just caught stealing a fire extinguisher. Now Mark is grounded and spends more time at home, which is horrible because he is always around scrutinizing everything I do. He spins around on his unicycle outside, commenting on any outdoor activity I am trying to do peacefully, like twirling sticks or creating a utopian valley in which my soldiers can work and play free from war. "What are you, a baton twirler or something?" Mark says, or, "Aren't you a little old to be playing with soldiers?"—and if he isn't observing me he is firmly slotted on the most comfortable part of the couch, limbs alighted on all the pillows, watching boring military-themed TV shows like *M*A*S*H* or *Hogan's Heroes*.

Or he puts together models. They come in boxes in interconnected pressed plastic inside sealed cellophane. He bends over his desk and airplane-glues bumpy green tanks together. He puts them in dioramas of grassy fake moss and cotton-ball smoke. He places soldiers fighting around the tanks, crawling across the tundra with blood gurgling out of their wounds. I sneak into his room and very lightly touch them. One time I walk into his room while he is painting a nuclear missile. There he is, crouching over the deadly weapon.

Wow, that looks pretty good, Mark.

"I got the paint all wrong, and don't talk to me. It's going to screw up my concentration."

Can I stand here?

"Yeah, just don't suddenly make any movements."

So I stand there, statue-still, trying not to stir the air, and watch him paint a red star on the side of a warhead.

Besides TV and models, Mark keeps himself busy reading comic books in his room—*Powerman, Iron Fist, Daredevil, Master of Kung Fu*—always bulbous men in bulging shirts who hit people and kick through doorways without any flouncy capes or ray guns or irradiating rings or purple powers, which, of course, I like.

Now my brother sits in his room drawing comic books of a superteam he made up called the Rebels. I feel like he is going through a very significant artistic transition. His heroes used to be ordinary in their superiority, square-jawed and caped with determined, shaved faces. But the Rebels are grittier. They're an edgy urban superteam, living hard switchblade lives in a place far, far away from our suburban home. They live in the dark, unpredictable streets of New York, where anything can happen! They are a gang of tough, streetwise, smart, and apocalyptic kids. They all have ratted hair and spray-paint splooshes on their T-shirts. They fight the evil deeds of the Teamster, a scary crime king. He wants the Rebels offed, but they always get away with their amazing city-inspired powers:

Vermin—who controls roaches and rats
Stink—who can influence people and ferret out criminals with her aromatic powers
Slime—who has the power of trash
Pigeon—who can fly short distances
Airshaft—who can create violent windstorms within cramped, small spaces

—and *Roxanne,* a beautiful, rapacious woman who can immobilize people with her power of orgasm.

He is getting very intense about his team. It's the first time I have really seen him focus. I walk by Mark's door, and he sits there on the floor reading *Powerman* with his legs up, taking notes and perfecting his sketches. I just watched the Tuesday-night lineup and I am feeling witty. Here is a perfect, airtight time for me to burn him, I think.

Aren't you a little old for comic books¿

"Yeah. So¿ Do you still cry yourself to sleep at night¿" he says, calmly, never turning around. I stand there, baffled. I scramble to my room. Anything he says to me resonates, always. He is at his peak of power, and I have nothing—just me with my homo knees, without any superpowers, no flouncy capes, no pulsating rings.

I do cry myself to sleep every night. I thought I did it so silently, though. . . . I cry because as soon as I am prone and the light is perfect, tears loosen out of my eyes. In moonlight through the Delmar blinds, or at dusk when the weather chills and breezes snake through the storm screen, I cry and repeat a phrase like *Why me why me why me,* or, *I don't know why I don't know why* because those phrases lock in the freshness of longing.

My brother is fourteen and I am ten. In the droop of his shoulders and cave of his chest, he looks as prepared as a paper doll for the cigarettes and Rolling Stones T-shirts to come. Mark has access to older people that I do not have. He is really good friends with Ken Fenning, who works at Burger Chef but is also our baby-sitter.

Ken Fenning is never called our baby-sitter, but I suppose if we were all girls he would be called this. He comes over to "hang out" some weekend nights if my parents go out. We used to have a senior-citizen exchange student with us, Frau Freund. She would hobble around and hum wartime folk songs. I loved it when she baby-sat us because she made doughnuts. When she went back to Germany my parents had to find another adultlike presence for those rare times they went out at night to Christmas or Memorial Day parties. Now, though, my father seems to be at a successful job because my parents purchased a VCR, retiled the shower in the master bedroom, installed a skylight, and go to cocktail parties often. On Fridays, my mother always adjusts her blond hair and settles big chunky jewelry on her chest and my father beeps for her in the car and she rushes out, wafting out the front door in turquoise earrings.

Ken Fenning was a wrestler in high school and has a thick neck and veins that trace down his forearms. My parents arranged for him to "hang out" with us because my brother hates the word "baby-sit" and Ken is cool. He is the son of my parents' friends from my dad's business. I don't know exactly what it is that my dad does. I know it has something to do with Styrofoam packing peanuts because I saw one near him once.

I do know he is no longer in the military. All his equipment and uniforms are in two big cardboard boxes in the basement. Once I went down to the basement and cracked the packing tape to peer into them, and only saw a layer of nicely folded, dull green cloth. Worn, old, bloodied, blackened from shellfire—I couldn't tell. The clothes were silent. I don't know if he killed anyone, or if he saw death or guts at all.

Ken Fenning has a Camaro and is a manager at Burger Chef, an occupation I do know because I find it a very interesting job—hamburgers with cheese cooked and stacked in roiling, foily chutes under an orange light. He wears short-sleeved, white button-down shirts and glasses. Ken is amazing because he is confident with his job and his ever-present fast-food-burger odor coming off of his body like fresh paint. He has a lopsided smile and his glasses shade his staring eyes in a cool aquarium blue tint. Ken comes over, and he and Mark go into his room and play albums loudly.

Somehow, it is acceptable that an eighteen-year-old is hanging out with a fourteen-year-old—probably because there are always soccer coaches and pool lifeguards and lawn-mower boys yelping and gawkily walking around the neighborhood, and when they all get together to play football in someone's yard, the range of ages is made invisible.

Ken and Mark usually go out front on days there is no game, and in the dark they throw a Frisbee or a football. If I look out the window, through the blinds so they can't see me, I will see their bodies, almost indistinguishable in the dim light of the passing rush-hour cars. They bend and jump. "Hut! Hut! Hut!" they say. "Go!" they scream, and they run for a reception, catching it and pretending it is a goal or touchdown, or that they are scoring points toward winning something. Cars and hollers, cars and hollers.

Sometimes I go over to Troy's, watch the *Creature Feature* from 5 P.M. to 7 P.M., and come home, and Mark and Ken are already watching TV, so that means they control the channels. It is so unfair. I complain but it is useless. Sometimes Ken Fenning feels like he has spent too much time alone with Mark, and to ward off weirdness, he invites me along when they hang out at his place. He lives in the rented basement of the Pearsalls' house and you enter through the sliding glass door. His floor is uncarpeted and he has three blue beanbag chairs, a TV, and a short, brown dorm refrigerator by his twin mattress. His place has an ashtray odor. It's Thursday night, when Mark and Ken's favorite show, *Slater,* is on.

Dirk Horsely, an actor very recognizable from *Love Boat* and its spinoff show, *Aloha Paradise!,* plays a private investigator in gritty, urban New York, contracted out to help solve unsolvable crimes. The opening credits show him grabbing on to the swinging ladder of a helicopter, running away from a smoky exploding car with Chuckie, his secretary (played by the beautiful Penny Petrie), bothering his haughty boss (played by the famed older actor James Wholegood, who himself played McCabe in *McCabe,* which they show in repeats on channel 20) ("Is that James Wholegood?" my dad said once when we were watching it), and slowly dunking his head into a bubble bath with a cigar in his mouth, which really happens in one episode. Then, the montage ends with him saying that great line "You flick my trigger!" in his southern accent. Slater (Horsely) wears this thick cable-knit white sweater with a floppy wraparound belt. He walks into funky black-populated clubs and looks for drug dealers to give him leads to crimes in his sweater and cowboy boots, while everyone around him is wearing fedoras and chains and satin shirts and black women with light-blue eyeshadow are dancing behind hanging beads. And, as usual, he'll get in a fistfight. Usually Corndog, his streetwise friend who is black and talks jive (played by Thalius Smith), will come in and throw a saving punch. "Corndog, you flick my trigger!" Slater says, and Corndog will always say, "You be talkin' jive, Slatah!"

Mark loves that show, and it is one hour when his cruelty cools, when his mind isn't researching a way to insult me, and he slouches in the family room, or, if we're at Ken Fenning's, in one of Ken's big blue beanbags with his chin in his chest, mouth partially open.

"Mike! Hey! Get the Cokes in the fridge, man!" Ken says, sitting next to Mark, eyes fixed on the TV, his legs embedded in the third beanbag chair. I get up and go over to the refrigerator, leaning over Ken's bed, where a magazine is crammed in the crack between his mattress and the wood-paneled wall. It is folded over so I can just see a cylinder of skin. I think it is a leg, covered with hair. A masculine leg, and then a pubic bush, and then, disappearing behind the curve into the wall, a sliver of the beginning of a wide penis.

I focus on that curved naked shape, but I know I cannot hover there long, so I cough. Coughing always works to stop time. In the span of those little fake chokes I scrutinize the penis sliver, the hugeness of it, mounted in dark hair, a crooked raised vein lacing down the side. That is a man. I store this information and walk over to them, crouching and sliding the soda cans over to the two. *Slater* starts, and I am in God's green favor, because the scene opens with Slater in a pool with a big drink in one hand and a girl leaning on his arms, running her fingers through his chest hair, so I get to see Slater's body, and it's okay to stare and devour his body with my eyes because it's television, and everyone looks as if they devour when they watch TV.

Yesterday on the way home from work I saw three black-and-white ads with sexy steel-faced men with giant flexed jaws and bodies rippling with muscles, their hard, shellacked, shiny bodies selling underwear, cologne, crewneck T-shirts, whatever. Advertisers are beginning to treat gay guys as they've treated women for years, drowning us in envy and then selling us gym memberships.

And as if I need to promote to all citizens of the earth how little self-esteem I possess, I decided to try to call Jack just to make sure, beyond a doubt, that he doesn't like me. He answered the phone— "Yeah?"—from his studio, and I said, *Hi, it's* [full name], so he didn't have any way to be confused. He was totally stiff on the phone. Polite, like he was giving me technical assistance with my stereo. I should have understood from Jack's overproduced body and smile that he was all promises, all sellable cardboard promotion posturing.

Benny woke me up on Sunday and we walked to Houston Street to look at couches, and saw signs for gay plays with naked men wheat-pasted on boarded-up Bowery buildings: *12 Naked Men! Naked Men Singing! Naked Men Again!* On one corner, above us, there was a medical assistants' school with an old, sad sign with dead captured moths piled behind it blocking the light. Next to it was a series of windows, a classroom, and a hospital gurney pressed up against the glass with a Resusci-Annie doll lying under the covers.

What a weird sight, I said. *A naked Annie in bed like a prostitute in Amsterdam.*

"What if you saw me up there just fucking the doll in bed?" Benny said.

That would be weird, I said.

"I would just be there," Benny said, "humping the Annie doll with this grin on my face and Annie's blond hair would shake all over the place in mannequin fidgets.

"Fuck that Jack guy," Benny said after a long pause. "He's an ass-hole. You can do so much better." We kept walking and I was grate-ful he said that.

My brother came up here to visit. He was doing work for some phone-communications expo. He came to my apartment with a blazer on and his name tag pinned to it, a little bar code below his name. "It's pretty cool because you can just walk through the scan-ner at the front door of the conference and it reads your bar code and bleeps."

"Your brother is totally hot!" Benny said the minute Mark went to the bathroom to take a shower. "It's funny," Benny said. "I saw him looking at me and he grabbed his crotch!"

I smiled at the intricate organization of Benny Sexworld. In Benny's head every man is horny for him. And Benny is so con-vinced of it, even when it is an absolute impossibility—my straight rugby-shirt brother, for example. In Benny Sexworld there is a hot, hard erection under every zipper. Gay guys, married men, profes-sors, fathers, everyone is subject to Benny's little "you want it" comments, to his prickling, exploring, advancing hands. The uncanny thing is that so far no one has socked Benny in the face for his comments and pinches and slippery fingers. He gets away with everything he does and it makes me so angry sometimes, but I never say anything, because I would look jealous that I am not down people's pants. Maybe I *am* jealous.

Mark got out of the shower and got dressed and sat down with us and we got really stoned. I didn't know he still smoked pot. We just sat there and watched infomercials and syndicated shows, completely cemented to the new orange couch in the living room. Benny kept groaning like he always does at various males on the television: Knight Rider, JAG, Scott Bakula, *Baywatch* guys, even the flash-cut, flexing arm of a musk cologne ad. "Nice shoulders!" he says. "Smooth skin," he says. Benny must always vocalize his longing. His creativity is both irritating and marvelous, like looking at an impossible, tacky miniature that someone made in a grain of rice. My brother sat drinking beer, and at first I was nervous about Benny's constant assaults, but then Mark started joining in, the way straight guys do now: "Yeah, he is pretty good-looking. . . ." That, of course, provoked Mr. Horny more.

"Yeah, he is, isn't he," Benny said, and sneerily smiled. Mark started asking questions about gay sex. If there is one thing that straight guys and gay guys can meet minds on, it is how much we want to have orgasms, and since gay guys have a lot of sex, straight guys have this congressional-boys-club kind of respect for us. I kept silent and listened to Benny describe the world of gay sex as if it were Candy Land, men everywhere with their gumdrop nipples and candy-cane erections.

"Do you look at guys' penises when you're at the urinal?" my brother asked.

"Sure!" Benny peeped. "If there is some weird businessman who yanks out his dick in his weird Perma-Prest suit, you sort of want to see it, you know? Do you?"

"Yeah, right. All the time. Do you pick up guys at urinals?"

"Sometimes. Yes—I sucked someone off in Bloomingdale's last spring."

"Gay guys get sex all the time."

Yes, maybe gay guys are in a stunted adolescence because we weren't allowed to be assholes and fuck each other all the time in high school.

"I bet you had a lot of sex in high school, Mark."

"Not really."

"I am so sure that is a lie! I bet you brought home so many girls!"

"But we didn't have sex sex . . . I mean, I wasn't an idiot. . . . I didn't want a kid."

"That must suck, yeah. . . . Well, in a way, we don't want AIDS, so it's a lot alike."

We do all these stupid voodoo techniques like sucking and not swallowing. And then feeling freaked out later on.

"You don't fuck?"

"Sure!"

"Do you do, like, weird stuff?"

"Like what?"

"Like leather stuff?"

No.

"Yeah! I do a lot of role-playing. Last weekend I had to pretend I was coaching a B-meet swim team and shaved a guy's pubic hair."

How specific, Benny.

"I know! Mark, I bet you role-play all the time with your wife. Like, I bet you pretend you are a woman and she's a man, or I bet you pretend you've been really naughty and she puts you over her lap and spanks you and rubs your ass."

I can't believe Benny blurted that out. "Yeah," Mark says, and I look at him and his face is suddenly slightly filled with more energy, and he's nodding his head, and I know that this means he knows I told Benny about Ken Fenning. Mark remembers that incident, and he knows I know, and he is now expressing, in that reddish nod, that he does not consider what Ken Fenning did to be abuse or gayness or anything. There is this pacifying tuck to Mark's eyes, and that means he understands that Ken Fenning never played around with me, and his eyes convey relief that nothing ever ever happened to me. That I just quietly dodged Ken Fenning while he reigned over us that weird year when we were kids. I surge with love for my brother.

Manager

I have been on the highway a few times. It runs around the edge of Springfield like an intestine or a dike. Near one of the exits, I never know where, is the amusement park Storybook Kingdom. When, sometimes, we go to a different mall besides Springfield Mall, you see it on the side, in the trees: a huge orange mushroom, the top of a red carousel, and a green caterpillar head with sideways eyes and two large front teeth. The rest of the amusement park is in trees. The last time Ken Fenning was hanging out with us he said, ducking into his Camaro, that he would take us to Storybook Kingdom.

I have never been there, but my parents insist that when I was younger we did go, but this always gets me very angry, because if there is one thing that is true in the world it is that I would remember going to an amusement park: complicated aqueducts of water, piggy characters with foam noses, loony sounds, older Dirt Bike Kids with girlfriends and farmer tans and cutoff T-shirts, the crush of crowds, the smell of dried soda, the sleepy drive home curled in the bucket seat. We had all sorts of vacations, and I remember them well. Not only because they were a break from the endless greenness of our subdivision, but because I am the youngest and always have to wear life preservers or bibs or hats to make myself half-price. I feel as if I have been doing it forever, much longer than Mark, who isn't that much older, but whom I have never seen having to wear a Waterland Wonder Vest or Wacky Duck Pontoon or Freddie Fishhead.

I never go to Storybook Kingdom. My fucking brother, by the time Ken arranges it, is already far enough into the seventh grade to realize how absolutely gay Storybook Kingdom is, so we never go there. "Storybook Kingdom is for queers!" he says. Instead, Kenny takes us to his workplace, Burger Chef, for a behind-the-scenes tour of the kitchen and the assembly of the Spaz burgers (three stacks of meat patties layered with a perfectly circular bun) and Chocolate Fluffy shakes.

One Saturday Troy and I are eating sticks of butter on my porch (I did this only once, because I got the worst shits about six hours after the following incident) and Ken Fenning comes up and asks if Mark is home to see if he wants to go see *Return of the Jedi* and he does not invite us. He's wearing cutoff shorts and an AC/DC tank top. Mark materializes behind the screen door. "So let's go," Ken says to him.

"No," Mark says, in this voice that sounds very dramatic.

"Okay, fine."

Ken Fenning's face fries into red and he crouches down and says to me, "Tell your brat brother that maybe when his tantrum is over I'll come over and pick him up." I look down and there is a gap in the leg of his shorts. I can see his thick testicle sac, and then he stands up and walks to his car.

When Ken sits us at home he will use the word "fuck" in a sentence as soon as my parents leave and pull out *Playboy*s. He and Mark look at them but they won't show me.

"Hey, Mike, fuck, do you want to see some beaver?" he says.

"No he doesn't," Mark says. "I bet you don't even like girls!"

No, that's a lie. I like girls, I say, and I can hear the words "I like girls" as three outside sounds that my body makes, coming out of me like loose, disembodied stones.

I don't want to see those books anyway. I say this very dramatically. I am feeling very pious these days. I go to my room and play with my electronic games, like Merlin and Simon and the Electronic Detective. On their glossy boxes, the instructions say that these games are designated for my age range, which makes me feel very secure and abiding and I contentedly smile while I press their little buttons.

I can hear Ken and Mark roughhousing downstairs, grunting and struggling—"You idiot!" "Screw you!" They laugh and throw each other on the floor and I can hear Mark's chesty exhalations. Then their voices move into breaths that sound full of meaning. The central air kicks in and blows passionately. This is when Ken gives Mark his Massage. I sneak down the stairs to watch them.

I have to float down the stairs like a weightless praying mantis, placing equal amounts of weight on all four limbs, testing each carpeted stair for creakability. Then, finally, on my toes, I move down the last ledge and into the foyer, delicately padding past the hall closet lined with Hopi-inspired grasscloth wallpaper. I reach the end of the hall, which opens into the kitchen, and, to the left, the TV room, and I lean one huge eye past the doorway.

There is Ken, with Mark over his lap, facedown as if Ken is going to spank him. Mark is writhing around cursing, curling like a Chinese fortune fish, pinned between Ken's arm and knees. Ken has his hand on Mark's ass, and he is vigorously rubbing it in circular motions, rubbing Mark's heinie through his jeans. I'm gonna give you the reddest Indian ass, Ken says, and Mark is grimacing and then his face softens—like a Bad News Bear. Like a tough kid on an *Afterschool Special* who isn't as tough as he seems to be. Like a kid with a lotta love to give on CBS *Kids Break,* and he laughs.

Powerman

"What are you reading?"

"Nothing."

"A comic book?"

"Uh-huh."

"What did you say?"

"Yes. A comic book."

"Oh. Is it *Iron Fist*?"

"No."

"Is it *Powerman*?"

"Well, obviously not if it isn't *Iron Fist*, since they're a team."

"What is it? Let me see—"

"Stop! Don't crease it! It's the *Hulk,* okay?"

[silence]

"Hey, Mark, who is stronger: The Hulk or Powerman?"

"The Hulk. Duh."

"Come here."

"I'm reading."

"Read over here."

"I'm comfortable."

"Come on, come on."

"No."

"I want to show you something."

"What?"

"I got you something today."

"The *Slater* sweater?"

"I'm not going to tell you!"

"Where is it?"

"Hold on. Close your eyes."

"Okay, okay."

"Okay, open them."

"This isn't it."

"What do you mean, this isn't it?"

"THIS ISN'T A *SLATER* SWEATER! That's what I mean."

"Yes, it is!"

"You idiot."

"It's the sweater. The guy at Bonwit Teller said that tons and tons of people have come in there and asked for a *Slater* sweater from that show and—"

"You are such an idiot! A *Slater* sweater! The one he wears is white and has a big collar and rope tie and this has *no* collar and buttons!"

"It's the closest I could find."

"What—did you get it confused with Ponch? You idiot!"

"Screw you!"

"Screw you!"

"Fag!"

"You're a fag!"

"Bite it!"

"You bite it!"

"Do you want an Indian ass?"

"No!"

"Yes, you do, I can tell!"

"No, I don't, you pud fuckoff!"

"I'm gonna give you the reddest Indian ass!"

"Get off!"

"You deserve a break today."

"Get off of me!"

"Too late."

"Stop!"

"Ah, stop whining like a girl."

"Ahhh! Fuck you! Ahh! Ahh ha hahahaha Stop! Hahahahaha! Stop! Ha ha ha ha ha ha!"

Hold your penis, pull back the sides at the, no . . . at the top."

Okay.

"What sites were your sexual acts?"

Sites?

"Yes. Oral? anal?"

Oral.

"No anal contact at all?"

No. Yes. Well, I mean, do you mean in my life?

"Yes."

Well, I have never had anal sex without a condom.

"Did you in your previous sexual relationship?"

Yes. I mean, I did wear one. He did.

"Are you HIV positive?"

No, I don't think I am.

"What do you mean?"

I practice safe sex.

"Which means what?"

I have protected anal sex and oral sex without ejaculation?

Dr. Linde, like every doctor I have had recently, touched me coldly when he checked me and, with his stiff impenetrable silence, generated a paranoia in me that has now blossomed into full-blown AIDS panic.

When a gay guy goes into any clinic, it is assumed that he is diseased. Guilty before innocent, and you spend your time trying to plead your case with a doctor who doesn't look you in the eye because he is disgusted by you. At least that is the way it is in your AIDS-panic brain. Even if the doctor is sensitive and well-trained and wears colorful kente cloth clothes and gives you free condoms, AIDS panic makes everything a mockery.

I suddenly feel so careless and irresponsible and guilty when I am in a clinic—all those words clearly describe me like a brochure. It's always the same when a gay guy gets into guilty AIDS-panic mode. We will never marry, we just spread disease. We are the lowest life forms on earth. We are the cockroaches behind the paneling. All we do is freak out about being dirty, get tested, think we are clean, and then become slowly dirty again. You feel free and then become repentant for having too much fun. Clean then dirty, slutty then repentant, over and over, in feverish flashes, a perpetual loop of torture.

Dr. Linde swabbed my urethra with the dryest cotton swab ever created by man and then gave me a "qwik strep," and my sore throat wasn't strep—some other infectious thing, which means I got it off of some man's plank. Probably that mistake of a one-night stand, Eddie. Or Jack . . . or Rod . . . or John. God, I am a dirty, guilty, diseased freak. "We won't know the results for two weeks, but take these antibiotics anyway," he says, and gives me a bottle of fat yellow pills.

I walked out of the clinic into the leftover trash of a street fair on Amsterdam. I don't know what everybody was celebrating. No one had swept the streets yet. Cups, flags, wrappers, a piece of dead fat chicken with clearish blubber smeared across the sidewalk. I walk to the subway and pass a woman sucking on a jumbo

Sprite in front of me. She turns her fanny pack toward the front, thinking I am a criminal. I glide down into the dark subway on the dented escalator.

I have been tested for gonorrhea of the mouth, gonorrhea of the dick, syphilis, and HIV. Here it comes, the panic, with all those thoughts about life after a positive result: having to rearrange my messy life, to carry around one of those weird oblong pill organizers, to learn to be optimistic all the time. Be positive, Mike! Be positive!

All our lives lead to disease and death. I think about that horrifying moment, two weeks from now, when I get my result, and walk back to my apartment, tell Benny, watching his face grip tightly, listen to the hollow voices of every single person I reveal the news to. I feel as if I already know the answer, I can't stop living out the trauma in my mind. Soon the sickness in me is mental and planted deep deep inside. And I shuffle through the memories of all my sex acts. Me having sex, naked, with desire, kissing and close (God, how stupid and attentive and full of energy I look), and I measure each encounter by the robotic risk factors listed on brochures and Web sites and posters.

And no matter how many little safe-sex habits I have formed, I can just sit in a chair and I will feel like my skin is shrinking on my body or that I am being covered with this chilly, chilly Saran Wrap and I think that I may be dead. I cannot walk one step without trying to construct that step as the step of a person who is HIV positive. I am HIV! I am a plus sign. Every step is a monitoring, a glandular recognition of my new, brief battery life.

Gerbil

There is a decomposing opossum lumped in the curb by Katawchuk Creek. This part of the street isn't in front of someone's home, and the animal-control van keeps driving by it, so I watch it rot over the entire span of eighth grade. It deflates, and its colorful fur loses its blue-white glow and brindle. A pool of worms surfaces at its raw ribs. It smiles wider and wider, teeth baring until the teeth are all that is left. After a rain, it settles into the cement of the curb, as flat as a tire tread, and then, like tires do, it flattens on the road and disappears.

Cable installers are drilling into the ground everywhere, their bright purple and yellow hieroglyphics spray-painted on the streets to mark their digs. They are always working. On the way to school they bow down to the ground in matching jumpsuits, never looking up, never loitering, always concentrating on sluicing through the green lawns.

I walk home through the Katawchuk Creek shortcut, which is gored with a cement sewer trough that I used to plug with branches and sand when I was eight or so, so immature to me now. Ninth grade is coming up, and I heard from some source, from the subdivision folklore, or from my own waking nightmares, I don't know, that in high school, if you forget your gym clothes, you have to participate in your underwear. I believe this because I am religious. I walk home with my trombone case and stack of books, fearful of tough teenagers and of God. If someone calls me a fairy or someone loogies my locker, it is God. If I am tripped in the halls, my books skating across the dry hall like hockey pucks, it is God. If I am masturbating in the bathroom and suddenly flash to the sickening image of Frau Freund's fat ass, it is God. These are the tools of God. I understand now that experience is part of a larger tablet of God's laws. God is here and He is very insane.

I have a small scoop of doubt about the underwear rule, but I know that God can detect skeptics, and He will twist reality and make me play dodgeball in my tightie whities anyway even if the rule isn't initially true.

I sit on the trunk of my brother's blue Camaro. My parents got him one and no one notices it's the same kind of car as Ken Fenning's except for me. Ken Fenning is long gone from our lives. My brother is old and has girlfriends. My legs are warm from the radiant tailpipe, and around me are the cement driveways and trimmed azalea hedges, the efficient sewers and repaved streets, washed cars, white curbs, and forest-green trash bins. In the houses I can hear at least two different families wiping dinner scraps into the trash, rinsing and racking plates into their wide-load dishwashers. The dishes clink. Water showers out of the nozzles into the tunnels of stainless steel, into unseen drains and pipes, flushing and merging, into the deeper dug septic tanks, and then the water pumps into huge electrified sewage plants planted into the capable suburban earth, which is itself made of its own tectonic, scraping plates.

I know that high school will be more of this: me in the school halls with a pit of dread in my stomach, me playing trombone heartlessly, me having my sinful, fleshy sex dreams that make me feel when I wake like I lost something, me looking at jumbo jets overhead, imagining some lonely guy in a seat who looks down at me.

The sun quickly lowers behind the Parkses' house across the street and I hold myself woozily afloat with that schoolish swell, that funereal, autumnal, pencilly, papery Back to School! zing in my stomach. There is no option but school. I can do nothing else. I will never, never rebel. I understand I have no choices, just a series of grades and colored textbooks to absorb. I will endure ninth grade, and the grades to come, like scars.

I cannot confirm the rumor about wearing underwear in gym class because I bring those precious polyester shrouds diligently every day. I ball them around my hands to pad the hard trombone handle, and walk to school occasionally bending down to check for their presence.

Gym is not fun. Our teacher, Mr. Spartina, is a chesty man with a southern-sheriff kind of accent and a red, red face and a wide forehead. He screams very loudly and on the first day places us in a grid formation on the gym floor, where we are supposed to sit for roll call every day. I have to sit in the front of the grid because everything in school is done in alphabetical order.

"I want you to duplicate yer name on these three-ba-fahv index cards!"

I start writing my name over and over, and Mr. Spartina comes over and rips it out of my hand and says, "No, no, no, Albo! What are you, some kinda artist? This isn't art class!" And everyone laughs and I don't even really understand what is so funny but I do already know, after only two minutes of the first day of the first class, that I will be made the class's pansy example. Of course, as if I'd won an unlucky lottery, there is nobody else in my class with a last name that begins with A, B, C, D, or E, and so Todd Flamadio sits behind me. Todd Flamadio has a huge, muscular quarterback body and he is only thirteen—it's like he squatted one day and strained until his pituitary gland exploded and socked an early burst of adolescence through his frame.

"Hey!" he says to me. "What the fuck do you have on your socks?" I have these socks with green snakes on them, and when you pull them up they elongate. I thought they were really neat.

They're snakes.

"They look like frogs!" Todd says. "Albo has frogs on his socks!" Todd says.

No, I don't, I say, but Todd has already publicized this tabloid version and it is unstoppable and it spreads through the grid of kids and everyone wants to see and they crane their necks and laugh.

I do have a group of friends now. Alex, Troy, and Bernhard. I wear my snake socks with them and they don't say anything and we throw a Frisbee around after school. On the weekends we sleep at one another's houses all the time. Mostly we go to Troy's because he has a new wide-screen TV or we go to Alex's, whose dad works night shifts at the newspaper, and we run around throwing food at each other.

We are eating Mama Celeste personal pizzas at Alex's and we stack them on top of one another into an oozing five-layer cake. Alex cuts it and pulls out a slice like a pie, and a bridge of mozzarella stretches across the plate. "Hey, guess what? Cheese is solid B.O.," he says, and we laugh and laugh and laugh.

Alex has two dogs. His house is never clean and the shades are always drawn so that his divorced dad can sleep. Alex eats Patio burritos all the time and his refrigerator is stacked with them. Bernhard's parents are French, and he doesn't wash his hair as often as other kids, so he has chunks of dandruff the size of fingernail clippings. He lives in the same town-house development as Alex and Troy. All of their parents are divorced, too. They all have many, many pets. We don't have pets.

"I don't want dog doo everywhere!" my mom says. I tend to agree with her, because one time I was over at Alex's playing Frisbee and I slipped and dog shit smeared all the way up the side of my jeans like a Poo Bedazzler. We had a hermit crab named Felix. I always wanted to pet it, but it would shy away into its shell. One time I put Windex in its water tray, not to kill it, just because . . . and it turned gray, dried, and died. We also had gerbils once but they, too, died. They were named Benny and Denny. I kept them in my room next to my bed, and they would scurry under the fluffy coils of cedar chips every time I walked into my room, so I never knew what they looked like until after the accident.

Every night before I go to bed I put on a really sad song like the B-52's "Dirty Back Road" or Pat Benatar's "Don't Let It Show" and light a thin candle my mother got for me and lie on my pillow and cry so that my tears will crest to the song's final verses. Then I will say good night to Benny and Denny and go to sleep.

Alex and Troy and Bernhard and I play this game where you throw the Frisbee at someone to tag them. It hurts when it hits you, but it's funny to see someone get conked with the Frisbee, so we do it anyway. We are in the woods and I am waiting for Alex—and I am the last one caught. He sees me and I am running and laughing. I reach a mossy clearing in the forest and Alex stands there, ready to throw it. I feel something sting me on my shin, and I look down and there is a bee, and it is joined by a zigzagging clump of more bees. There is a hole by my foot in the moss, and more bees spit out of it like popcorn, twirling around one another and I scream *BEEEEEEEEEEEEEEEEEES!*

I scream and run and run. I run to Troy and Bernhard and Alex, standing there. I am panting and have my hand up to my chest.

"You scream like such a girl!" Alex says, and I try to stand with my legs further apart and not feel the sting on my leg.

That night I am really tired and I light a candle and listen to "Fall," the last song on Berlin's second album, and I cry like always and fall asleep. I dream of men again, all in a row, and on the end is Mr. Spartina with his strangely hard, paunchy belly and he is motioning for me to come over to him so that I can press my face into his stomach, and I am about to, but the scene begins to flicker, and I am half awake, with light playing over my eyelids. I open them and see a flame at my face. I see Benny and Denny's cage aflame. I forgot to blow out the candle and it tipped over and the cedar chips are on fire. I shoot up out of bed and look into the blackened cage. Little Denny is a knotted crisp, curled into the shape of a charcoal briquette. Benny is scratching the corner of the cage, his body incinerating. I inhale a breath to scream but decide to say "No! Fuck!" with masculinity.

I run to the bathroom and fill with water the pink bucket set aside for vomits that my mom keeps under the sink and run back into my room and douse the flames. Benny sits there, wet and flat, breathing rapidly, not making a noise.

He lives for two weeks, but his paws become flesh lumps. His little front legs lose their fur and then fall off like treated warts. He tries to spin in his creaky, charred wheel, but his stubs keep falling through the wire. Creak, creak, creak, thump. Then, one morning, I wake up and his body is splayed out on the side of the cage, motionless.

I go to school that day and in gym class Todd starts calling me a fag because we are in the middle of a flag-football and "fag" is a word just one letter away from "flag" and he can't resist. I am filled with indignation because I am experiencing death today.

Just stop it, Todd, I say. *My pet died today.*

"What pet?" he asks.

I had these gerbils—

Todd begins to howl so loudly that he erases my *Shut ups* and everyone else's increasing whoops as they find out I have pet gerbils, and once again I am confused, because I did not know that this was the time that America is in love with the idea that fags put gerbils up their butts for pleasure and have AIDS. I don't know this.

"Hey! Albo has a pet gerbil!"

No, I don't, I say. *It died,* I say. Everyone laughs and laughs and laughs. I walk over to Todd Flamadio and he backs away. "Ahh! Don't come near me! You've got AIDS!"

We play basketball. I hover on the edge of the court, with its inscrutable crop circle of lines and markings. The world is unreal with its flurries and sudden changes. Who knows what will happen next, who knows what strange gesture I make that will bring attention to me, who knows anything. I am dazzled by it all.

I feel lucky, though, because I am not on a team with Todd. The kids on my team are erasable and invisible, like Troy. Charles Inning and Jeff Wrenn. They have mom haircuts and don't yell loudly. They treat me like a veteran—empathetic, but not too close. I am passed the ball and I grasp for it and I dribble it in this chance to prove I am gerbil-free, and I pass it to Jeff Wrenn. "Good pass!" he says to me, and I am so grateful.

When I get home, Mom has set out six chicken breasts to be grilled. On her portable kitchen TV, a newscaster mentions AIDS and asks Lisa Lakepotter, who has the story, to describe how it is spreading through gays. Her words are incomprehensible to me because I am busy watching the footage of men crowding a street in San Francisco. They are sweaty, old, with steel-wool mustaches and leather vests. It's a parade, sometime before the disease, and then the image shifts to a doctor's office—a hollowed-out man with big eyes lying on butcher paper, skin as pale as the dry clinic walls.

"That's too bad," Mom says. "Could you light the grill? I feel sorry for their families."

I walk holding the white tray of breasts through the family room to the big black grill on the patio. When I reach the sliding screen door, I step through to the patio and turn one eye to my mother. *I feel sorry for the people who can't choose to be that way.*

"I do too," she says, and I quickly step outside.

My test results were all negative. I know that in a few months I will fill myself with AIDS panic again, but for now I can't hide my elation. It's bad, I know, and I should try to be sober and repentant like a little naughty mule in a storybook who learns his lesson, but I don't fucking care. I am clean again, I am free again, and I am tossed out onto the beautiful world with its blinking traffic lights and trees and buildings and honking cars and Eric, Eric, Eric. That go-go-boy guy, that shining planet who is beautiful and has a body hard as a credit card.

I saw him when I went to the gold old Wonder Bar last night, sitting on a tall stool by the video screen showing porno. Eric sat next to me and smiled, and I saw his eyes look into mine. We are curious deer, silently sniffing each other.

"Hey! What's up?" he says.

Not much. I'm sort of bummed it's the end of summer.

"The swan song of summer," he says.

The swan song, right right. He grabs my knee. He wears a vintage red Members Only jacket with speakers embedded in the shoulders. *Cool jacket,* I say.

"Yeah, I got it at the Salvation Army for, like, three dollars."

Do the speakers work?

"Yeah, don't you remember this thing? It was totally hot when Walkmen first came out. It's a Walkjacket."

A Walkjacket, ha-ha! That's so cool!

"I know, and it still works. You just hook up your Walkman to the jacket and it plays through the speakers. Here, listen."

What are you playing?

Missing Persons.

I love them! I can't hear anything.

"You have to get closer," he said. And so I put my ear on his chest and smelled the inside of his neck, and it was as if he had vaporized and entered my body and gently massaged me from inside. His hand moved up to my waist, and I sat there for a while listening to "Destination Unknown" and his heart beating. Someone walked by, a dark silhouette I recognize. The figure turns and looks at me like I am a relative. I quickly realize who he is. He doesn't have his Nike hat on now, but I had sex with him at Ozone. I also realize that I am wearing the exact outfit I wore that night. I look away and ignore him.

"Hey, let's go hang out on the couch," Eric says. We sat and he stretched his arm out behind me. We talked about Connecticut and what drugs are good. We looked at each other seriously, conspiring over a burning bomb we were trying to pretend wasn't between us. We spoke about objects and music, and I don't know what I said my favorites are because we just slowly closed in on each other and kissed. It was the warmest, most pleasurable kiss I have ever had. We kissed.

Then we talked for a while about how we wore our tube socks in junior high school. He wore them pulled up, which means he was sporty. He moved to New York from New Jersey five years ago. He lives in the same number building and number apartment as me but, weirdly, four blocks away. "How crazy," he says smokily. *That's so weird*, I say. "You have a great smile," he says.

Thanks, I say. He is silent but fills those silences with his smile. We are both kind of drunk. He is probably drunker than me. He invites me to his place.

We walk to his street. He lives with this guy Blaze and they trade off sleeping on the couch or in the walk-in closet that is curtained off. It's kind of a cool deal. Communal. Whoever gets there first gets the bed. Blaze walks out of the closet space and I am introduced to him and I am very, very friendly, asking him *What do you do?* and saying *Wow, what an interesting name—I bet you get that all the time.* He stands there with eyeliner around his eyes and talks about how he wants to design CD jewel boxes. *That's so cool,* I say, and he says "Yeah," and smiles slightly, and then says, "Good night" and slinks into the closet.

Eric turns to me, twinkling. We make out on his couch with the lights on, two windows opened to the street, presenting us like a moving diorama.

Aren't you going to close the curtains? I say, and he says, "No, I think it's kind of hot," meaning sexy, and I say *Cool* again. The last time I said "Cool" this much in my life was when I was seven and into the Fonz. "Ayyyyyyyy! I'm the Fonz!" But I don't care.

I keep thinking, while I am naked, that Blaze is not making any trips to the bathroom, which is weird, I think, because I always make trips to the bathroom. We fall asleep.

I wake up and Eric is on top of me and says, "Won't you be my neighbor?" I laugh. He tumbles off me. "You know what I feel like listening to? China Crisis."

Oh my God, I used to love them. They totally define my junior year of high school in Springfield, Virginia, which is this suburb outside of D.C. Where in New Jersey are you from?

"Ridgefield."

That's where my officemate is from, weird. I know whatever about the name game, but did you know Gina Kapadopolis?

"Gina Kapadopolis? Yeah, I think she went to my high school."

You're kidding!

"She's sort of short and has big hair and wears lots of lipstick?"

Yes!

"Yeah. She went out with my friend Taylor."

Really? When you were in high school? How long?

"I don't know, like a month or so."

Did you hang out with her?

"I guess. I don't remember."

Taylor. What is Taylor's last name?

"Law."

What? Law? L-A-W Law?

"Yeah."

Taylor Law.

"Yeah. We used to hang out in high school."

You guys hung out? What did you do?

"Drove around and smoked."

I am fizzing with magic. He doesn't really remember anything, but I am in awe of the minute thread that connects us all. His eyes are closing and he is dozing off and I know I am supposed to leave.

You know, it's cool if you want to sleep in my bed if you want, I say in this concierge tone.

"No, I like to sleep alone, I am a really light sleeper. Thanks, though," he says, which completely makes sense, because so am I, and I respect his honesty and need for a good night's sleep, so we kiss goodbye again. "I'll see you," he says definitively, and I walk down the street and see these two Dominican kids kicking an airless soccer ball against a wall, and a man smoking on a milk crate and a pretty girl with lots of eye makeup on and wearing a fake fur, and I love all of our lives.

Hazer

It's tenth grade, I am in high school now and I am still in band, and I am still carrying that stupid trombone in its clonky case. We are trying to raise money to take a band trip down to Florida for the Eastern Seaboard Mid-Atlantic Symphonic Band Competition, and we are told we have to sell things door-to-door to raise money. Our bumbly bandleader, Mr. Payne, who has organized this trip for over twenty years, tries to muster the energy to explain our plan: "So pass these around the room. These are your order forms. You only get one order form. If you lose the order form you will not get another order form."

The product we are selling is cheese and sausage. I have to walk around my neighborhood and knock on people's doors and ask them if they want any cheese or sausage.

I make no sales. I knock on ten doors and stutter softly and everybody looks above me as if there is a storm coming and then says no. I go home every night and my parents ask me if I have made any sales and I say no. This is when America is in love with the idea that without pain there is no gain. No pain, no gain, no pain, no gain, so anything that feels inarguably insufferable and wrong and humiliating, like going door-to-door selling stupid mail-order food that nobody wants to buy, is just a way to succeed. "You need to try harder," my dad says when he gets home from his mysterious work. He empties out his pockets on the kitchen counter, clinking keys and change and Chap Stick. "You have to go out there and think 'I am going to sell this cheese and sausage. I am going to make it happen.'" Whatever job it is that my dad has, it is one where he wears suits, comes home smelling of files and lip balm and fluorescence, and knows these pain-gain things.

He must have suffered pain in the military, crawling around in the mud in boot camp, some power-mad captain making him do extra push-ups, horrors of war too horrible to mention. And he has gained, too. He has a car, he pays for me to eat, he has no regard for five dollars (because I steal five dollars out of his wallet often). He is even gracious enough to pay for dinners occasionally. Once we all went to a Vietnamese restaurant with his work friends Bill and Gary. A big grill sits in the middle of the table, and waitresses bring raw food for you to cook yourself. Bill, Gary, and my dad laughed about what a boob Jimmy Carter was and sizzled their Vietnamese meat.

The next day I am standing at my locker and unloading my large stack of books, blank order forms neatly in its shelf space, and I feel something approaching behind me. Something big. Something glacial. Some emergency of approaching electricity, and I turn around and Jason Hazer walks by—his atoms ricocheting off the lockers and walls and people and me. I am left breathing heavily in his radiating wake.

Jason Hazer is a year older than me and attends the same school, but it seems as if he lives in some exotic part of Springfield I have never known about, some leafy, gated, curvy Copenhagen where there are hardworking, naturally blond people who have charming houses with colorful shutters and grandmothers who wear traditional clogs. His hair is dirty blond and spiked, not wet mousse-abusey—he does it the cool way, the way the guy in Big Country does it, dry and tall so it moves like wheat in a country field.

He is just plain old hot. He won the Most Individual Superlative because that is the power of Jason—so popular yet never stopping being himself: An Individual. For example, he was listening to U2 when everybody else was yammering on about the J. Geils Band, and he was the first person in the world to turn up the collar of his OP shirt, and then when everybody in the world was doing it, he was the first person to crease that fucking collar back down.

If you see him in the halls, an unexplainable cataractal swell immobilizes you. I see him and I am just washed over by him—his body shaped perfectly in his clothes, and dark eyebrows and amber-waves-of-grain hair. But then he'll be holding the hand of Tasha Bartok, or one of those other girls with wide hips, base-slathered faces, and oily smiles that silently say, "I'm on the Pill because I'm getting fucked by the hottest guy ever created!"

But still, he seems alone. I sometimes imagine he has a tough homelife, his mother working at a roadside greasy spoon really late, his father dying long ago of black lung, his little armless sister with an angelic face who needs help eating, his house an old, paint-peeling, uninsulated two-bedroom with a midnight train tooting by his window, and him in his grotty room, doing sit-ups, looking out the window, tears welling up in his eyes. There is some secret zoned in him that only I detect. I think, "I can find and unravel that sad knot in him nobody else can get to. I am the one." I suppose Jason represents something symbolic to me, something about ambition and desire and self-esteem, blah blah, but my attempts to get near him always make my cells jigger. Jason fits in me like a spine.

Listen to the sound of his name. Jason . . . Hazer. . . . Jay Sun Hay Zer. It has that sound to it. I swear, if I had the power to try another path, I'd run away from high school, find some charitable program in which I would go to Africa and learn what linguistic anthropology means, live with the Ndembu tribe for a year studying the spontaneous hair-matting of old women during burial rites, befriend some batty British anthropologist, kiss his Guggenheimed, Fulbrighted ass, get a grant, go to high schools across America to study the linguistic components of popular people's names, and I'm sure that I would find that, morphemically and phonemically, the syllables, vowels, and consonants of the name "Jay-Sun Hay-Zer" make up the purest, most perfect linguistic construction of popularity.

I write a poem about him in my private red spiral:

There is only one kind of eye
and it looks
and pierces
you look
your eyes
blue pools
that I must swim in.

Oh Jason. . . . Popular people like Hazer always feign innocence about their power: "I don't know . . . I'm just friends with a lot of people" (it was the one sentence I desperately snatched up as I was walking by his locker). The cliques are strong as walls in high school, and I am not one of those who say, "Oh, our school really didn't have cliques like that. Everybody supported each other." I see the cliques clearly. They are there and it is a fact in this balkanized world.

I have to scratch and claw my way to the top. It is a rough road, but I do it. It happens very very quickly, and I am blurred with ambition, so I can't quite articulate each small step I take up the ladder. It's almost as if I move intuitively up the chain like a salmon or a leaf-munching bug. I mutate to cope with the changing grades until my junior year, with my sharp claws and layered haircut and proper Nike canvas sneakers, and I rise to the highest phylum.

I start out as a band geek, with my trombone and fearful face. One time I wear jeans with a hole in the knee and I am walking with my friend Terry Sparrow (who is unpopular because his name is a girl's and a bird's) and I am telling him how the hole in my jeans makes my knee sweat and this burnout girl hears me. She has blond hair in wings with brown roots, black black mascara, and a Rolling Stones baseball shirt (over which she has placed a long white carpetbag sweater with big pockets at the hips), and her jeans are tucked into brown knee boots. And she is smoking!

"Your knee sweats? Huh, only fags' knees sweat," she says, and exhales. I just look ahead and keep walking. But I burn her, because I just take my middle finger, put it in my pocket, and walk away.

This middle-finger maneuver is very satisfying. I do it all the time to Mr. Reer, the trombone teacher, when he shakes his head and says he doesn't understand what is happening to me. "Did you practice this at all?" he will say to me, and I blubber, *Well, yeah, sort of,* lying so completely because I never, never touch that dumb trombone. If I do pick it up, I blow into it and every note sounds as meek as an amplified me. Mr. Reer just looks at me as if I skip class and score dope for my angel dust addiction. He knows I am lying and gives me a long talk on dedication and practice. He also uses the "No pain, no gain" phrase. "Look, Mike, you can never progress if you don't practice at least thirty minutes a day. The trombone takes commitment. No pain, no gain." I nod dutifully, positioning my secret fuck finger under my thigh.

I pack my cheese and sausage bag and walk through the new con-dominium development on the other side of the Springfield Plaza. I haven't been here since it was being built, when Troy and Alex and Bernhard and I threw Frisbees around the plowed, flattened dirt. Now it is a development called South Sea Forest, complete with a tiki-theme thatched-roof gazebo and bamboo shoot signs marking the handicap parking spots. This is the last area I have not not sold cheese and sausage. I walk up to the first door, white aspen wood swirling with its black knotted eyes, and I am staring at the eyes when I knock on the door and Jason Hazer answers the door.

I am selling this cheese to go on this trip to Florida with the band?

He stands there, listening. And I am trying not to look at him because that way, somehow, this entire meeting will not register in his memory. *And I was just wondering if you'd like to buy some of this?*

"Let me ask my mom," he says, and leaves the doorway and I quickly glance into the house, and it has a long, mirrored foyer and a fig tree in a Chinese wine-carrying jug at the end of the hall, glim-mering under a skylight. He comes back. He is barefoot, and his measured, long toes come forward to me. "Nope, sorry," he says, and I say, *Thanks anyway!* And he closes the door, and I feel a little good because "Thanks anyway!" is kind of, slightly, a cool thing to say.

I walk home preparing to see him at school, perfecting my "Hey, what's up?" head nod. Like a mountain climber I will use this meeting as a precious wedge. I will dig my fingers into this small crevice and climb into familiarity with Jason Hazer with all my strength.

The next day I go to school and look for him between every period, but I don't see him for weeks. I wait and wait, and when I finally do see him, it's been long enough for him to ignore me socially in a completely classy, understandable way.

There is this one burnout girl in band named Tammy who often wears long, flowing coats, a black fedora, and a long, diaphanous purple scarf (or simply shawls and clogs) and a layered, divided cascade of feathered hair, and I befriend her. She has a burnout exterior, but she is a good student and very organized. Her three-ring notebook, stickered with Deadhead skulls and Molly Hatchets and Foghats and Peter Framptons, is meticulously divided into sections with colored tabs and tiered labels. She sits behind me, in accelerated English, Jeff Wrenn sits in front of me, and the teacher calls us the Triumvirate because we three always raise our hands to talk about the light and dark imagery in *A Separate Peace* or the use of rebirth and death symbolism in *Light in August*. Tammy always smiles and says, "Hey, good morning" when she walks in. One day after class she asks if I want to hang out, and we go driving around in her Honda to 7-Eleven and Fair Oaks Mall and Friendly's. We talk about TV and make fun of other people.

I meet her burnout girlfriends: Rachael, Stacey, and Natalia.

They think I am friendly and fun because I'd rather talk than get in their pants. Soon they are always picking me up in their low, smoky cars and we drive around listening to Led Zep. These are wise, wise women. They reminisce about their lives like they are forty-year-old secretary-divorcées. "Remember when we went to Jack Santos's grain punch party?" one will say. "Aaaaah!" the other two will say. Or they will just say, "Wooooo!"

These girls are full of stories, but they don't tell me directly. I just sit in the car and slowly piece together that they have already tried pot, have given hand jobs, have crashed through windshields in two separate drunk-driving accidents and lived to tell about it, and have swallowed pints and pints of jizz before high school, down their sixth-grade milk-mustache mouths.

They have done it all, and now they are bored with their social life and don't want to do much at all, so we just sit on car hoods with six-packs, or we go to the Chesapeake Bagel Bakery because this is when America de-ethnicizes bagels and it is suddenly okay for good conservative Christians to eat something associated with dirty Jews. We go there and have Bagelnuts ("It's a bagel and a donut rolled into one! A Bagelnut!"). They have me wear Hush Puppies and faded jeans with torn, frayed cuffs, and encourage me to quit band. It is assumed but never said that I am not into girls, and they abhor boys now anyway.

They rehash stories all the time: One time, one weekend, Tammy gets together with Peter Cavera at his tenth-grade birthday party. Everyone is drunk and passed out, and Peter drags Tammy up to his room and pushes her down into his crotch (a casual hint for her to blow him), and so she does, but she jerks back her head when he comes.

"What's your problem?" he says.

"Fuck you!" she yells, walking out of the house, him yelling back at her, "Fuck you! Why don't you come back when you grow some titties!"

She gets in her car and drives drunk across town, stopping at 7-Eleven for some Virginia Slims and then driving to the McDonald's parking lot, where Rachael, Stacey, Natalia, and other burnouts lean on cars and smoke until cops drive by and shine their lights. The girls bring Tammy over to a more private area bordered by Dumpsters and wait for her to give them details about the blow job. Tammy thinks about it for a long while, and then says, "It's like sucking on a clean finger."

"Did you deep-throat it?" Stacey asks.

"Yeah."

"What happened? Did you gag?"

"No."

"How?"

"I just opened my throat," she says. Years later, now that they are all masters of blow jobs, they tell the story again in front of me and they all laugh and scream, and I sit there, quietly, thinking about how Mr. Reer demanded I do that in my stupid trombone lessons I finally don't have to take anymore because I seem fulfilled to my parents with my accelerated-English-class girlfriend, Tammy. I think about giving Mr. Reer head and opening my throat for him. I get a boner in my cords.

Some time midway through sophomore year, there is a shake-up in the burnout power structure. A rebel faction called Punks is making its presence known. Tammy and I decide we must mutate. Tammy cuts her hair, squishes gel through it, and it is suddenly spiked. She tells me to cut the sleeves off my rugby shirt, and she cuts my hair into a short do with a high front cowlick. We go to parties where guys in basements thrash around to really bad music. They have crew cuts and wear green army sweaters with patches on the shoulders and talk about the power of the white race. I stay upstairs with the girls and the more effeminate guys, and I meet a girl who calls herself Bitch and who has one pink sprig of hair right in front of her head. She is really nice, actually, and the best thing about knowing her is saying hi to her in public places like the hall or something.

Hi Bitch!

But, even though Punk has character and solidity as a movement, and even though Tammy and I show promise as future perfect punkers, we both agree the music sucks. Tammy and I crave bouncier music that has melodies—New Wave. We hang out with Leslie and Jenna and go to underage clubs and record stores and buy Yaz records and compliment Leslie, who is really big, by telling her she looks like Alison Moyet. Leslie wears lots and lots of bracelets and streaks her eye makeup in swooshes up her temples. Jenna is a crossover New Wave–popular girl because she is beautiful, has an asymmetrical haircut, and always says the same thing about everything: "Bonus!" The four of us go to these dumb sock hops together after football games and dance to Billy Idol, U2, and the Go-Go's, my favorite band. "Bonus! It's the Go-Go's!" Jenna says. "Now they're playing Modern English—*Bonus!*"

There is a very radical shift in history going on at the time—Molly Ringwald is growing in recognition, R.E.M. and the Smiths are showing up on mixed tapes, vintage clothing is being bought. I wear a thin leather tie one day to school and swiftly melt into the mod crowd, the more presentable New Wavers who wear vests, plaids, and buttoned-up collars with brooches. We all have long bangs and gain power by our involvement and visibility in the arts. This gives me a kind of cool visa/green card to be able to befriend the smarter and stylish popular people, respected by the burnouts, mods, and lunkhead football jock types, and I become popular.

All of this happens in two months.

My brother is a senior now. He doesn't bother me as much—mostly because he is busy dating. He is old-school popular: Budweiser, classic rock FM. His friend Steve wears a fedora and carries around an electric bass. Mark is a senior and there is a great opportunity for me to network with the people who know him and become more popular myself, but I never see Mark or anyone I should know. The senior hall is big and far away, and actually I am a little confused about where exactly these seniors are, but I know he is popular because we had our house T.P.'d twice and he brings home girls at least once a month. The girls always have drastically different hair lengths. Jennifer with short, close layers that she constantly combs to maintain their alignment like a Zen garden. Linda with long sun-tinted hair that comes down in clumpy tassels over an underbrush of brown. Shauna with her hair so spun up and hairsprayed that it is impossible to figure out what color it is—it could be black, it could be blond, but its lacquer of spray creates a sheen that blinds the retina to all spectra.

Mark has a party because my parents are out of town at a wine-tasting weekend with the Fennings. I spend all my time up in my room with the portable TV, and I can hear the thick choruses of people at the kitchen table, and the plinking of quarters into the chug glass. I defiantly go downstairs for more Fudge Jumbles and Mark grabs me in this brotherly drunk way that makes me blush. "This is my brother, Mike!" he says, and everyone says hi. Everyone is really, really friendly. This girl Sandi, who is orange with self-tanning cream, comes up to me and kisses me on the mouth. "You are such a cutie!" she says. She takes me off to the patio and asks me who I listen to. *Well, my favorite group right now is Berlin.*

"I love them!" she says, and squeezes my arm. She smells like baked makeup. Gordy Archnow jumps in front of her and picks me up.

"Mark's bro! Mark's bro!" he says, and twirls me around over his shoulder. He carries me around the party and keeps saying I am a really cool kid. This inflates me and I feel like he can truly see the way I will be when I am older, because he is so much older and drunk, so he is perceptive. Then he grabs the back of my head and kisses the top of my head with his sweaty face. It is very wet.

I go back upstairs and watch *The Sea Gypsies,* this amazing retelling of the Swiss Family Robinson story, where a family is stranded on an island and must fend for themselves through storm (man vs. nature, not man vs. man or man vs. himself). Mark goes out to his car, I hear it turn on and then off and then on again. I run to the window and Mark sits in this girl's car, and it huffs in neutral. I watch the car for a long time. All I see is a forearm and a shoulder moving through the dark car interior. I can tell they are having sex by the motion of the limbs—circular motions, sudden stops, figure eights, numerous strokes. Their skin keeps moving and moving. It reminds me of colonoscopy footage they show on the those weird surgery shows late at night, because you just see these flesh balls and beating organs and you cannot place their location on the body.

It is junior year and I have cultivated my popularity to the level where it is possible for me to move in and out of cliques fluidly. Of course I have to cast a handful of friends away like wet rags: Troy and Bernhard (not Alex, because he falls into the copper mine quarry and dies). But it is worth it . . . because I have befriended Paige and she is a friend of a friend of . . . ¿ That's right—Jason Hazer.

Hi Jason!

"Hey, Albo."

I start hanging out with this whole new circle of popular people who think I am funny, like Pete Shane and Jeremy Loud, and I stand at their lockers. I achieve a kind of second tier of popularity. Second-tierers are not as luminous as Jason Hazer or Pete Shane or Tasha Bartok. We are more moonish, reflecting their light well when we stand next to them. Tammy achieves second-tier status through an intricate, pioneering bi-school attachment plan: Her boyfriend is well known in nearby Lake Katawchuk High School as an award-winning track-and-field athlete. Even though that school's inner ecosystem is completely unknown to us here at Springfield HS, Tammy delicately drags her boyfriend to sporting events, which gradually spreads his popular residue over our high school and onto her. I beam with pride for her.

For me, second-tier status means I don't have to have a girl-friend. I can just beam in my Surf Naked! long-sleeved tee and that will be enough. The higher tiers make you look as if you are productive and get good grades, and if you look it, than you can be it. You always smile here in these tiers. You can blur your faults from scrutiny. I am just popular and that's enough. I am thankful for my second-tier status because I can enjoy all the benefits of my position without ever having to become a figurehead. Pete Shane, I notice, has so much responsibility. He can't jerkily grab his front pockets if he panics that he lost his BMW keys, for example. He must say hi to everyone, he must always have his Vuarnet sunglasses accessible, his rust-colored check shirt must be rolled to a particular area of the upper forearm and stay there.

The look of the upper tiers is strictly comfort style. Sure there are goths, punkers, New Wavers, Madonna wannabes, Deadheads, burnouts, cowpunks, heavy-metal satanists, but above all that, in the upper tiers, clothes are chosen only for the sake of comfort— all-cotton, softness, Polarfleece, Gore-Tex outerwear, crewnecks, clammers, cableknits and surfwear, even though the surf is three hours away and is lame, low, cold, and Atlantic.

Now I am a senior, it is spring, and have about one month to enjoy my caste climb. I stand at Pete Shane's locker at break, I drive around with David Spears and crazy Carla Gavelbetter, I skip school twice with Jeremy Loud. We go to the train tracks and smoke menthols and he confides in me that he really wants a long-term girlfriend. Jeremy is going to go to West Point next fall, but he likes me because I'm weird and represent the art world, so he can freely look at the sky and say things like "Wow, the stars are cool."

I go to three parties: one at Neil Hayden's, who likes John Cougar Mellencamp and is short; one at Jenny Carver's, where I do Whipits with Todd Flamadio and he tells me he always thought I was cool before he passes out facedown; and one where there is grain punch. I say hi to Lara Kelsie and she says hi, I do my hilarious Pac-Man imitation and everyone laughs, and I join a game of quarters and bounce one quarter perfectly into a shot glass and make everyone drink.

Jason is always strangely absent. Someone will casually say, "Hey! Where's Hazer?" And I will bristle up like a bionic hare to listen to the bit of information about him while trying to look as bland as possible, holding my large red plastic keg beer cup. Jason has become a pure urge, and when I fantasize about him I am fantasizing about all men, about future men, about the larger idea of future and my body negotiating its vast, possible plains. Somehow I have to express this to Jason. And so I try his eyes. When I look into them for the brief seconds I have with him—in the halls or when he stops briefly at Pete's locker, I try my best to fill my look with information about this barren future of mine that is hungry for scenery.

I kind of stop hanging out with Tammy, but she has a boyfriend now and she doesn't call me either. She is angry because I am hanging out with Pete Shane and the guys, and she used her status to get a boyfriend. I do not feel bad at all because I have worked very, very hard to get where I am, and I know, even though I have never been in one, that when you are in a couple, everything else looks more fun. Still, Tammy scowls at me in the halls now. One time I am at Pete's locker telling him about how I thought I had to wear underwear if I forgot my gym clothes in seventh grade (I lie and make it years ago), and Tammy walks by and sticks out her middle finger and says, "How is the air up there, Mike?" A bitter reference from an old Bangles song on their obscure first album. It is a well-placed, puncturing jab.

"Boy, she sure got you," Pete says, and leans back, his streaked long bangs sifting gently over his right eye. I just laugh nervously. But under the nervousness is the easeful, summery feeling that I am popular. My head is clear, classes are suddenly easier, teachers glint and grin at you. I skip history and no one notices. I look and feel better because of popularity's constant spa. I hear about parties without even investigating or asking. My senior-year science project is The Human Aura, which takes me about two hours to construct—a white piece of cardboard that people stand in front of and I record the colors I think they give off. I effortlessly get an A.

Then, in that fear-making warmth of spring, that lost longing and gusty wetness of school-grounds grass and weak crocuses of front yards, death comes. The *Challenger* space shuttle explodes, and these three burnouts I don't know very well get in a drunk-driving accident and two of them die and one of them is hospitalized. Our school holds a silent prayer during my fifth-period trig class for the kids and Christa McAuliffe. That very same week Q107 has this contest that declares whatever school can turn in the most postcards to the station will win a free concert in their school by Wang Chung, the then top-10 pop group from England. Our entire school bonds together: "Let's do it for Brandy, Aaron, and Lao-Ting!" We work very very hard, writing extra postcards during ten-minute break and lunch. And we do it. We win! Somehow we convince ourselves that by winning the contest we are doing a really important thing for those poor dead and injured burnouts. In actuality, we are pretty much celebrating their commitment to their roles as burnouts in our tiny, gross little microcosm, since they actually did burn out—what burnouts are supposed to do.

My mother is very well informed about the accident. "I was talking to Aaron's mother in Supermart. Apparently the car hit a five-hundred-year-old oak tree and it took off the top of the car in seconds, and sheared off their torsos completely. Could you light the grill?" She is always informed. Supermart is a hub for macabre information. Often when my mother goes there, she comes back and tells me how Angela Wetwel's son just lost his cheeks to a rare skin disorder or specifically how much of Tricia Slosser's leg was turned into pulp when her brother ran her over with the lawn mower: "It was completely liquefied. She must have weak bones."

Anyway, that Friday, we all drive two miles to the school in our cars that our parents gave us, park on the side of the highway, and march into the gym. The national news is there. John Blond, voted Class Clown, and his girlfriend, Best Dressed Carla Gavelbetter (she's so crazy!), stand beside me. We wear T-shirts that say "I♥Wang Chung" to show our support for Wang. Scott Holiday comes on from Q107 to tell us how psyched he is to be there, and then they come on, and they sing all our favorites: "To Live and Die in L.A.," "Dance Hall Days," "Everybody Have Fun Tonight, Everybody Wang Chung Tonight," and my favorite, "Let's Go, Baby, Let's Go, Baby, Come On!"

We know we will only like this band for about three days, and then we will throw them into the trash heap of popular culture, so it makes this moment even more urgently fun. We all scream for the band, but we hate them. We are all dizzy discovering how ironic and pointless the world is, and it makes us very friendly. We sing along to every song. We don't even know any words. It doesn't matter—we lip-synch them as badly as they would on *American Bandstand.* Tammy comes up beside me crying with laughter, and we both scream, "All right! Wang Chung! All right! Wang Chung! Wang Wang Wang Wang Wang Wang Wang WANG WANG WANGWANGWANGWANGWANGGWANGWANGWANG-WANGWOOOOOOOOOOOOOOOOO!"

Wow, it's Beach Week, which is actually just a weekend, and I am invited to come along and stay at Pete's condo, with all the most select men. Jeremy Loud and I drive in his dad's Taurus. When we get there, everyone has divided the rooms. There is one bunk left, and I have to sleep in the room with Phil Clausen, who snores, John Blond, who fucks his girlfriend in the room all night, and Todd Flamadio, who has become fat and bloated and gets drunk all the time. The first night he hallucinates where the bathroom is and pees on my suitcase. He apologizes the next day. *Don't worry about it, it's cool. It's cool,* I say.

I spend most of my time sitting on the burlap-brown beer-soaked couch, or out on the balcony, looking out onto the surf or seagulls or sunsets. I am allowed to be moody and look at beauty because, remember, I am considered artsy. Inside everyone is singing along to mixed tapes of unifying graduation songs about how we as seniors have to overcome a larger oppressor—"I fight authority, authority always wins!" and "We don't need no education!"

Jeff Wrenn and Lynn Flushing also come out to the balcony often. Jeff is very skinny and has bushy brown hair in a mullet cut and a horsey face. I have seen him in classes since sixth grade—his face as familiar to me as streets like Garfield Court or Forest Boulevard that I have passed every day going to school since first grade. He wears a white wide-necked shirt from Costa Rica. Lynn wears an Indian-print skirt with a plain T-shirt. Her hair is frayed and blond. They listen to folk music. They are very calm and sift through parties, saying hey to everyone and then sit in corners and smile. On the last night of Beach Week we go for a drive in Jeff's blue convertible and blast "My Name Is Luka" really loudly and park at this dead end and watch the sunset. "Beer bongs are so stupid," Jeff says. We talk about the future, about whether there is a God. Jeff and Lynn are both basically agnostic.

Back at the party, the crowd is drinking from the keg. Paul fills up my red cup. They pass around this beer bong—a funnel with a thick tube running from it—and all the guys chug down six-packs of beer poured into its foamy top. Todd Flamadio does ten beer bongs that night.

Todd, like, how, like, do you chug all that? I ask him, and he turns and pulls me into him with his fat-muscle arm, his fat beer face, sweaty and smelling like a frat floor. "You just open your throat, Albo!"

Todd is disgusting, but I look at him and imagine he is Jason Hazer. I can do this kind of easily because one time I walked by Jason's locker and Todd had him in a playful headlock. Jason's fibers are intertwined with his. So, in a dance of imagery, I can shift Todd into Jason and then shift Todd away. When Todd Flamadio puts his arm around me and squeezes my shoulder with his alcohol-pudged hand, I bloom inside.

"Hey, Hazer!" someone says. I look behind me, through the keg cups held by unimportant humans. There is Jason. He says hey, in a wetsuit, holding a surfboard as if he just emerged from the low surf of the Atlantic. Jason Hazer. His hair is styled messy and shows the traces of former trends and spikes and angles, little ghosts of pubescence dancing on his head. He is luminous, and I step away from Todd and pull at my poncho to try and find a cool posture. He says hey to me and I say *Hi,* and he asks me a question but fucking Todd starts screaming "Wooo!" and I do not quite hear him.

I go out onto the mellow patio. Jeff and Lynn are talking about the universe and whether it ends. "Hey, Jason!" Jeff says, in this lovely, friendly style. Jason steps out onto the porch. I am stiff. Of course, I have been such an idiot, I think. Jason is a mellow-patio person! "How long've y'all been here?" Jason asks.

Two days, yes, I say. He talks about the surf, which gets us talking about the tide, which gets us talking about the moon, which brings us right back to the universe and whether it ends.

Jason comes with Jeff and Lynn and me to Wok on the Beach for Chinese food and I am thankful for that because spending a long period of time with him gives volume and color to the mythopoesis. I see him chew a straw, order food, pull open a door—all acts full of imagery and symbolism. He and Jeff talk the entire time, and I cook up a giddy, ticklish conversation with Lynn, clutching her like rubber. *I used to be totally into the B-52's, too! Remember Garanimals? I still have my patrol belt!* And Lynn is laughing with me. Jeff mentions college. He is going to McGill in Montreal for environmental science.

Jason nods. "I don't know what I'm going to do yet," he says, and I take it upon myself to try to sympathize. I am going to go to the state college two hours away. *I am so confused about school,*

I say. "Things have a funny way of working out," Jason says to me, and smiles. That night back in my bunk bedroom, stocked with five of us second-tierers, I listen to Phil snoring and Todd snoring and John and Carla humping and I whisper that sage philosophy to myself:

Things have a funny way of working out.

ric, tall and hazel-eyed guy with polyester shirt unbuttoned and tight brown cords and snakeskin belt. Eric, with thick rings and piercings on his upper ears. Eric, with actual glimmers coming out of his comic-book eyes. Eric, who hugs and sits on the laps of all the drag queens and leathermen, of all the other vested, tight vinyl guys. Eric and his clipped beard and walk-in skin. His body that you want to fall into, a body that defies physics by giving off more energy than his medium-build, well-situated self seems capable of.

In the innocent, blind old days, I would just observe some crush like Jason Hazer from far away down a hall, and I would have to find a way to describe the fullness I felt. Now I get to touch my objects of affection. I am in an escalated, hands-on, petting-zoo version.

I told Gina I knew Eric. I tried to act really calm about it. "Oh, my God, Eric Rush? What the fuck? He's gay? I believe it. He was totally weird."

He said you went out with his friend Tay—

"Taylor Law? What did he say about him?"

Well, nothing.

"Where is he?"

I don't know, he didn't say.

"Is he married? Is he fat?"

I don't know.

"I can't believe this!"

So, did you know Eric?

"Barely. He was totally weird—he never said anything. Is Taylor in New York?"

She spent the rest of the day on the phone with her friends talking about Taylor Law.

Eric Rush. I didn't even know his last name. A name of cool mint air freshener. I went to see Eric as a go-go boy at Freon, which has this Anne Rice cyber-fetish night, whatever that means. This year, it is hip to remember being goth. Last year it was New Wave, and the year before that it was the classic-rock look. For Freon, you have to wear eyeliner and black clothes and swirl your hands around in twists and gothic flourishes to get past the doorman. Benny and I had put on eyeliner and I felt really stupid. I tried to be goth in high school for a week by wearing a trench coat and slicking my hair back, but I stopped because I couldn't afford to get any accessory brooches and crucifixes, and anyway it was so *hard* to maintain every day, and you always had to wear such long-sleeved shirts and the cuffs fell down too far over my hands and got caught in my trombone case.

We walked in and they were playing something industrial—acidic guitar sounds with wrench clangs, steam pipes, shift bells, and oiled cranks—because in the post-apocalypse, according to industrial music, factories are still in high productivity. America during an apocalypse is still strong enough for stupid singers wearing torn hosiery and white pancake makeup to make millions of dollars in the music industry.

Freon has two levels. There is a ground floor with a long bar and cement walls and these small cages hanging from the ceiling with little candles flickering in them for a dungeon effect. The basement area is bigger, with a stage and speakers on either side acting as blocks for go-go boys or posing drag queens.

Benny and I walk down to the basement. The people around us seem so much more a part of their costumes—high collars, powdered, egg-white faces with fake beauty marks, all these dusty vampires billowing around the space. On the stage, above all the ghostly goths: Eric—with a white face and charcoal around his eyes, his swerving body licked by lights. I pretty much just want to have sex with him again right there. Eric has a practiced slumpy posture—jacking his arms back like a girl field-hockey player. I look at him and could easily slide my body into the memory of having sex with him last weekend. I am standing there, absorbing the visual information of his body, collecting the sensory input of his moving flesh in front of me with the stored memory of my past sexual activity with him. I'm plotting those points onto the basic grid of my head to try and achieve some sort of robotic euphoria and it works. I feel engorged with him. I stand there thinking of that scene and pant like a hot dog. Benny just looks at me and says, "Why don't you just kill him, Mike? Then you can shellac his body and prop him up in your room!"

Eric is part of a long lineage of go-go history. He is historic. I thought about him onstage and I thought about the larger idea of go-go dancing as theater and the larger idea of theater, and the theatrical experience. It suddenly saddens me to think about theater, about audiences sitting and watching a rehearsed experience to feel something they aren't quite feeling at home. I stared at the drag queens up onstage with Eric. One queen was doing that old "my microphone looks like a dick, watch me suck it" act. Everybody laughed, including me. How stupid and bawdy our senses of humor are—ha-ha-ha a man dressed as a woman being lewd. Everyone gets off on this sort of thing, from the dark goth drag here at Freon to RuPaul, Mrs. Doubtfire, Tootsie, Fabio, Richard Simmons, Milton Berle—all mixed-gender buffoons. It's been in the air since Shakespeare and before, everyone laughing and squawking and throwing their pennies in the Globe Theatre at the drag-queen Ophelia or Desdemona as she simpers and whimpers like a woman is supposed to. History is everywhere, even at Freon.

Benny and I go downstairs to get more stoned. Eric comes clomping down the stairs, in his leather g-string and chaps. *You looked great up there,* I say. "Thanks," he says, and hugs me.

"You got a haircut!" he said.

Yeah, it's a little uneven. The hairdresser guy in the middle of my haircut said, Your hair is so forgivable, and I was like, Oh my God. Ha-ha, I laughed.

"It's all the locks," he said, and ran his fingers through my hair.

All the locks, I repeat. *Hey, I talked to Gina.*

"Really? Oh yeah, how is she?" Eric says, and then Benny comes up. "You do look hot," he says to Eric, and then reaches around and curves his hand under one of Eric's buttcheeks. Eric smiles and I stand there with a fake grin, because I have to pretend to be full of free love. Oh God, what am I doing? I am so flooded with him. I am doing an incredibly heroic job staying away from him, or being unattached, but then I start thinking about kissing him and my dry attempts crumble like an earth dam.

MONTAGE ONE (1987)

Senior summer is a haze of pleasure. You glide into your popular June oiled and forgetful. You live a constant montage of upbeat soundtrack interludes, flash-cut shots of speedy wind-blasting car rides and John Cougar Mellencamp tapes falling in between the seats. Of school bells, and echoes of lockers closing in halls, or saying "Boy I totally have senioritis," while you carelessly throw your backpack over one shoulder and jingle your keys. Of sneaking into neighborhood pools at night with Blake Walter and Kelly Tanshaw and you see her legendary breasts, blue and warped, under the water.

You blur into your own graduation, driving insulated cars with the A/C at full blast, putting your robe on over your beachy blue khakis. You swing your tassels, hold up diplomas, nod to "Pomp and Circumstance." You drink keg beer, lip-synch Def Leppard, smell Polo cologne.

You work the summer before college at the Springfield Mall sock kiosk, Sock It to Me! Jeff Wrenn works at the pet store, Snips N' Snails, and his girlfriend Lynn Flushing works at T.J. Maxx. You go eat at IHOP with them every night after you close. You make Jeff laugh and milk comes out of his nose and then you are laughing even more. You drive around in Jeff's red Honda and play New Order and 10,000 Maniacs loud, smoking Capri cigarettes. Jeff keeps putting his hand on your shoulder when you get in the car.

You fake-smoke Salem Menthols, you eat mozzarella sticks, you drink black cherry sodas. You kiss Jeff hello and goodbye now because you are socially loosened by late nights giggling, astrology, and the vague lesbianism of Tracy Chapman. You get in the backseat of his Honda, kiss Lynn first, and then lean over to him and feel his cool cheek on your hotter cheek. The kisses get closer and closer every night, until you press lips quickly and feel his spit there, drying in the whoosh of air as you run to the door.

You detect Jeff everywhere—in mown lawns, in the sissing sprinklers, in the bank's digital displays of temperature and time. Jeff's clavicle, Jeff's forearm, Jeff's hand grabbing your thigh in passenger seats. Jeff's face and body ripples into your face and body. Jeff's hair in a bi-level cut, his beach-striped shirts and bland pegged jeans and no-sock Docksiders and long face radished with acne. Jeff sticking out his tongue when nobody is looking. The protruding tongue, which, in your needful, swallowing eyes, is beautiful.

You speed through parking lots, you breathe in August car exhaust, you get a gust of nervousness from dorm-assignment letters or from Back to School signs in store windows. There is a five-kegger at Bethany Storch's, everyone is drunk, and Jeff asks you to sleep over. You walk to his house nearby and cars pass and you wonder who will see you. Inside he wrestles you to the floor—ha ha, I got you. You go up to his sloppy room, scratchy yellow birds screeching in a cage, a ferret and gerbils skittering in their cedar chips. His parents sleep down the hall. Just say it, he says. *Are you kidding?* you say. Just say it, he says. I am so scared, you want to say. *I'm not saying anything. . . . This is so stupid—I feel so stupid.* It's not, come on. Say it, he says. *No! . . . Is . . . I can't. . . .* He tells you to write it down and hands you paper, and you write down the shaky phrase, and he takes the paper and crumples it up.

And you start your diary.

August 5th, 1987

Dear Diary—I'm at the Chesapeake Bagel Bakery with a coffee and a Bagelnut. There is this powerful booming thunderstorm outside with rain as hard as knotted rope. It's almost as if I had created it. The five conflicting fronts inside me are converging . . . this will be a thunderstorm of intensity, a strong song to the changes I have to take,

the climax of my innocence

I may still be a semi-virgin in some eyes but . . . Shit, if this is stolen and read by some stranger—whoever you are reading this account of life by an oversensitive bisexual and slightly poetic young man, you will be enlightened into the extremes of my lifestyle. I don't care if a million people say the first time doesn't really change you. It does. It may be slight, but it does.

The party at Bethany Storch's was HUGE. I was crazy, dancing all over the place with Pete Shane's girlfriend Denise. It was fun. Even Tasha Bartok came—Jason Hazer went to California to go surf for real. She doesn't even look fazed in his absence. Her face is completely smooth and smiling. We dance to the Eurythmics, "Would I Lie to You?".

Then the cops came—Lynn, Brian (this junior guy), and me went to wait in my car, we had to leave because the lady cop kept yelling "Let's go! Hguh!"

"What a fucking dyke!" Lynn said. So then the party got totally busted—it was like Mardi Gras on the street—people everywhere. And we went to wait in front of Jeff's house. We smoked some cigarettes and waited. Then we went back and the cool people had stayed—Jenni, Neil, Pete & Denise, Lynn, John Blond, Carla, Bethany, Debbie Dyner, Steve H., and Jeff. We went out front and talked about doing mushrooms together sometime soon. I went out back to the patio. I felt like being alone and smoking. Jeff came out to get the matches I stole from him. He asked me what I was doing out here.

Smoking, *I said.*

In that soft voice he sometimes gets he said, "You can smoke inside." I don't know, the way he said it was a major turn-on. Then he goes, "Do you want to sleep over? We can walk to my place. You'll totally get DWI if you drive."

I thought that maybe he was being polite so I said, If you'll have me.

"What?" he said.

If you'll have me.

"I will," he said, smiling—then he walked away, touching me on the head. I laughed, it was kind of funny.

After a while the "cool people" (high school is so stupid!) started

*leaving and Lynn wanted to go home. As we walked to her car, she
asked if I wanted a ride home and I told her I was sleeping over at
Jeff's, and she said, "Oh scary—no—I would be afraid if I didn't
know Jeff had a bunk bed." She went on like this, insinuating. She
has been such a major bitch lately, always dragging Jeff off to talk
alone. I can totally see through her laid-back exterior to her completely clingy needy center. We were standing in front of Lynn's car
and they got really silent and started looking at each other so I
walked off. I let them do whatever they do as they say good night. I
walked out of the cul-de-sac and let them continue their stupid relationship. I could hear them talking in that chirpy low tone and then I
heard Lynn's car driving away. I must have taken quite a long time
because I walked for two thousand miles until I heard Jeff's footsteps
jogging up behind me. Jeff caught up to me and said, "I'll give you
fifty bucks!" like I was a hooker. I just laughed.*

*We ran a race down the hill to his development through the night
like one final blackened flight. I won. I didn't know if I liked cheating on Lynn or being this "other person." It kind of made me laugh to
be even in this position.*

*We walked into his house. Jeff's parents aren't very friendly. I met
them both and you get the feeling they are about to divorce. He gets
his curly dirty blond hair from his mom and his thin body from his
dad. His mom wears a lot of turquoise jewelry and I said to her,* Oh
my God! My mom loves turquoise. She bought a lot of it in
Las Vegas when we lived there.

*She just said, "That's nice," and stood there and then left the
kitchen. They went right into their bedroom, which is upstairs and
really far down a hallway that bends and has three towel pantries.*

His parents have a private den room with couches and pillows all over that overlooks the Jacuzzi and the woods. Jeff's room is close to the stairs—and you can hear his pets skittering around from the den. I sat stiffly on the couch and he lay on his back on the carpet. All of a sudden he jerked up. We saw these freaky glowing eyes of a possum. I said, Oh my God, *and he went* "Shhh." *We went over to the door, slowly creeping like we were animals ourselves. He put his arm around me and we watched it, it watched us. I felt my breath untangling at his touch.*

"She must have rabies," *he said, exemplifying his love and vast knowledge of creatures.*

Why? How do you know? *I said, curling into his arm.*

"Because she's coming close . . . they never do that."

Gross, *I said.*

The opossum left us and we sat down again—I on the couch, he on the floor with pillows (he took his hand off of me). He told me we could talk loudly down here because his parents' room is almost soundproof. I was lying on the couch, he was on the floor right below me—he kept twisting all over, burying his head in his pillow, and moaning.

What is up with you? *I said, laughing.*

"I'm so agitated!" *he said. All of a sudden he jerked up again and asked me why I was on his couch. He tried to pull me off of it and tried to wrestle with me. We ended up on the floor rolling around, I had him for a sec, but he got me in the end. He dramatically screamed that I sat on his nuts. I told him I was the King of Karate. He laughed. I kept pretending to be totally tough in this jokey way. He tried to give me a wedgie.*

And then it happened. We had this incredibly twisting conversation and I told him how I am what he thinks. I had to write it down, I was shaking, I was so nervous, and it came out of me in shaky quick letters. I looked at him, he softly knelt down and looked deeply into me. He said, "So am I."

We quietly went to his room. He put on the Cocteau Twins Treasure *album and I held my breath that he knew the beauty of* Treasure. *Yet I was beginning to feel absolutely foolish and awkward. Almost immediately, Jeff began getting ready for bed. He took off his shirt and pants. He stood there in light-blue underwear. He does have an incredible body. I felt even more awkward—I did not want to stand there and strip in front of him. I took off my sweatshirt while he sat on his bed and then I took off my jeans. I was in my Surf Naked! T-shirt and underwear. He said I could sleep up top.*

I said I had to go to the bathroom. I went there and looked at myself in the mirror. I began silently screaming, What the hell do I do? *I pissed and ran some toothpaste through my mouth, and washed my face with cold water and went into the bedroom. . . .*

MONTAGE TWO (1997)

I am lying here, remembering everything. I remember graduating from high school and then the memories flip fast and tatter. An orange-carpeted college dorm. Well-lit atriums, study-lounge Snickers wrappers, wet dining-hall trays, the vague, sad waft of pasta sauce. Sweatpants, hot breaths, shared showers, toiletries in a bucket with my name on it: Mike.

Students in libraries, the leaf-blowers in fall, girls in simple ponytails. Dozing, dozing, professors lecturing. Cold marble steps and the *Aeneid*. A feeling of ambition. The fat, bloated face of my roommate Rog Blackburn, getting drunk with a pizza-box pyramid behind him.

Lecture classes, wooden seats worn like driftwood, the endless curlicue doodles in the margins of notebooks. My two women friends, Keerstin and Il-Sook, their dorm suites with their night-day-office makeup tables and posters of naked men cradling babies. Drunk and dragging Il-Sook home in her crooked sweater and flats, pit stops for pukes.

An empty cafeteria at night. The Lesbian and Gay Student Union Dance, and Benny with big eyes and a turtleneck and soft, chin-length hair. Our nervous dry sex, our one time holding hands, our quick drift into friendship. Thesis notebooks, final projects, a crowded pointless graduating procession, a shish kebab dinner with my parents, and then moving back home and sleeping in my little stripey room on my twin mattress, Cracker Jack pillowcases and scratch-and-sniff stickers still stuck to the bedpost, still scarred with my dead cousin's X's.

Driving to gay bars in Washington, D.C., and standing there, feeling awkward in my clothes, going in and out of clubs, over and over, trying to perfect an unknowable, alluring, bulletproof self. A shapeless sports jersey. A mock turtleneck with blue and green stripes. Tight red velvet pants, wild seventies shirts, gelled wet curlicue hair, V-neck T-shirts, jeans with holes, jeans with no holes, chokers, crosses, wires, white.

New York. The hand-me-down desks of nonprofit organizations. Xeroxing or dozing or both. "Coming out" to my parents on the phone and their delayed, satellite reactions. The glow of a belief in simple love. I will find a perfect boyfriend within the first year I am here . . . a Todd or a Dan. Or Minh or Pedro. Or Bertrau or Simke. Or even Basket or Almond. Anyone.

Ecstasy, pot, crooked coke lines, tabs of LSD. My shivering strychnine face, my hungry french-kissing face, my sweaty fascinated face, my dry mouth. *I'm okay, I'm sorry, I'm going to get going, I'll see you around. That's cool, whatever. That's cool, whatever.*

New York for four years. Tight worn Izods, corduroy pants, pilly V-neck sweaters, parachute pants, Members Only jackets, finished-sleeve heavy-metal concert T-shirts. Me sleeping with numerous men, each with their clothes and smells and unique and separate heads, me holding each head with their bodies in their beds. Futons, springs, floors, pillows, heads . . . men men men men men men. Then Martin, then Ian, then John, then Rod, then Adam, then hip-hop clothes, then Jack, then Miles, then gross Eddie.

Here I am, lying here with Eric next to me, in his bedroom. Let me never have to remember him.

August 5th, 1997

Benny and I went to Wonder Bar. The Wonder Bar is annoying. I am sick of it being so full of crap—always tinkling with cheap Vegas artifacts and seventies beads and garage-sale paintings. I was very drunk—full of tequila, two beers, and a Cape Cod. I had a huge glass of water from the nice Greek bartender. Then I saw Eric and George and went up to them. Eric kissed me hello. I said *Hi* to George with extra excitability. *You look great!* I said, and I wasn't lying, I was surging with love for him suddenly. "How are you?" he said, smiling. He's never smiled at me before. Then they turned and whispered very seriously. George slapped me on the arm. "See you man," he said. *Oh! Bye! See you!* Blaze walked up and I said *Hi* to him and he looked at me and didn't say anything. I don't understand Blaze. He either forgets he even met me or has no sense of progress in meetings. Especially since I was so friendly to him. Blaze is at least supposed to say, "Hi, I'm sorry I forgot your name . . ." But he doesn't—he drifts off like a moan. Eric sat there casually, like this kind of behavior was fine. With these people it's okay to stand silent as cornstalks and wave in the wind. I must learn to be less talkative.

I tried to smile, nod, and drink to stay connected to Eric, but we were interrupted by a drunk woman who looked a lot like Gina; her name was Victoria. *She looks kind of like Gina,* I said. "I can't really remember what Gina looks like," he said. Victoria said she liked my shirt—I was wearing that Surf Naked! T-Shirt that I had brought from home. She told me she was married to a gay guy named Pepe or Jaime or something but got divorced, so now she's out just having fun. "It's very very rare to meet nice people in this town!" she said, and then she beamed at us and said what I was afraid she would say: "You two are lovers?" My face felt sunburned.

"I love him," Eric said, and put his arm around me like we were golf buddies. I stood there and I seriously think I said, *Duh,* and then I tried to dispel his statement and I said *We all love each other in this crazy town,* and then she turned toward Benny and Tony. They were totally stoned, so they were fascinated by her. I got stoned, too. No one has any drug but pot these days.

Is there something wrong with Blaze? I said to deflect the huger curiosity I have about George. He said that Blaze is going through some sort of personal porn phase and gets together with guys every night—if he comes home he always takes up the bed. I am trying to imagine Blaze cradling someone's face with uncontrollable passion—I am getting a bit aroused.

Somehow I naturally arranged it so that Eric and I would leave at the same time from the bar. We walked out and Eric hiked up his jacket. "I hope I don't have to sleep on the couch."

You can come to Boston, I mean my place, if you want, I said. I don't know why I said Boston.

"Thanks. I can't. I'd love to. But I know we'd end up getting together." He looked off into the long horizon of delis and liquor stores. Then, in this politician tone, he said, "I've got a boyfriend."

Okay, I said, and I thought of George and how every time I see him I become hyper-animated to powder over my guilt and anxiety. Hiya, George! Woweee! I am a Little Bubbly Tugboat! Honk! Honk! I am a Bubbly Tugboat!

I think I said, *I'm glad you are so honest.* But that would mean that I actually told someone the way I felt instead of running home and writing it down.

We walked down Avenue B, and I was ready to part with him when we got to 4th Street. He said, "Wanna walk me home?" or maybe, "Are you going to walk me home?" I don't know. And then we started walking, me talking about pollution, telling him that thing that Rod told me—how we have been mutated and poisoned by our detergents and plastics, how we are too contaminated to have traditional relationships, all because we live in polluted, overcrowded, complex systems. He didn't ask me one question, and hummed along next to me through the streets. We got to his door. "Do you want to come in and watch *Aladdin*? It's my favorite movie," he said, and I said *Sure,* and we went in, and the toxic radiant uranium inside me burned.

So we went into the apartment, softly. "All right!" Eric said. Blaze wasn't there, thank God. *Oh, you've rearranged this place, it looks nice.*

"Let's sit in the closet," he said. He pulled open the curtain—a lumpy bed of checkered sheets, leather pants, dirty shirts, and an orange feather boa filled up the closet space. Eric climbed over it and turned on a TV and VCR crammed into the back. *You have two TVs?*

"Sure—I hate Blaze's taste." Eric put on the TV. He put in the video and the glow of a cartoon sunrise in animated Arabia fell over his face. The whole little room was blue. I watched him watching it, and his big hazel eyes repelled the light with their glass finish, his blond hair absorbing the blue tones. I could have watched him the entire length of a film feature, but I forced myself to turn toward the screen and become interested in the dumb, dumb Disney plot. Eric and I sat there on the huge expanse of his bed, not touching each other. I was going crazy, so I decided to unplug and get up and go to the bathroom. I washed my face, looking at my aerobicized, drunk body. When I came back, Eric had stripped to his black underwear. . . .

August 5th

When I got back to Jeff's room, I couldn't see anything. I began to mumble how I'll never make it to his bed. I heard him whisper, "I thought you fell down the toilet." Ha-ha-ha.

I can't see a thing, *I said.*

He goes, "Here is my hand." I felt for his hand I inched closer he was leading me down next to him. It was me that guided myself beside him though. Somehow I knew where his lips were, and I kissed him. We kissed, it was the warmest, most pleasurable kiss I have ever had, we kissed. I went on top of him on the bed, and I sup-

pose I was moving quite rapidly, making too much noise, because, he said, "Shhh." We kissed more and more, I felt his whiskers on my face and neck, I felt his tongue, his mouth had a slight tobacco taste, it was wonderful, I grabbed his hair, I touched his face, he moaned in my ear. When I did this to him, he whispered, "Oh God." Aha. He was running his hands up my back. I played with his mouth with my hand, he kissed my fingers, then pulled my index finger in and began to suck extremely erotically hard, I smiled. I slipped off my shirt and felt his chest—it was tight and defined—he ran his hand down my leg, squeezing my thigh and butt. I unzipped my pants and let them go. Somehow he began to pull off my underwear and with a little struggle it came off, he did the same to himself and then he pulled the covers over us and we squeezed ourselves together very hard. I reached for him and fondled his long, upturned erection, I went down on him, but did not stay there long. He reached for me and felt me, sticking his finger up my b-hole at the same time.

I sat on the bed and Eric's attention had suddenly turned to me, I don't know how, and not the movie. I can't remember really what happened, but we started kissing. We kissed and couldn't stop, both of us sitting up and breathing heavily. Then I flipped him on his back like an otter and scooped my hands under him and buried my face in his collarbone and then his armpit—he smells so great, burned rubber, and he pushed his face into my shoulder and sucked on my ear. He loves to have my fingers up him, and I can feel something hard up him, like a little stone or bone. I sucked him off a long time. His penis is perfect and I can suck it for a long long time.

He brought me up to his lying body. I sat with my legs straddling his face, he began to give me head, it felt so good, but I could not orgasm. So after a while I pulled out and we caressed and kissed some more, before he switched places with me and moved down on me, beginning again. It felt incredible . . . it was not fast enough so I helped his head while stroking his hair and pushing down.

I rammed his dick deep into my throat so that it became this new inflated, familiar rubber tongue, as warm as my mouth.

Then he turned onto his back and I began stroking him very hard. He took my hand and corrected me a little. I suppose he wanted me to go slower, I did for a while, but then I sped up again, it took a while before all the muscles in

His body felt so warm and correct there over me, he pulled out and propped himself up with one arm and jerked himself off and said, "Just lie there. I'll do it all," and drove his pelvis into my ass, his dick flopping between my legs, and came on me in short spurts and

his stomach and chest clenched. They were hard and he breathed. He climaxed and I stroked him to it. I cleaned him up and we embraced on top of each other,

we squished his cum between us like denture cream. He put two fingers up me, and sucked me and it felt so good and I made these cooing sounds.

marvelously moaning simultaneously. Jeff reached down for my erection and sucked me, his mouth creating a tingling suction, and he lifted his eyes up and looked at me and I stared into his eyes.

He said, "You are so hot" to me, and I said *You are too,* and pushed his mouth back down on my dick and he started choking but he did it anyway, and his spit made my thighs slippery and I squeezed his head between my legs

I felt the strength of his mouth on my erection and the workings of his jaws and his mind all down there for me

and then I felt it coming and lifted up his head with my hands and he wrapped his arms around my waist

Jeff's head jerked up and down and up and down and I wanted him there and I came and came *and I came and came* and shot all across his collarbone *and squeezed his biceps until it was finished. Then I whispered,* I want you, *to him but I don't think he heard me. I wanted to say more, but there was never a good, solid clear moment to,* God, please don't be the love of my life, Eric, because that means my life is closed now.

August 5th, 1987

Jeff put on a sweatshirt torn at the sleeves, showing his belly button. I thought I would be seductive and got the old Rolos in my pocket that we could feed to each other. He didn't want any. I leaned over

him and he rested on his back with his arms under his head. He was quiet for a while, then lit a cigarette, and then told me how he had been having sex with guys since he was twelve. He leaned back on the couch and told me about this older man who would pick him up outside of his parents' terrace in Gwatheemalah (Guatemala), and they would drive to his huge estate and they would have sex and the guy would yell at him and Jeff would storm out of the veeeya (villa) and once they were both in the town square and Jeff had to pretend not to know him. Jeff ached for those times again, and he exhaled the smoke.

I kissed his Marlboro Lights mouth. "I am so excited to move to Montreal. It'll be good to be independent, where no one knows me. Like, I love having a car now, I can go anywhere. You know the weirdest thing happened . . . I was at Dupont Circle in the city and the car was running and I was waiting at a traffic light and this guy got into the car and we ended up totally getting together."

I didn't say anything. "What?" Jeff said suddenly. "Look, Mike, we're not attached to each other."

Look, I know you've got a lot on your mind, *I said, looking down and bending my arms in stupid spirals.* But I love you.

"No, you don't. You'll be fine. I am just your first."

August 5th, 1997

Aladdin was still playing and then he ordered food from Stingy Lulu's—and he paid for it. I ordered a mixed green salad and he ordered penne with chicken. "Open wide," he said, and gave me a bite. He was very quiet.

Did you know that garbanzo beans cause neurological disorders? I said to him out of the silent, cool blue. He smiled and drew me toward him. Then the phone rang. It was George. "He always calls this late," Eric said.

Eric and George talked about the cute joint birthday gift they were making for their friend Sahara. Eric looked up into the thick blue of the video. I heard Blaze come in, bang around, turn on the TV in the main room, and pass out in front of the set, snoring. I was stuck in the little room while Eric mumbled to his boyfriend. I started dozing off when finally Eric hung up the phone.

"I feel really bad." Eric said. "I'm a dick."

We're young, Eric, I strangely said. And then he said he was going to bed and I said, *I'm going to go,* and he said, "All right." And then he said, "I'll walk you out," and I said *No, stay in bed. I'll tell you a story while I put on my shoes.* And he lay there— drunk, I suddenly realized. *Once upon a time there was a Prince who fooled around with this, um, other guy—*

"And that Prince had a boyfriend," he said.

And he and the other guy had a thing going on and the guy who wasn't going out with anybody wanted to tell the Prince character that he liked him a lot and would never ever want to jeopardize his relationship and he just wanted to tell him that . . .

I started to really believe it, too. It must be what it is like to lie about murder in a court of law. That selfish passion, the blood-hungry desire to strangle George out of Eric's life can be covered up, made to look like genuine feelings of concern about their relationship. Like a good murderer I can really believe it, too. I can clean my guilty self spotless, wipe off my bloody machetes, get the red flesh out from under my nails, become innocent even to myself, turn over my face into a wide, open, plaintive O.J. grin.

I convinced myself that Eric and George were in a more important world than mine, and while I was storytelling to Eric, I got cry-mouth: that involuntary yawnlike contortion of the face as you supress huge, huge tears. I have absolutely no control of myself around Eric, which means it will end soon because my attraction to him is at too high a temperature, and bacteria die in heat. It will end the way weak insects end, how a happy childhood ends, or a sitcom ends and then begins its sad, paler life of endless repeats in syndication.

August 12th, 1987

Dear Diary—Right now I'm in the family room and my mom and dad are on the porch having a dinner party with the Fennings. I just went outside to say hi to them all. Mr. and Mrs. Fenning are so so boring. Mr. Fenning asked me if I was going out tonight. "You've got a girlfriend to entertain, I'm sure," he said, and I just said Yeah *really fast and ripped out of there.*

So many things are happening at once—I am swallowed by events. This hot August is spiraling inside me. Yesterday, Jeff picked me up and we went to see The Karate Kid, Part II *(ha ha) at Whiteriver Cinemas, which was also playing a matinee of* Friday the 13th Part V: A New Beginning, *which we were going to see because they don't check for IDs there, but Jeff said, "Who wants to pay to see a bunch of T&A?" Lynn had to go to work so she couldn't come. Then Jeff and I went to his house. In the daylight it's even more awesome. His parents must be completely wealthy—their huge town house sits way back from Keene Mill Road. You have to drive down a long grassy driveway that has lantern lights along the sides. He says they are in international trade, which can apparently be quite lucrative. We went over to the patio and hung out by the Jacuzzi and smoked.*

    It's been a month at my dumb job, and the only thing that quenches me is that Jeff works at Snips N' Snails in zone three of the mall. All I can think about is Jeff. I didn't know what to think at first, but now after our intense night I am pretty sure Jeff definitely feels the same. Am I trying to fall in love with him because it is plausible now? If I am, I'm ashamed. I remember I had always thought he was unattractive until the day Lynn Flushing (she was in my government class last spring) went on and on in this note about him and how she is in love w/ him and how he is great and how his body is exceptional because he was a gymnast when his family lived in Barcelona (he says "Bah Thee Lonya" and other Spanish words authentically) & etc., and then Lynn started dating him. She is really cool and down-to-earth about it. Lynn's growing out her bob. She has a natural spiral perm. She told me this really scary story about how she tripped on acid and then found out it was PCP. She began to believe her body was a stack of anatomy sheets in an encyclopedia and she lay on her bedsheets and freaked out. She was only thirteen. She got really angry at Jeff when he told her he wanted to get some tabs of acid. She gets very serious about it and held my arms with her hands and made me promise never to try it.

    Jeff and I are totally connecting, our conversations seem to last for-

*ever. He has traveled so astonishingly much. Besides being so absolut-
ley hysterically funny, Jeff is fascinating. He reads voraciously. (Topics
came up in AP English last year that he knows all about, e.g., Jean-
Paul Sartre, Irish people eating.) He is an almost expert on animals and
wants to be an environmental (sp?) scientist. He has all these birds and
a ferret in his room. He knows Spanish extraordinarily well, he collects
these weird Peruvian gourd carvings. He has this cool way of walking,
with this hulking curve to his back and his legs turned out in Charlie
Chaplin feet. He laughs in sudden spurts. He is very good-looking,
though he has a problem w/ complexion (look who's talking!). Long
nose, big deep blue eyes, long hair, and these lips that I want to touch.
That is all I think about. Touching those lips. Kissing those lips . . .*

Musings

*His eyes are jeweled and shallow-water blue and forever. His
eyes' brows are dark and streams of chocolate—these two rivers that
surround the candy of his face. His ears are like tan sheets that were
thrown in a corner. They have an odd, peaceful aestheticism about
them. Like they were just thrown on and have this asymmetry that
makes them totally symmetrical. His eyes see me seeing me seeing me
in them. His eyes are the folds of mirrors, the cracks in glass. Jeff's
jade eyes, the jade Jeff eyes, blue jay, two robin's eggs, two pieces of
crystal bells of blue and tiny shrieks that come between changing
notes in a song. They are like two roller coasters side by side sharing
that same candy metallic glitter color that gets hot in the sun. Two
blue eggs, frying and crackling and hissing and spouting icicles—his
eyes look at me, but do they look there? Is there an invisible wall (to
me) that makes it so it looks like he is not looking at me when he is
looking at me? I just see these two ice cubes and bubbles of blue*

crayon air, two bluish rain forest ferns and I pick them like a botanist.
I found a new species but they are poisonous.

Dear Eric,

It's been a week and you haven't called. I called you and left a message and you didn't call back.

Gina told me you were silent and mysterious in high school. I can see you, leaning on the fake buck fence in front of McDonald's Happyland—in your trench coat and black high-top sneakers and layered "Hungry Like the Wolf" hair, smoking Salem Menthols because that's all they have at the High's Kwik-Mart. You probably never called anyone. You have leaned on fake fun zones your whole life, never having to say a word.

You got C's in school but you were good in art class and made tiny portraits of Bono or Midge Ure or David Sylvian in the margins of your civics book. You hung out with Taylor Law, a hugely popular guy in school, and you stood at his locker and made jokes about school spirit. You never said anything to Gina, but one time she was talking to Taylor about the John Cougar concert and you licked your finger and stuck it in her ear. "Gross! Gross, Eric! What the fuck did you do that for?"

You just shrugged your shoulders, "It's a wet willie," you said.

I am furiously trying to make up your past. Here on 6th Street, in my small, small room, window to an alley, to other people's music and flickering televisions, you are changing and I want to anchor you, get you down to one manageable conglobated mass of made-up details. You will be pure, beautiful white skin all the way through, like boneless chicken breast. You will be monstrous in size—bigger and bigger, skyscrapers and scaffolding, scooping me up with your scaffolding arms.

But you haven't become a complete illusion in my brain yet. You still have a smell to me. That's when you know your smothering memory has taken over, when the smell of someone goes.

But your face is losing familiarity. There is a carnival that just popped up in the lot by my apartment building. Tilt-A-Whirl, a Ferris wheel, stupid booths, and a loud spinning rocket ride, lit up, flashing louder and louder, tossing out lines of light, hooting and wheezing me to sleep. I just realized that I am not sending this to you. Once you get to descriptions of carnivals, you know not to send.

August 20th, 1987

I walked to Snips N' Snails after I closed the kiosk last night and caught Jeff walking out of Raffeter's Everything Is Ten Dollars. "Hey," he said, "I was just going to try to catch you."

Really?

"Lynn got really angry at me and she was supposed to drive me home—could you drop me off? I'm really tired."

We drove around for a while and listened to my China Crisis tape. *Jeff told me he feels really guilty about Lynn, about cheating on her.* "I'm a dick," *he said, looking out the car window, the streetlights casting movable beams onto his face.* No, you're not, *I said.* We're young, Jeff, *I said, but I really mean that we can't help doing what we are doing, bound together by shared desires.*

I can't help the way I feel either, *I said.*

"You will," *he said.*

And I said, Why do you keep saying that?

Jeff just smoked his cigarette and looked exhausted.

I feel for you, *I said, and he began singing that Chaka Khan song and I said,* Shut up, I mean it, *and then I almost started crying, the corners of my mouth turning downward.* You haven't even seen where I live or anything. *And Jeff said kind of sarcastically,* "Okay, you're right. I'm sorry for being such a dick."

But then Jeff said he wanted to see my house. We drove there and then Jeff and I parked between the Fobriches' and the Perspers' across the street from my house and he began to stroke my leg. . . . Soon he was down my shorts and I was telling him to stop (oh my God, if the neighbors saw us I will die). He said he had to leave. I said We could go to my room, on the side of the house, *he said no way w/ my parents there! Finally I said I was going and had my body ½ out of the car, he says he'll go down on me right here, right now. He told me how "solid" I was and how muscular (which I found odd) and then talked about my erection and how I should be proud of it, it was embarrassing! He moved out of the car and we walked to the side of the house, then to the other side of the house, way in the back of the yard by the sewer, and we did it. It was so . . . pagan, so* Light in August, *very primitive and sensual.*

I made a mixed tape for him. UFM . . . Ultimate Fuck Music. Sade, David Sylvian, Alison Moyet, Roxy Music . . . only the best. One side is called Smoke and the other is called Sex. Why the hell am I so crazy about this dip who collects Peruvian gourd carvings and keeps rodents in his house and smokes?

Dear Jeff,

I've been thinking about your how you feel guilty about Lynn—and until today I didn't really understand why you are so mixed-up. Now I do. You have got to tell Lynn what's going on—in your cruel magician's hands she thinks that you are hers. She talks about moving to Montreal and just working while you go to school. . . . Is anyone free from your web of lies?

You have never just thought about yourself, EVER, have you? Jeff, I can't ask you to even try to tell me what I am doing wrong in this mixed-up blender of a fucked-up romance when you don't even know what is going on inside you. You are a dishonest child, Jeff. WHAT DO YOU WANT FROM ME?

August 22nd, 1997

I am a puppet. Eric was go-go dancing again at Freon and I automatically bounced down there googly-eyed and wooden. What is wrong with me, do I have any self-control? But a few minutes after I got there, Eric came up to me, kind of drunk. He pulled me into the bathroom. "I need to get my dick hard to dance," he said—some sort of excuse to make out with me, and he sucked me off with me sitting on the sink and my feet propped up on the toilet seat. When I have sex with him now, I can't even enjoy it because I am busy trying to remember the moment, the fleshy moment of it, so I can hold on to it. Because we are simply "fuck buddies" to each other. Casual casual casual. "Casual" is this word that means you are supposed to open up your head, take out your brain, and not blink while you have sex and then feel completely free. "Casual" means you cannot amalgamate memories or the fondness that comes with memories about anyone: "Casual" is supposed to be fun. Fun fun fun.

I said, *I love you*—I couldn't help it. He said, "I love you," and held me with his body. "You've got a hot body," he said, and I thought about his hotter naked body in front of me, the even line of light hair traveling down his stomach.

When we walked out, Benny was there with this weaselly smile. "Where did you go?" he asked. I told him I was in the bathroom with Eric, but I couldn't get the elated smile off my face. Then Benny, of course, had to inject himself into the moment. "Yeah, Eric is flirting with me, too."

Eric climbed onto the block, wringing his stomach muscles around in circles. He danced face to face with some tatooey man. "Oh my God, Eric is such a flirt, look at him," Benny said. I wadded up my wet cocktail napkin. I threw it at Eric and he turned and waved. I laughed really loudly as the industrial music suddenly stopped in a steamy hush. *Haw!* I screamed.

I can't believe I threw my napkin so desperately at Eric. Obviously that is a poor form of self-control. I wanted to throw it at Eric like I threw bits of sticks at Jeff's window that time so long ago and made him talk to me and told him I loved him. It's been ten years and I am still holding bits of things to throw.

August 22nd, 1987

How good I've become at departures. The kiss, the faint farewell, then always, always the sinking of the stomach and then the nothing of leaving. I am going to college on Tuesday. Mom and Dad are driving me there. I will soon be washed in the light of an entirely new landscape.

New ideas.

New loves.

Still, I am shackled to this town, to Jeff and all he possesses within me.

Jeff's parents are away in Argentina for a week. At first knowledge I glowed with the seductive possibilities: food, candles, strawberries, "Lorelei" playing on the porch. Jeff rising out of the Jacuzzi's bubbly aqua. Every day after I close the kiosk I go to Snips N' Snails and he isn't there. I go down to T.J. Maxx. "He's with his fucking friends in the city," Lynn says angrily.

Lynn and I went to HoJo's—we talked about Storybook Kingdom. "Jeff and I went there once," she said. "We took pot brownies and laughed for so long." She mentions him in everything. And I am nothing. I have no memories with him, only moments of passion. She said she is going to some function with him and his parents at the Ken-

nedy Center when they get back. She decribed the stupid dress she was going to wear. I told her his parents freak me out. "Chuck? Anya? They're actually pretty cool."

They were really cold to me when I slept over there, *I said. I saw something piercing in Lynn's eye.*

August 25th, 1997

It is the end of August and I have been sitting at a booth all morning for work, pretending to be full of cheer. We have a booth at the Lesbian and Gay Marketplace Convention at the Hilton on 54th Street. I don't really know why—to promote liver awareness, I guess. No one stops at our table. The convention is a big, disgusting celebration of money. It is to celebrate how capitalism has found ways to cram products and advertising into our new, lavender, baby demographic beaks. It seems as if the only result of creating a gay identity was to become a legitimate part in the gross exchange of money. Magazines with buff men on the covers to give us body-consciousness problems. Disco divas wailing over itchy beats. Vague AIDS symbolism in ribbons and posters and Keith Haring contours. Black-and-white calendars with biceps embracing other biceps. Stonewall, Gay Games, AIDS Rides, Red Party White Party Black Party. Triangles and Rainbow Flags and T-shirts and Condoms and Celebrate Pride! Celebrate Pride! Stick us through the ATM machine for some fast cash and Celebrate Pride!

Here is the number Eric gave me. As is evident from his

wide John Hancock, Eric is like a founding father—he promises a glorious union, but after he conquers you and plows through your land, he leaves it clear-cut and plagued with Old World poisons. Look at his mean, pinpointy "R" and "I". . . they speak for him. They should have warned me against his words like "You are so sweet" and his compliments about eyes and smiles. Eric is only an advertisement for himself, smiling and offering a lovely vacation package to a verdant land that doesn't exist. A Floridian scam.

I got back to the office and Gina was sitting at her desk buffing her nails. *You look like a stereotype of a secretary, Gina.*

"Have you talked to Eric? Did he tell you where Taylor is living?" Gina asks.

No, I haven't. I don't think Eric knows.

"Why?"

I don't know.

"He is so weird. He probably is so drugged-out he doesn't remember."

He's actually pretty thoughtful.

"God, you must want him pretty badly."

He's sort of shy.

"It amazes me how you go for someone you ultimately cannot have. Why don't you try to like someone who likes you back for once?"

I hung up the phone on her. I am sick of people blaming me, saying that I am choosing something that is wrong. What a bunch of self-absorbed, self-help crap. I did not "choose" this—this just happened. *Fuck you,* I said over the wall. I said it semi-softly because I didn't want another fucking demerit from Joyce. I don't know if Gina heard me, but we spent the rest of the day in a freeze, not looking at each other, brushing shoulders on the way to the fax machine as if we did not exist to each other at all.

August 27th, 1987

Oh God so much happened. Night has attacked in its blackened manner.

Sunday night I went straight to the mall to see if Jeff was working. He wasn't. So I went to his place. Jeff was in his room, getting ready for bed. I looked up at him and thought I had to act fast. I grabbed some sticks and began to throw pieces at his window, but they didn't reach and I never got his attention. I decided I would not give up. I had come too far. He turned off his light. I had little time. I pushed through the gate and walked into his backyard. Now I could get a few good throws in. Finally he came to the window. "Who is it?"

Me.

"Steve?"

No.

"Jason?"

No.

"Mike?"

Yup.

He came downstairs and we sat in his living room, smoking. He told me I was naïve and I told him I hated what was going on with us. He told me about the times in stupid Gwatheemalah when he would go out all night (when his parents were fighting and never came home) and how he met a man that became very close to him. He was twelve, the man was twenty-six. The man had a big house with a pool and a courtyard in the center. They had a month-long affair, but then Jeff had to leave. He never said goodbye to the man and he regrets it. He said all that and then looked off. He lost his virginity at 12 w/ a man. He told me that things would change. That I won't be as heart-wrenched over the next relationships I have.

He thought, quote, "That we could have a relationship, but now we see how different we are." My heart was ripping.

"My lover in Mexico, Yarlano (¿) once told me the Mexican expression for an affair. 'You see,' he said to me, 'there are los catedrales, *the cathedrals, your wife, your partner in life, and then there are the little huts surrounding the cathedral,* los hornitos, *and you may have many little huts, many* hornitos *of lovers.'"*

I'm a hut? *I said. I said I was angry at the way things were, how he didn't need me and how I wanted more and* How the hell am I supposed to change my nature to become less sensitive? *when he was giving me all this shit. He was very silent for a while, when finally he spoke. He told me that what I said was important but I would change my mind. Finally I screamed at him,* I don't want us to come back from college, and you give me a gift, have a party, and then later—

"What do you want then?" he interrupted me.

I don't know. I want to be close to you all the time, I guess, I don't want memories! I hate memories! *I said.*

"Are you okay?" he said.

I'm fine, *I said. I just smiled because I didn't want him to fucking ever see anything ever again even though I was steaming inside. I walked out into the backyard, and Jeff followed me, asking if I wanted a ride home, like I was some kind of invalid. We walked into the parking lot behind his house and he hugged me and it felt disgusting, the kind of hug you get in an airport from someone proudly going off and leaving you behind. A fake embrace. Then a horn started honking. I looked up and Lynn was sitting in her car, honking her horn, the shrill sound blasting. Jeff ran over to her car. I kept looking up to see if his parents were going to come out, but they didn't wake up, which is surprising because Lynn would not get her hand off the horn. Everything was so dark and quiet in the town houses. Jeff got her to stop honking and was saying something in a calm voice, but Lynn started her Honda, and Jeff jumped away while she jerked the car forward.*

"I hope you both die of AIDS," *she screamed, and drove off.*

August 27th, 1997

Eric and I met at the Wonder Bar by accident. Well, I had sort of stuffed the probability box by being there for four hours thinking he would stop in the bar. I had been rehearsing what I would say to him, but it's 4 A.M. and instead we went to his place and wordlessly had sex. Blaze was in the other room, passed out with the remote in his hand again. We had sex in the closet again. George called again and they fought again and I looked at the fascinating wall again.

He hangs up the phone and suddenly sits up. "Hey, I want

to get some smokes—I'll walk you halfway home."

Oh. I say. *Sure, cool.* I say.

Eric and I walk. I am wearing that zip-up jacket with crazy seventies geometric designs on it. I hate what I'm wearing. I feel as if it's been out of style three times over: the end of the seventies, the end of that kooky time in 1990 when Deee-Lite was big, and now. We reach the colorful community center on 6th Street—painted with a Lego-bright mural that curves around the doorway with a ribbon of text saying "500 Years of Oppression." We stop next to my building, by the corrugated aluminum walls they've put up for construction. I bring up Gina, just for one last attempt at a shared universe. Then we talk about his work as a go-go boy, about Björk, and about gay marriage, and then I say:

Okay, here is my serious sentence. I am into you. That's it.

"You're so cute. How exactly do I respond?"

Oh, nothing, just "Groovy" maybe?

"Okay, here is my serious sentence. I like you. You are really such a great guy. But I'm with George right now . . ."

Oh my God, I know I know, you are getting the wrong idea about what I mean.

"What does 'into' mean then?"

I like you. I love you. I like the night we had and everything.

"Between like and love."

No . . . I guess so. I can't explain anything right now, I am so tired. I'm sorry.

"I'm not really into being a dating monster right now."

Oh, okay, I understand.

"I am a slut."

That's . . . fine . . . I am too.

"Did Benny tell you we had sex?"

Oh. No.

"Does that bother you?"

Uh.

"It does bother you."

Not . . . whatever.

"You know, I like hanging out with you. . . . Do you want me to platonically call you or should I not for a while? . . . We see each other out a lot."

No . . . call me, I want you to.

I am simmering. I feel like I have been electrocuted. Somehow, though, I am able to make a mummy out of myself, and allow that dehydrated, charred outer layer of myself to spew dried dirt clods of conversation. We talk about brain patterns, health food, macrobiotics, and this woman with big tits who works at Angelica.

We kiss and then I make us kiss again. And then we kiss and decide how great it would be to be friends, oh do you still want to go to that new fag night, sure, sure, great I'll call you tomorrow, great, okay, okay, bye, bye.

I walk into the apartment. I am so tired. My hands and arms are tingly, like they are battery testers. Wet Benny walks out of the bathroom in a towel. "Hi! Hey! I just got home!" He is smiling with his fucking wet face. "How come you're home so early?"

I don't know.

"Was he weird? Was he not into you?"

I don't know.

"Maybe he wants something different than a relationship right now, you know."

Uh.

"Well, good night," he says. "Wake me up when you get up."

I can't sleep, of course. I guess I am filled with anger. I think about throwing something down really violently and then yelling, but I cannot pull off that kind of European seriousness for that long, so I decide to make some coffee and drink it all and poison myself with carcinogens. There is the faint blue glow of morning outside. The light is sick and thick. Birds chirp. The coffee gurgles in its plastic Dutch space-saving machine. When it's done, I pull the pot out and stand there.

I walk into Benny's room. He is awake. "Hi!" he says. I just stand there. He is naked, drying off with a towel. He has his portable TV on *Access Hollywood*—"A Salute to *Baywatch*!"—and the blue ocean light flickers through the room.

"Oh my God, I can't believe it but I have crabs again! Isn't that hilarious?" he says.

I walk up to him, in this furious gypsy silence. He looks at me curiously. I pour the coffee on his head. "No!" he screams, and then he makes these puppylike yelping sounds, the brown coffee staining the mattress and steaming there. A breeze blows in the window, and with the breeze, I hear the distant sounds of more birds, and morning, and the caws of kids in playgrounds outside, or possibly of the seagulls of *Baywatch*.

I'm in the Springfield Plaza parking lot waiting for my parents to come back from the Summer Blowout Sale. Hair Fashion, Bil-Bar Vacuums, stupid CVS. The Fantasy Garden restaurant where Tammy and I went before the Sweetheart Dance in tenth grade. The Shell gas station has already set up a decorative scene for Chrismas and it's September. A cold front is blowing the robes of Joseph and Mary. They are billowing. Across the intersection, the Lutheran church says:

SPEAKING THE TRUTH OF LOVE

Today in my house with nothing to do but sit around, I found pictures of my mom and Grandpa Joe and Aunt Millie and Uncle Ted and Grandma Maude all in their fifties' clean-lined skirts and slacks sitting on lawn chairs and resting pilsner glasses and shots of gin on their knees. In one picture, Grandpa Joe stands over his wife at their golden anniversary, wearing the same pants that are right now fit over my crabby crotch.

There are lots and lots of pictures like this—of Sunday cocktail parties in clean uncluttered houses, with wood paneling and red-coffee tables and atomic clocks. The beginning of time. Propagation. But only clothes and gay grandsons are left.

Everyone is pairing off and propagating—everyone I know. Gina came singing into work and gave her two-week notice because she

234

and Costas are getting married. She pretended as if we had never fought. She said that she and Costas had brunch with Taylor Law and his fiancée, and he is getting married in a month. "It's so weird!"

Jason Hazer is married and having children. I talked to Tammy about it today (she's getting married, too). My old fat preteen friend Troy Tumfeld, I just heard from Tammy, has apparently been going out with this bank teller, Chris, for a year. His mother set them up. Everyone is gay AND married. Even homosexual pedophiles are starting families—Ken Fenning is married with one child, one on the way.

I talked to Lynn Flushing on the phone. She called my parents to get my number in New York. We started giggling like we were at HoJo's. She lives with her Coast Guard husband in Nova Scotia. She sounds so calm, like all drama within her has been washed out to sea. I try to sound more mature, too, laughing about our histrionic night in the parking lot as if I wasn't still seventeen, in love with the wrong guy, blubbering, and pouring coffee on people. She says she talked to Jeff a couple of years ago, but lost touch with him after attending his ceremony of union in Chicago.

God I am itchy—these dying crabs are on my body. They are probably noticing that I am becoming lucid about my sordid sex life: "We are losing our host body! He will want to have a fulfilling relationship soon! Quick, itch! Remind him of how much of a whore he is!" Those fucking crabs have traveled far—from Benny to Eric to me. Or was it me to Eric to Benny . . . or George to Eric to Benny and me . . . or George to Benny to Stephen back to Benny to Eric to me . . .

I dozed off in the car for a few minutes. I had this dream that I am lying in my childhood bed and a pear-shaped man is lying on his back, on top of me. The vague, fruity figure wants me to suck his dick and I don't want to, and suddenly Benny appears from inside the closet, board games and winter coats tumbling out with him. "I'll suck him!" he says, and he does.

I left this morning without even talking to him. I passed by his bedroom and he was in there with cool towels on his body, spreading aloe gel on himself. Benny scorched me, I scorched him back. Now I feel bad though. We'll be friends again—he will say he's sorry and I'll say I am sorry, out of relief and out of embarrassment over our trite lives. We'll go out to an all-you-can-drink brunch and put our arms around each other and say loud things about how men stink and men are whores and men should never come between friends, men suck, men suck, conveniently forgetting we *are* men.

I have never dated someone for longer than one month, and that was Benny, yes, Benny—oh my God I dated Benny. It was in college, when we were both flossy and skinny with our little chests and fleshy faces.

If you were to query my friends to discover why it is that I have not had a successful relationship, you would have to deliberate among them like a juror. Here are some that I have tried to gather together from the crowd of responses: "Don't worry, you'll find someone" . . . "It's weird, you know, you have to love yourself first" . . . "You need to love yourself before someone else can love you" . . . "You go for stupid guys, Mike" . . . "You're what? Twenty-seven? You're still young, Mike" . . . "It's a mysterious series of circumstances" . . . "You have just happened to have not been in the right place at the right time" . . . "It'll happen when you least expect it" . . . And I listen to the huge litany of reasons and I am supposed to ruminate peacefully over each tired piece of advice.

"The difference between you and Eric is that you are so indirect," Gina said to me. "You don't ask for anything from anybody." She said that and I felt like a deep, deep well with dead, flat water at its bottom, and she is right. Eric is wrong for me, and of course I like him. He appeared in a flyer for Freon the other day and I sat there looking at the picture as if it were a little Narnia. "I love you, man," he says to me, and then goes off to dance on the block and goes home with George. He puts his arms around me and we go into the exclusive bartender bathroom and we kiss and then he sucks me off and I say *I love you* to him and he says "I love you" and I know it is all wrong. I should not like him, but who is there to like? I can't see anything but flatness. Flat magazines, flat walls, flat blankets, flat stomachs, flat storefront facades. Flat things pull toward me. And in their flat way they love me. They say I love you with their tongues flat in their mouths and their flat flat monotone voices. WHAT IS WRONG WITH ME? WHY AM I OVER-OBSESSED WITH SURFACES?

Okay, right now I have the ability to cleanly, statistically analyze my sexual life into a pie chart, and I feel as if this ability is only going to last a little longer before I fall back into my mindless sexual trough, so I have to write this down fast:

I've slept with a hundred people (rounding down), all men. The biggest wedge could be dramatized by me sitting on a bed, listening to someone's drunk snores, trying to figure out if I should leave or stay, whether I like this person or not, whether I am polite or in love, and never deciding. Another, slightly smaller wedge of men could be considered so disgusting that I want to retch when I think about their greasy, spindly, clammy, sour-smelling bodies on me. And then there is that thin, thin sliver of guys with all their promise and beauty, with all their eyes and lips and boyfriends. In this sliver, I sit there putting on my shoes, the sliver guy tells me he has so much going on or how intense his boyfriend is and then I try to say something significant and weird to him to be memorable. I try to become the perfect erotic memory for him, the smiling, undemanding, weightless *Whatever!* boy, and then I slip out the window like a tissue.

Then imagine a two-week period of me aching for this person and then that ache waning and then it ending. Then in three months I see him coming down 7th Street. "Hi, how are you? What's up? I'm fine, I'm tired. I know, I can't wait for Friday, too! I'll see you later!" And I wonder if he is still working things out with Craig or Andre or George or if he still has so much going on, if he feels any residue for me, because if he does I am sure I could feel things for him, too. I turn back and look at his body walking away.

And then a year later, I will see him again, somewhere more adult and professional, like buying wine in work clothes in Midtown or coming out of a gourmet health-food store with fresh snap peas and twenty-dollar fillets of Chilean sea bass in his hands, it doesn't matter, and maybe we will say hello, maybe we won't, it doesn't matter, but he will make me peer into that old, once-hot memory, make me peer into it like a refrigerator in the dark that hums.

I am tired of walking the streets, humming and staring at architecture, settling into a subway seat and looking at every face just in case someone to love slips into the car while I wade in potential tears. (Because it could happen anywhere! When I least expect it!) I am tired of trying to find love and then trying to not find love but secretly still trying to find love while looking independent and least expecting it. I am tired of being the one who tries and fails while Benny looks at me, smirking sympathetically. I am tired of being told I can only be happy if I find a stable tube-shaped guy I am quietly unattracted to and we move to a gentrified section of San Diego and have jerky, quick sex that he cleans up swiftly with a towel that smells like Tide.

I am getting total cry-mouth, and I keep darting looks up to the store to see if my parents are coming, to give me time to recompose. I am sad both because of Eric and because of what he represents: the more global fact that I am not in love and I can't seem to find that. I am polluted. It's this part of me that is a ball, an error, a lump in my left breast, and I want it excised or burned out. It's a knob deep inside me that is ten years of Jeffs and Erics and all the clotting that comes with those guys collected into a ball. This deeply contaminated part of me thinks that I'm not fulfilled unless I find some guy to drape myself on. This parasitic lump thinks that I need a movement or a boyfriend to settle into. I want this lame, wobbly, needy, dumb, deep part of me poisoned and removed.

And the hilarious fact is that I am just one of a billion polluted people in a plaza of pollutants. I see it now. Outside of my safe, cooled car encasement, in the litter of ATM receipts and frozen-yogurt lids and quivering Blockbuster bags, are billions of polluted people in their cars, spewing exhaust into the air, listening to their woozy music, crying to themselves. A sprawl of plazas and driveways and homes, of home after home. A smooth, curvy meshwork, glowing with parking-lot lights, dirty grand-opening flags, warm red drug-store signs, and all the polluted people, barely connecting, but never alone.

I don't need Eric. I don't need anyone. I mean it this time. Nothing is wavering in me. I am free. I am a veteran with my tattered flag, crazy craggy face, and crabs, strong, trying to be alone.

HERE

You better watch out, I am the King of Karate.

I'm the King of Wet Willies.

My brother used to do that.

Gave you wet willies.

Yeah . . . no, no, don't, DON'T, gross, it feels so wet and you feel like you can never get it out. What are you doing?

Giving you a wedgie.

What is this?

This is your brother, Mike. I'm actually your brother in disguise.

Wow how scary, what a role player you are; you must be in the drama crowd.

Shut up.

[pause]

So why do you think we came over here without Lynn?

I don't know, what do you mean?

I don't know.

[pause]

Why don't you know?

I don't know. It's not like I wanted to intentionally exclude Lynn.

Why?

Why what?

Why aren't you happy?

I didn't say that I wasn't happy. I'm happy. No, not happy. I don't know.

Why are you depressed?

I'm not. I don't know.

Come on, tell me.

I guess I'm bummed a little because I had met you and Lynn and every-one so late—the end of senior year, and I hate myself for it.

Oh. Yeah that's too bad.

What is the deal with you and Lynn?

It's platonic but we do some things but not anything serious.

I've decided that I am probably going to be a virgin for the rest of my life.

I'm sure you will eventually have sex with something.

I have this philosophy about horniness. It's my horny theory.

What is it?

Well, once I had this dream that I was having sex with this glob of flesh. It was just a ball of skin and I realized that sex is something separate from the body. I was having sex in the dream with this, like, girl and it was, like . . . I closed my eyes in my closed eyes . . . and she turned into a glob of skin and so did I but I still felt really horny. It was like we were . . .

Not sexes.

No, we had sexes, but it was like our genitals were in our whole body and not in one specific place. We were like these piles of horniness. We were like these two bogs fucking.

Well does that mean you would have sex with anything?

What?

Does this mean you would have sex with dogs, guys, your mother?

No. It has nothing to do with that. I just mean I think that sex is something that spreads further than where your body takes up space. You're confusing . . .

[pause]

Well, then finish it.

Finish what?

Finish this philosophy. Obviously it pertains to your identity.

No, I was just making a statement about my horny theory.

What does this say about your sexual identity?

Nothing.

Well, if you could have sex with anything in this room, what would it be?

I would . . . I don't know. I would build a complex machine that would